S0-DUV-168

The

BIG

RED

SUN

PQ
2672
A64
G713
1971

The

BIG
RED
SUN

Daniel Larany

*Translated
by
Robert
Bullen
and
Rosette
Letellier*

PRENTICE-HALL, INC.
ENGLEWOOD CLIFFS, NEW JERSEY

Design by Linda Huber ●

THE BIG RED SUN by Daniel Larany,
translated by Robert Bullen and Rosette Letellier
Copyright © 1971 by Prentice-Hall, Inc., for this translation.
Copyright under International and Pan American
Copyright Conventions
All rights reserved. No part of this book may be
reproduced in any form or by any means, except
for the inclusion of brief quotations in a review,
without permission in writing from the publisher.
ISBN-0-13-076166-4
Library of Congress Catalog Card Number: 70-134203
Printed in the United States of America   T
Prentice-Hall International, Inc., London
Prentice-Hall of Australia, Pty. Ltd., Sydney
Prentice-Hall of Canada, Ltd., Toronto
Prentice-Hall of India Private Ltd., New Delhi
Prentice-Hall of Japan, Inc., Tokyo

FRIDAY ●

● ● ● THE TRUMPETS NEARLY threw him out of bed.
● ● ● Georges Benachen thought the loudspeaker had
● ● ● been placed under his pillow. Unconsciously, even
before his eyes were open, he hummed the refrain from "To
sail the open seas one depends on the helmsman," that haunt-
ing anthem to the glory of Mao Tse-tung: "The fish cannot
live out of water, the cucumber vine cannot give up its ten-
drils, the revolutionary masses cannot abandon the Communist Party, the Thought of Mao Tse-tung is a sun that never
sets."

He looked at his watch: seven o'clock. Through the window of his room on the third floor of the Hsin Chao Hotel,
he could see the first workers who, under the furls of enormous red flags, nonchalantly set out on their daily job: the
demolition of the ancient wall of Peking's "Tartar City."
Over the loudspeaker a shrill female voice was spelling out in
Chinese the morning editorial of the *People's Daily*.

Another day began, another day of waiting, as vain, he was
sure, as all the others which had passed since he arrived in
Peking. There could be no leaving the telephone. Miss Wang,
his assigned interpreter, had been quite positive about that.
"I'll call you to let you know if the meetings you asked for
have been set up. But, as you know, our leaders are very busy
these days. Their time is precious. It's entirely consecrated to
the service of the masses."

Miss Wang waxed sententious. She loved to mouth solemn
formulas and pedantries—something Georges was pretty used
to by now. He was special correspondent of *African Will
Power*, a left-wing Algiers weekly, and he had lived for five
years in the intimacy, sometimes heavy, of Third World
leaders and Francophone intellectuals—characters who considered themselves the last defenders of fine language and
who did honor to the education which had been so lavishly
heaped upon them.

Barefoot in his pyjamas, his eyes swollen by sleep, he walked
the immense corridor which stank of mice and of the acrid

2

wax peculiar to hotels in Communist countries. Behind a small desk the bellboys read the *People's Daily* editorial, using the same accent as the loudspeaker voice he had heard earlier. In bad English he ordered tea and toast. On the way back to his room, where he would wait for his breakfast and an unlikely call from Miss Wang, he picked out some brochures by Chairman Mao and the last three issues of *Pékin Information*, a weekly digest in French of all major official news published in China.

In the most recent issue he found a few lines about what had brought him here to the capital of China in the midst of the Cultural Revolution:

> Representatives of the peoples of Africa fighting for their liberation arrive in Peking.
> Comrades Diego Tombalouwou, Chairman of the Liberation Front of South Angola, John Seymour, Delegate of the People's National Army of Zimbabwe, and Ahmed Abdouldawe, Chairman of the People's National Movement of Somalia, accompanied by their wives, arrived Wednesday in Peking on the invitation of the Chinese Committee of Afro-Asian Solidarity. Greeted at the airport by comrades Wang Wang-li, Vice-Chairman of the Committee, and Chen Fu-chu, Secretary of the Revolutionary Committee of Peking, the valiant African combatants against › Imperialism and Revisionism were cheered by representatives of all segments of the capital.

There were small red flags and those of Zimbabwe, Independent Angola, and Free Somalia, laboriously put together and confidently waved by the "masses"—some two hundred strong mobilized for the occasion—at the dark-skinned visitors in resplendent *boubous*. (The national costume is always better; if you don't have one in your own country borrow *djellabahs*, they were told at the Chinese Embassy when passing through Cairo.) The signs were written in French, in English, and in Chinese: "Salute to our comrades of Zimbabwe, of South Angola, and of Somalia fighting for their liberation!" Then the canned tirades, the banquet of nine dishes at the House of Hosts, the visit to the day-nursery of Textile Factory Number Two—all this was part of a ritual that Georges, an asiduous reader of the Chinese press before his trip, knew by heart. It was thanks to the help of an old friend from the Law School and *Cité Universitaire* in Paris, and of a colleague of the New China Agency in Cairo (not his only job, Georges suspected), that he had succeeded, to his own great surprise, in obtaining a visa.

This visit, however, was but a cover. What really gave his coming quite another coloration was contained in a few lines in *Le Monde*. It was small credit to Georges that he had learned it all by heart.

> Tokyo (AP) . . . Posters displayed yesterday in Peking proclaim that Chen Wu-hsieh, member of the group of the Cultural Revolution in the Central Committee and acting Chairman of the Chinese Committee of Solidarity, is a counterrevolutionary who follows the bourgeois reactionary line, according to Japanese press correspondents in the Chinese capital. It is the first time that Chen Wu-hsieh, so far considered personally very close to Chairman Mao and Prime Minister Chou En-lai, and one of the most important theoreticians of the Cultural Revolution, has been attacked by name by the Red Guards. The posters indicate that the man formerly responsible for relations with the liberation movements of the Third World inside the Central Committee of the Chinese Communist Party has already been the target of numerous accusation rallies but that he had refused so far to engage in satisfactory self-criticism.

4

Chen. . . Georges remembered the little man with ferret eyes behind large glasses, during that long evening in Algiers.

What in the world could have pushed him, this official of the apparatus, trained to the most rigorous discipline, for whom secrecy had become second nature, to display such confidence and sincerity toward the almost unknown newsman Georges then was?

"I'm telling you this, Georges, because you're a friend, almost a companion in arms, because both of us have studied in France, because there comes a time when one has to talk to somebody. Within a few months we shall witness unbelievable events in China! A revolution absolutely without precedent! He is going to dismantle the Party. Leave us without defenses at just the time the Americans, with the active complicity of the Russians, think they have a free rein, and under cover of intensifying the Vietnam War, are preparing to attack China herself. Should the worst happen, and I'm convinced it will, there will be some of us in the Party who will react in order to save the revolution and Comrade Mao—in spite of himself, if need be."

The man had talked at length. He had given Georges a fascinating tale of the rivalries within factions and between personalities which, still behind closed doors, were tearing apart the high spheres of Peking: the growing influence over a bitter and aging Mao of the small group of "ideologues" directed by Chen Po-ta, his former secretary, and Kang Sheng, a turncoat functionary of the Third International; the complex game of the military, who used Marshal Lin Piao, ailing and considered ineffectual, to eliminate the influence of staff chief Lo Jui-ching as well as the security services he had for a long time directed; the complicated quarrel against Peng Chen, then Mayor of Peking and considered abroad a likely candidate to succeed Mao himself. "If I told you this evening," he went on, "the name of the man who will write the checks for the operation, you wouldn't believe it. But take it from me, the Stalin-Trotsky fight of the twenties, the great purges of 1937–38 are nothing compared to what you're going to see in our country very soon."

These unexpected and unsolicited confidences brought a flattering notoriety to Georges. Up to then his reputation had been that of an intelligent if perhaps too enthusiastic apologist of African revolutions, the very type of "engaged" intellectual whom his old drinking companions of Saint-Germain-des-Prés did not take very seriously, one who steered an uneasy course between Bourguiba, Boumedienne, and Nasser. But this interview with Chen made it possible for him to write for his weekly a long report in depth on the political situation in China. Covertly, carefully protecting his source, he had announced, with approval in advance, the coming leftward move of the Maoist revolution, citing Lin Piao as one of the principal beneficiaries of the operation, and putting his readers on guard against all preconceived ideas which would tend to compare the evolution of the Chinese Party with developments underway in socialist parties elsewhere.

The article was a hit. The "Moscowteers" attacked it violently. They recalled that the author was a character eminently suspect in their eyes. He had broken with the French Communist Party over direct aid to the Algerian National Liberation Front (FLN), which he had done so much to defend. He had known the right time to betray Ben Bella, and so maintained himself in Algiers after the coup, while most of the French "red feet" * of his ilk had had to scurry about for refuge elsewhere. The praises he heaped on Peking "leftism" constituted a new manifestation of petit-bourgeois opportunism which had earlier brought about his expulsion from the Party.

On the other hand, "bourgeois" specialists on the China question adopted him as one of their own. *Le Monde, Problems of Communism,* and *The China Quarterly* reviewed his

* Translator's note: "pieds rouges" (red feet) as opposed to "pieds noirs" (black feet), a popular pejorative for the French settlers in Algeria.

article. For this perpetually needy man of thirty-five, who neither war nor political battles had been able to raise from obscurity and most of all from loneliness, it was, if not glory, at least a very honorable notoriety. Remarkably, the Chinese themselves seemed to appreciate the article, as if he had done them a favor with these revelations so knowingly measured out. He had been invited quite often to the sober dinners of their overalled diplomats. And he had been led to believe that an invitation to Peking was being considered.

But of course Georges had not given out Chen's most dangerous disclosures. Perhaps his discretion was less creditable in that he had not taken them seriously at the time. Chen had said softly but without hesitation: "Some of the comrades responsible and I too know that we might have to take refuge in a friendly capital like Pnom Penh where we can openly proclaim, free from imperialist and revisionist interference, the objectives of our fight, and where we can denounce the betrayal of the revolution by Peking opportunists. To be sure, we'll be called lackeys of imperialism, and so on. But it will be of little importance, because we know that in reality Mao agrees with us. And besides, there will be such confusion in China that no one will take these accusations seriously any longer!"

The reception the Algerian government gave at the Aletti Hotel in honor of Chen's delegation on his grand tour of Africa lasted well into the night. The Chinese, casting off his habitual regard for security, had drawn Georges aside into a window embrasure and talked to him privately. Perhaps it was Chen's high rank that made this possible. On saying goodby, he pressed Georges' hand at length. "We'll see each other again. Come to Peking. I can help you have an interesting trip, very interesting, believe me. I've read your book *From the Fetishes of Revolution to the Revolution of Fetishes;* I know our goals are the same. That's why I talked to you as I have. Make use of what I've told you, but be careful. You will serve our cause—which is also yours." Then he turned on his heels and rejoined the knot of Algerian leaders who were beginning to be visibly nettled by his prolonged absence.

A few months later during a stay in Paris, Georges could see that his new reputation had now surfaced among the intelligentsia of the left.

Except under the name of "Mr. Marcel," he never knew the honorable agent from SDECE who waited for him that grim day in January in the office of the chief of the Alien Control Bureau at police headquarters, where he had been called during one of his brief trips to Paris, "about matters which concern you."

Mr. Marcel was a placid sort, fortyish with a paunch, quite sloppy but on the whole agreeable. He drew on his pipe, plainly aping the character of Simenon's Inspector Maigret.

The chief was called into another office and left them to themselves. They found a number of topics of mutual interest. It took no more than an hour to convince "Jerôme Vasseur, alias Maurice Benhaïm, alias Georges Benachen, born in Versailles October 30th, 1933, holder of Tunisian passport 29007 KB, domiciled in Algiers, calling himself journalist and man of letters, without visible means of income," that it was of primary interest for him to cooperate actively with the Paris Bureau as he had done on other occasions in other countries. Georges' dossier, which just happened to be in Mr. Marcel's briefcase, was bulging with the usual mixture of real and fake information—hearsay and photostats of letters, telephoto shots of meetings which Georges had believed were forgotten, and incriminating testimony taken from fellow workers, rivals, and betrayed husbands. His well-paid job of placing FLN funds in a Swiss bank for their former treasurer Ben Khidder, then the help he gave Ben Bella's staff in preventing the transfer of these funds to Spain; a trip he took for the Algiers leadership to the

8

United States, and certain contacts he had made in Washington on that occasion (the subject of a special memo from the SDECE man in the American capital)—all of which would have certainly given his liberal friends the wrong impression. A few words thrown in casually by Mr. Marcel did the job of persuading Georges: Boumedienne might well have rid himself of Ben Bella, but he would not be so pleased if he were to read, in *Le Canard Enchaîné* for instance, whose readers are so fond of such information, that someone of his entourage had dined three times last week in Geneva with a certain "Colonel Ephraim," from Shinbeth—Israeli Central Intelligence—and that the topic most discussed was the political situation in Algiers, the army purge of the old *willayas,* and most of all the affair of the Algerian MIGS lost over Constantine owing to pilot error on their way to Egypt at the start of the Six Day War.

Not much, obviously, had escaped the vigilance of the fine fellows of the "Pool" or "Central," to use the terminology of the SDECE pros. Complacently if amiably, Mr. Marcel went over every little item in the dossier. As a man of experience, Georges showed no emotion. He knew very well what all of this led to, and the offer that was to be made him in a particularly urgent manner was no surprise, at least in broad outline.

But first Georges tried for appearance's sake to take a lofty tone.

"So, the laurels of Lopez keep you awake. . . . You'd like to get into a new Ben Barka affair. Who's the candidate for kidnapping this time—Bouteflika, or Boumedienne himself?"

Mr. Marcel did not blink.

"You're not far off, old man." Already, after three quarters of an hour together they were on the level of old working buddies, if not yet at the point of thou-thee familiarity. "But this time the client who interests us is not North African. He is someone who lives much farther away and whom you know personally. And the job is not kidnapping but to facilitate an

9

escape. Can't you guess? Someone you met a while ago in Algiers and who told you about wanting to get out of his country."

Georges was in the dark. His mind was far from the elaborate warnings of that curious Chinese he had met one evening, whose behavior had been so unorthodox. He had put the episode out of his mind as so many others like it, unusual but of no consequence, which had spattered his career. So Mr. Marcel had to dot the *i*'s and cross the *t*'s.

"Chen Wu-hsieh," he murmured very softly, as if already afraid their conversation was being bugged.

"You want him wrapped up in Peking, put in a crate, and freighted by Air France to Paris? James Bond is hardly a specialty of mine, you know."

"That's just why we're interested in you. Without any serious risk, you can help us. And we in exchange can help you make a trip which all of your colleagues dream of. Like everybody else you'll come back from Peking with a bestseller. All we want is for you to try to contact your friend Chen and give him a message. If you succeed, you will find deposited in your account at the *Comptoir des Banques Suisses* at Lausanne, under your own number K–20355—you see we're well informed—a sum of fifty thousand Swiss francs. If the operation proves impossible, you'll have had a lovely trip at our expense; besides, half the sum will be deposited before your departure to Peking and will be yours no matter what. So . . . what do you think of it?"

"It looks like a bad trip to me. I'm the one who'll end up carrying blocks of salt in Sinkiang, while you'll be downing drinks to my health at the Old Timer Café, or one of those other dives where you guys hang out, according to the detective story writers."

"You'll be sorry if you refuse, believe me," Mr. Marcel said quietly.

"Ah, threats! A touch of blackmail! As I expected. Certain things in that dossier—all of it fake I want you to know . . ."

10

Mr. Marcel nodded politely.

". . . if you dare send it to your colleagues in Algiers it would be, I admit, unpleasant. But much less so than a Chinese prison camp, or being sliced up by the Red Guards. Right?"

"The way things are now, the Chinese won't waste their time, unless absolutely necessary, arresting and trying as a spy an eminent champion of the African Peoples' fight against imperialism, colonialism, and neo-colonialism—Boumedienne's comrade-in-arms—and what's more, a personal friend of Mr. Abdouldawe and practically a member of his delegation on the official invitation of Peking. Chen is the organizer of the trip. It's inevitable that you'll meet him; you'll just have to arrange an interview. Therefore . . ."

"I don't need your help if I want to go to Peking," protested Georges. "You're so well informed, you ought to know that I've been invited personally by the Afro-Asian Committee. It just happened that the dates they proposed weren't convenient for me."

"They made it firm, this invitation?" asked Mr. Marcel. "Ever since the beginning of the Cultural Revolution, I'd wondered whether anything would come of this project. Tell me if I'm wrong. If so, we can talk about something else."

Georges had to retreat. He'd die for the chance to get to Peking at a time when the capital had become once again, for almost all of his colleagues, a forbidden city. And there was his urgent need for money—the expenses of his divorce and a very young mistress to keep.

Three more sessions were required, in an anonymous café on the Avenue des Batignolles, to settle the details of the operation. Abdouldawe, the extremist African nationalist, who was controlled ever so obscurely and indirectly, perhaps even without his awareness thanks to the subsidies so stingily distributed, would obtain Georges' inclusion in the delegation which he would lead to Peking. Once there, Georges would talk with Chen and inform him that, with the help of

Prince Sihanouk, who couldn't refuse De Gaulle in this area, he would be assured the right of asylum in Pnom Penh; that funds for expenses had been taken care of; and that, in short, a solution to the Peking anarchy, as anti-American as one could want, had been arranged, even if it could not be put into effect until the time was judged right by all concerned. It would be a twist of the wrist. The terrain was already prepared. Georges' job was essentially to give an "African" and "neutralist" facade to the operation. The real moving spirits of the game in Paris wanted, of course, to remain in the shadows.

Abdouldawe, in the name of the Coordination Committee of the Fight for African Liberation created for the occasion, was to invite Chen to Cairo. Nothing could be more normal, considering the role Chen played in the Peking section of the Afro-Asian Solidarity Committee. It would be during this trip that Chen would choose, not freedom—detestable formula, stupidly anti-communist, pro-American, and to be rejected with horror—but a temporary retreat. From Pnom Penh, a liberal capital, he would emerge at the hour of the greatest confusion in China with the sketch of a solution to rally most of the malcontents. Georges' job was to act on both Abdouldawe and Chen for the fulfillment of this grand undertaking.

All had been finely ground, slowly cooked, and wrapped up by the Far East experts of SDECE—a collection of Salan's former "Chinamen," half-breed fingermen retired from ex-French-Indochinese Intelligence and chased from Cholon after Dien-Bien-Phu, and serious intellectuals from the CIA who studied K.S. Karol and Edgar Snow. A complicated mixture designed more to unsettle Washington than actually to interfere in Chinese politics. Moreover, the character of the agent they chose—a progressive adventurer, a former member of the Jeanson network that was set up to help the FLN during the Algerian War, and an ex-Frenchman expelled by the Communist party—would eventually permit them, if it

12

happened to go wrong, to disavow the whole thing with a maximum of plausibility.

But that things would go wrong, Mr. Marcel assured him, was highly unlikely. After all, what did they expect from Georges? To "convince" a Chinese personality, who was already sold in principle, on the advantage of an eventual defection. To ask him, if he should succeed, to make contact in Pnom Penh with French agents, at a time when the intelligence networks of all the great powers would have nothing more urgent to do than to offer him their services.

Even in the eyes of Georges, who considered himself an amateur in this domain, this "mission" seemed pretty childish. So he was not surprised when, saying goodby for the last time after having downed three espressos one after the other in the café on the Batignolles, Mr. Marcel finally brought in his full artillery.

Georges had stood up. Mr. Marcel remained nailed to the long moleskin bench. "It's better," he had said at the first meeting, "that we not go out together. One never knows." This was one of the elementary tricks of the trade, Georges had thought, which gives the most sedentary of secret agents the illusion of living dangerously.

But this time Mr. Marcel pushed the comedy a little further.

"Just a minute," he said, "I almost forgot. Here's a piece of paper, an index card really, which can help you to know better our . . . mutual friend, the name of one of our contacts who lives in Peking. He might be able to help you. And another piece of paper which represents the sum of what we know about your eminent interlocutor in Algiers. Part of this information you could very well find in *Who's Who in Communist China* published by the Union Research Institute in Hong Kong. But only a part . . ."

The name was Michel Loriot, a French university man "who helps us out of some sense of patriotism. To top it all, a charming guy who has all China at his fingertips. Maybe a

13

little too much to the left for my taste. Don't bother to write down the name. You're sure to meet him; he hangs around the embassies. Entertainment is so rare there." Mr. Marcel went on quickly to sketch a flattering description.

Then he pulled out of his pocket, all crumpled and typed single-spaced, a sheet that carried the simple headline "Chen Wu-hsieh." Georges read it very attentively while Mr. Marcel absorbed himself in a crossword puzzle from *Le Monde*, rapidly filling in all the squares.

Chen Wu-hsieh. Born 1910, Huamgan Hsien (county) Hupei; father, minor official. Eldest of five children, three of whom died in infancy. Classical education. Sent about 1920 to Shanghai to be raised by an uncle who was a storekeeper. Runs away at the age of fifteen to join the forces of the Kuomintang then on a march to the north. Later he leaves for France as part of a work-study program. Enrolled immediately in Paris in the local section of the Chinese Communist Party of which Chou En-lai had been one of the founders. Meeting with Jacques Doriot, at this time international liaison for the French CP. Returns to China around 1930, after a probable stop in Moscow, where he is said to have married a young student named Yiminova from Central Asia and at the time in a Party school in the USSR. She is then lost track of. He is said to have been married again in Yenan, this time to an actress named Kou Feng-lien. On returning to Shanghai in 1932 arrested by the Kuomintang but escapes in time to participate in the Long March of 1933–1934 as a political commissar of a unit in the Second Route Army commanded by Ho Lung, with whom he seems to have cultivated, from this time on, a close relationship. He spends little time in Yenan, then capital of the Soviet Republic of China. There he is considered in turn as being close to Chou En-lai, then to Liu Shao-chi whom he assists on the workshop of the Central Committee, formed in 1947 and dissolved a year later, after which he was on the Federation of Syndicates. Head of mission in North Korea (May-June 1950, just before the start of the Korean War), in North Vietnam (April-June 1951), officially in the employ of the Chinese Syndicates. Part of Chou En-lai's delegation as secretary-general during the Afro-Asian Conference in Bandung (April 1955), then Chairman of the Chinese Committee of Afro-Asian Solidarity. After which sets up numerous missions in Southeast Asia, as well as in progressive African countries, notably at Accra and Conakry, where he is photographed, trying to hide his face (see attached) at the side of Sékou Touré the week after the rejection by Guinea in 1958 of De Gaulle's referendum for entry into the French Community. No certain record of his activities in 1959, but he is said to have been in Albania during this time to supervise the installation of a "training school of syndicate cadres" in Durazzo. In 1960 he accompanies Ho Lung (see file-card *Purges of Military Cadres*) and Liu Shao-chi to Jakarta for ratification ceremonies for the Sino-Indonesian Treaty of Friendship, and later closely associated with various foreign enterprises of Ho Lung. Assigned in 1961 to organize the People's Militia in Central China (only reference to any paramilitary activity since the Long March). In 1964 participates with Peng Chen (see file-card *Purge of Peking Municipal Committee*) in conversations in Peking with a Japanese CP delegation, then with the same Peng Chen in May 1965 on a trip to mark the forty-fifth anniversary of the foundation of the Indonesian CP four months before the abortive putsch and the resulting repression which decimated the Party. Next makes a trip to Cairo (October 1965) and

15

Algiers (1966). Elected deputy member of the Central Committee of the Eighth Congress in 1956 and member of the Committee for the Cultural Revolution in the Army in September 1966. Remains in favor, despite close relationships with diverse high personalities under criticism, purged, or arrested—something not yet satisfactorily explained. According to classified source M3, he is said to be member of directing group of Liaison Committee, Intelligence and Action Section, not under the Ministry of Security but directly under the Permanent Committee of the Political Bureau of the Central Committee of the Chinese CP. There he is said to have been in charge particularly of the supervision of certain special projects having to do with the eventual utilization of Chinese nuclear potential to its fullest operational extent.

Georges finished the paper and, without a word, gave it back to Mr. Marcel who returned the crumpled paper to his pocket and commented simply, "For your information, let me point out 'source M3' means 'moderately safe—not to be used without cross-checking.'"

"And so?" asked Georges.

"So nothing. I was just telling you. Just making conversation."

"Well, it's no longer just a matter of getting a simple opponent to leave China by legal means. The matter is someone who apparently possesses precious information on China's atomic potential. And the information interests you more than the man. Am I right?"

"We never try to impose our own interpretation, especially on our friends from the press," answered Mr. Marcel. "As far as I'm concerned nothing is changed. What we expect from you is what I explained before—to facilitate the departure of Chen if he still has the intention of leaving China. Of course,

16

if the fancy takes him to reveal the blueprint of their latest H-bomb, please take note. One never knows, it might come in handy. And we know in such cases how to show our gratitude. But this isn't the goal of your mission. There it is, my friend. This time I think we've said all there is to say."

But it was Georges' turn to remain seated.

"I'm sorry, but as far as I'm concerned, plenty has changed. A personality as eminent as the one in the biography I just read, romanticized or not, is certainly harder to contact than any functionary simply involved in promoting 'great amity among the peoples of Asia, Africa, and Latin America.' And the operation involves more risk. Consequently . . ."

"Consequently?" asked Mr. Marcel, puffing on his chimney, more like Maigret than ever.

"Consequently fifty thousand Swiss francs adds up to a ridiculous sum, counted against the risks and the odds. It's out of the question to do anything for less than 150,000."

"My superiors had foreseen your objection," responded the agent with an understanding smile. "They even estimated in advance the amount of your . . . claims. You see, they're not half as dumb as advertised by the press, among whom you number many friends I believe. Let me show you . . ."

He fished around again in his pocket and took out another paper as messy as the first. It was a deposit slip for 75,000 francs to the account K–20355 in the *Comptoir des Banques Suisses.*

"The other half will be deposited on your return. So you won't spend it all at one time—you journalists are such sieves. That's not bad for a messenger, eh?"

Right now this messenger wished he were somewhere else. He bitterly regretted that he'd ever got started on this dirty deal; the chances of getting out of it seemed ever more remote, the risks greater and greater. For one thing, the political disgrace of Chen Wu-hsieh, which occurred only a few days before he left Algiers, cast doubts on the whole laboriously rigged scenario. From now on, a meeting with such an individual, suspect and maybe already in jail, would run one up against insurmountable problems—especially if the responsibilities of Chen extended into the atomic domain. Georges paced his room from the bed to the window at least fifty times—exactly four and a half feet—until he realized that such agitation would only arouse the professional curiosity of the bellboys. At this point he decided firmly to renounce the whole absurd mission, to be sensibly content with the 75,000 Swiss francs already his. Reassured, or pretending to be, he became absorbed in watching the workers, men and women in blue overalls, as they removed one by one, by hand, the ancient bricks of the Tartar Wall.

The telephone rang. Miss Wang forwarded an invitation to a grand reception to be given at four o'clock that afternoon in the ballroom of the Hotel Peking in honor of the African delegation.

2 ● ALL PEKING WAS present. Which means that all one had to do was to follow the stream of cars to get to the immense yellowish building on the Chang An, a great east-west artery wider than the Champs Elysées. The traffic cops, wildly gesticulating in all directions, blowing their whistles without rhyme or reason, succeeded in creating the semblance of a traffic jam.

The guests were seated at small tables. Georges found himself surrounded on one side by a skinny Chinese officer, determinedly mute, identifiable only by the red patch on his collar and by his tunic of greenish unpressed cloth, and on the other by an obese Indian lady in a sari. Big drops of sweat pearled her cheeks and her nose, which was heavy with blackheads. The beads of sweat mingled with a pearl delicately embedded just above her right nostril. Georges' eating companions threw themselves voraciously onto slices of cartilaginous duck and blackish saltpetered eggs which made up the hors-d'oeuvres. Waiters in jackets of doubtful white filled the array of glasses placed before each guest with a saccharine red wine, a pink fruit juice, a lukewarm and watery beer, and, out of stone jugs, a translucent liquid which emitted a strange odor of excrement. Georges tasted it and, startled, nearly choked. It could well have been one-hundred-percent alcohol.

Facing him, a tall, skinny young man with blackish hair, long eyelashes, and a narrow brown mustache flashed him the sparkling smile of a dance hall gigolo.

"I see," he said in excellent French with a trace of a Slavic accent, "that you are not used to this maotay liquor. If you'll permit me some advice, take it slow. Nothing gives a worse . . . How do you say? Hang-up? . . ."

"Hangover," Georges corrected.

". . . than sorghum alcohol. It has to be said that there is a certain taste for rot here that manifests itself in many ways, not only in liquor, and yet I must say that the Chinese don't like maotay very much. They reserve it for us distinguished foreigners. But allow me to introduce myself: Alexandre Vassilevitch Zagachvili, first secretary of the USSR embassy. As my name indicates, I'm a Georgian, a Mediterranean let's say—like you, I think."

At this, the Chinese officer stood up without a word and went off, his mouth pursed in disgust, to join a group of his compatriots at the far end of the room. Zagachvili smiled as he watched him go.

"We are not very popular these days," he said under his breath. "Since they haven't yet—I say, not yet—received instructions to spit at us, they try to avoid us at receptions of this kind. As a matter of fact, our friend Ma Liang-fu, joint political commissar of the People's Army of Liberation post in Peking, who just left us, will be seriously rapped on the

19

knuckles. He 'failed in vigilance' by sitting at the same table with a revisionist like me. He is now—how do you say?—contaminated. He's good for two or three sessions of self-accusation and explanation. Well, they have time to waste."

It was Georges' turn to introduce himself: "Benachen, special correspondent of the Algiers *African Will Power.*"

"Ah! you are with the delegation!" interrupted the Russian. "Then maybe you'll have the opportunity to meet some Chinese. It's different with us unfortunate diplomats who are assigned here. Believe me, to contact a Chinese right now, even if you knew him before, is not easy. It can even be dangerous. Of course, in certain cases one is obliged to. But then you've got to be very careful and get detailed intelligence in advance. Anyway, here's to the success of your trip, to your mission! *Campei!*"

He stood up and ceremoniously touched his glass to Georges' before emptying his own maotay in one gulp. Georges did the same. Tears welled in his eyes as the acrid and stinking liquor burned his throat. The insistence of his companion on the difficulty of "contacts," on the success of his "mission" certainly seemed strange. I must be suffering from espionagitis, he thought, quite satisfied to find himself capable, under the circumstances, of some kind of black humor. But he had no time to pursue these reflections. At the table of honor, reserved for the principal members of the delegation and their hosts, a very fat little Chinese had just stood up and walked over to the microphone escorted by an interpreter.

"It's Wang Wang-li, the Vice-Chairman of the Afro-Asian Committee," whispered his Soviet friend. "The real boss of the committee, Chen Wu-hsieh, is in some kind of trouble right now, like a lot of people. But you probably know all this, being a specialist on Afro-Asian affairs."

Once again Georges had the feeling that his companion revealed a singular insight into his assignment. Young Chinese were going back and forth unobtrusively behind the tables, distributing to all the guests Chinese, French, or English photocopies of the speech Wang had just begun to deliver in a squeaking voice.

"Comrades, dear friends . . . The situation at the front of the revolutionary struggle of the peoples fighting for their liberation is excellent. Imperialism and revisionism are dying but still capable of desperate attempts. The peace-loving peoples, armed with the superweapon which is the Thought of Mao Tse-tung, this great spiritual atom bomb of our time, continue to return blow for blow. At this moment, in Peking, in this city where comrade Mao Tse-tung resides, the great guide, the great thinker, the great helmsman of the revolutionary fight, the visit that brings our African comrades here testifies to the immense attachment by all the peoples of the world to him, waiting for him to set the direction of their battle against imperialism, revisionism, colonialism, and neocolonialism. In the first rank of those who struggle in vain to arrest the wheel of history and, with the help of their servile alliance with the American imperialists and the Soviet revisionists, to multiply aggressions and provocations against Mao Tse-tung's China, are the reactionary leaders of India. Their provocations however will not go unpunished: 750 million Chinese, aided by all the peace-loving peoples, will repulse their aggressions . . ."

At the words "reactionary leaders of India," a dark-skinned dignitary dressed in a severe black jacket buttoned to the neck got up from his table and walked to the door. This was the Indian chargé d'affaires. His subordinates, among them Georges' neighbor, the fat lady in the sari, followed his example.

"It won't be long before it's our turn. Wait and see," whispered Zagachvili.

The speaker continued as though prompted:

"But the crimes of reactionary Indians and all other re-

21

actionaries would be inconceivable without the direct aid and inspiration of the American imperialists and, even more, of their lackeys and accomplices, the Soviet revisionists. The Kosygins, the Brezhnevs and company, inheritors of the anti-Chinese line of Khrushchev, have found in China herself faithful disciples, whose chief is the Chinese Khrushchev, the number one leader who follows the capitalist road in the bosom of the party. It won't be long before they, like him, will be thrown into the garbage can of history!"

At the expression "Soviet revisionists," Zagachvili stood up almost automatically and looked Georges straight in the eye. "I have to follow my chargé d'affaires," he took time to whisper. "If you are free, let's get together again for dinner at the Hsin Chao. We'll talk about all of this, the situation of . . . Chen Wu-hsieh. . . . If it's OK with you."

This time the bait was too explicit for Georges to ignore. He found himself alone at the table, the three eating companions having left in turn. At the same time as Zagachvili, all the Soviet and East European diplomats with the exception of the Rumanians and Albanians took their leave. Then, under the successive attacks of the Chinese orator against the British imperialists, guilty of the worst kind of atrocities against the Chinese in Hong Kong, against the French neo-colonialists, against the Western world in general, which was responsible for the extortions perpetrated against the peoples of Africa, almost all the diplomats present abandoned their places. Before the half-empty room the three African guests of honor, visibly embarrassed, took their turns at the podium and expressed, as rapidly and briefly as possible, their thanks for the brotherly help given to their cause by the government and people of China. Georges did not really listen. He began to wonder if his cover was as safe as Mr. Marcel had assured him it would be. The little café on the Batignolles seemed now so distant, as inaccessible as a lost paradise.

When he left the reception at six, he decided to take a walk before going back to the hotel. He needed to put his thoughts

22

in order and wanted to enjoy the end of a marvelous fall afternoon. The setting sun lighted the ocher and gold of the forbidden city. The famous October light of Peking invited contemplation and reflection. And without doubt the time had come for Georges to do some thinking.

With a gesture he dismissed the chauffeur who waited at the wheel of the ageless Chevrolet assigned to him. Aimlessly he entered Wang Fu-chin, the main shopping street of the capital, and headed purposefully away from the hotel.

Soon his eyes were caught by the giant poster-cartoons which ornamented the intersection. Liu Shao-chi, "the Chinese Khrushchev," and his wife Wang Kwang-mei were represented in the most humiliating and grotesque attitudes: licking the boots of Khrushchev, soaking up with delight along with him the repulsive juice which poured out of a rotting fish representing moribund capitalism, and then being crushed like so many turds under the vengeful boot of a gigantic and valorous Chinese proletarian. Other minor dignitaries of this hell of the Cultural Revolution also figured in the gallery of horrors. As he looked, Georges recognized the big glasses, the large forehead and prominent chin of the man he had come here to find, Chen Wu-hsieh. The caption was of course in Chinese characters. This newborn figure among the "ghosts and monsters" groveled and grimaced before a hideous caricature of a man in a tropical hat, the symbol of colonialism, who held out a sack of dollars to him. At his side a man with a hook nose, bloody hands, and a patch over his eye portrayed Zionism slaughtering the Arabs.

"Our friend has got himself into a fine fix . . ."

This remark, in French, startled Georges, who foolishly believed for half a second that he had been expressing his thoughts aloud. He turned. A great hulk of a European, dressed *à la chinoise* in a rather elegant "Sun Yat-sen outfit" of light gray, with a cap of the same color on his head, was smiling amiably.

The black hair, the slightly sagging middle, the cigarette

23

butt hanging from his mouth, the simian arms, most of all the enormous feet shod in the felt slippers worn by most city Chinese, left no room for mistake. Georges faced his official contact, Michel Loriot. According to his instructions from Paris, this was the man who was to help him in his mission.

"I've been waiting for your phone call," Georges shot at him in a show of bad temper.

"I thought it would be better to meet you by chance on the street. I was at the reception just now and was able to identify you by the picture in the front of your book, and I followed you. It was a good idea leaving by foot. Incidentally, I liked your book very much. It's ingenious, well put together. The whole treatment of the OAS is excellent, and so is the business on the role of the witch doctors as revolutionary cadres in Black Africa."

"Thank you," Georges answered automatically.

"But we're not here to talk literature, even anticolonial literature. Let's move along, OK?"

"Loriot is a dangerous character but efficient," Mr. Marcel had said. "To be handled with care. He's not a professional, but since you aren't either there is no reason why you shouldn't get along very well."

"Is he reliable?" Georges had asked.

"Never mind. He's well placed and he has an excellent cover." (Georges had little stomach for the word "cover," which, in the specialized jargon of the Service, "covered" so badly a multitude of sins.)

"Oh? What's that?"

"He is an 'expert' to the Chinese. He translates foreign language publications mostly. He has lived in Peking for two years. He has cultivated excellent relationships. Oh, he's a bright one all right, a real brain! And what an orientalist! I even think he translated part of the Little Red Book of Chairman Mao into French. Which gives you an idea of the confidence they have in him. And he knows our client Chen very well."

24

"If that's so," Georges protested, "why do you have to call on me? He seems infinitely better placed than I to see this thing through."

"Just because the position Loriot occupies in Peking would prejudice Chen against any move coming from him. He'd be more comfortable with an emissary from Paris, commissioned directly by us. Which is where you come in. Loriot is in charge of all the dirty work. As a journalist you know very well the difference between a permanent correspondent and a visiting one who arrives on the scene to reap all the glory, to get the interview the guy on the spot spent months setting up. OK, with us it's the same thing. You're the special correspondent in Peking, but with a double assignment—one from your sheet and the other from us. And even more, Chen knows you quite well, he trusts you, he's practically invited you to Peking . . ."

Georges trotted at the side of his taller companion who loped along in great strides. In his European dress—the dark suit he had put on for the reception—Georges felt conspicuous in the featureless, uniform crowd containing so many faces he had not yet learned to tell apart. He could find nothing familiar in the picture to cling to. The windows of the stores were covered by layer on layer of posters, the lettering of which was totally unintelligible and thus seemed all the more provocative. In front of each of the posters stood a compact and wordless crowd. Thousands just as silent cycled up and down the avenue. Gauze masks, once white, now dusty gray, hid half the faces of many passers-by, making them look like halves of invisible men or like shabby surgeons AWOL from their operating rooms. Georges, who had not yet had the chance to circulate on a Chinese street, wondered what brought on this strange feeling of dreaming and abstraction. Suddenly he understood. These Pekingese had no visible sex. In their dress, even in their walk, it wasn't easy to distinguish the men from the women. Only the very small children, dressed in quilted silks of reds, yellows, and blues, cast a note

25

of color here and there among the dull multitude. Georges reproached himself, while indulging these observations, for having absorbed too much of the bad anticommunist literature of the writers who had come here before him. You'll have to find something more original, he said to himself.

Loriot froze in front of the first poster, which was a kind of cartoon saga, a serial in twenty panels that covered the extent of a long fence. From the top pocket of his jacket he took out a pad and pen and began to take notes, calmly, like two of the people beside him. He paid no attention to Georges, who began to feel uneasy. Trying to put on a good face, Georges shifted from one foot to the other. He was bored. It was not at all the way he had imagined the meeting which he figured would hold so much risk, even before he had made the slightest move that could make him guilty in his own eyes or in the eyes of the Chinese authorities. But he thought, things being what they were, it was high time to get down to business and, if the risks proved excessive, to let his companion know that he could not count on him any longer, as he had virtually decided a few hours ago.

Suddenly he noticed that except for Loriot, who continued to cover his red notebook with ideograms, and him, they were alone facing the wall. Behind them a crowd had gathered in a semi-circle and were watching the two without saying a word.

And then in the first rank a very young man, almost a kid, pimply, moonfaced, with a mop of straight hair, raised his arms and shouted something, a sort of raucous, brutal command, at regular intervals as in calisthenics, to brush against gether, their fists thrust forward. In every right hand was the Little Red Book transformed into a physical as well as an ideological weapon. The "masses" in front used it, on command, at regular intervals as in calisthenics, to brush against the noses of Georges and Loriot.

"What are they yelling?" Georges asked.

26

To avoid being noticed he spoke through closed lips—as in bad spy novels, he thought with savage self-mockery.

"Down with Soviet revisionists!"

"Can't you tell them we're not Russian?"

"There's no telling them anything. They could get pretty mean."

"I suppose you call this nice?"

"Relatively. As long as they don't start beating us up."

But the circle tightened around them. About thirty men and women, most of them young like their chief and sporting scarlet brassards with gold letters, took positions between them and the wall of posters. The two Europeans were surrounded on all sides by tortured, grimacing faces, mouths agape. One might have expected to see their imprecations coming out in balloons, in comic-strip fashion. Faces distorted by hate—another cliché made real, Georges thought. The shouted slogans found their own tempo as a growing crowd joined the chorus. The street was now clogged and the traffic stopped. Soldiers had come to join the Red Guards. "Take a look," Loriot whispered, still as calm as before. "Here we have the cadres, the workers, and the military. They have realized the 'triple alliance' according to the precepts of Chairman Mao."

A Little Red Book skimmed against Georges' cheek, a fist pressed against his back—not hard, but physical contact just the same. Even more disagreeable was the warm breath from all the open mouths against the back of his neck; the cursing of the mob sprayed saliva all over his nose and closely pressed lips.

A rough scrimmage erupted within the circle of hate. Someone tried to plough his way through. There was silence. Then a phrase in Russian. Loriot gestured to show that he did not understand. A kind of oldish little girl, all bent over, bow-legged, iron-rimmed glasses on her nose, the shiny black hair, bowl-cut and straight sticking out from under a shapeless cap, began to read in barely intelligible French a question that had been written in advance in her notebook: "French imperialists, why do you come to insult the Chinese masses?"

Her voice grated like a door that needed oiling.

Georges got ready to answer. Loriot spoke first in his best Mandarin:

"We are not imperialists. I myself am an expert at the service of the Chinese people. My comrade is an Algerian combatant invited by your government."

"French imperialists," repeated the woman in exactly the same tone, "why do you come to insult the Chinese masses?"

Patiently, Loriot repeated his explanation, twice, three times, four times, only to have to listen inexorably to the same reproach again and again.

Another cadre—obviously her superior, as one could see from his manner, the better cut of his tunic, the three pens clipped to his breast pocket—then stepped forward. He also spoke in French, but almost without accent: "My comrades want to know why you try to penetrate our secrets of state and act as spies against us."

Guiltily Georges felt himself begin to pale. Was he discovered already? But he understood at once that, under the circumstances, "spying" meant Loriot's copying the subject of the poster in his notebook. He cursed his companion's lack of caution. "For an honorable correspondent, he's really gifted," he said to himself. But Loriot, who seemed a little worried a while ago, had regained his composure.

"We try to understand your great proletarian Cultural Revolution," he ventured, "in order to put Chairman Mao's teachings to work in our country."

The others began yelping their insults again. With a sign, the man of the three pens enjoined silence.

"What country does the comrade come from?" he asked pointing at Georges.

28

Before Georges had time to answer Loriot spoke in his place.

"From Algeria, where the people, hardened by years of victorious struggle against the colonialist French, admire, love, and venerate Chairman Mao and the great proletarian Cultural Revolution."

Georges didn't understand a word of this exchange. He had the feeling he was watching one of those "palavers," in the old adventure films, between the cannibals and the unhappy voyagers they are getting ready to devour.

But in movies there is always a diversion at the right moment to save the heroes: lightning strikes the witchdoctor, a helicopter lands in the clearing, or the U.S. cavalry comes on at a gallop. This time it was a tattoo of car horns. Four trucks had been held back by the density of the mob which kept the Europeans prisoner. Two astonishing figures were perched atop the cabs of each of the vehicles. Covering them were big paper headpieces, like the penitential hoods heretics of the Middle Ages wore on their way to the stake in an auto-da-fé. The vigorous fists of their guards kept their heads bowed low in an attitude of supplication and repentance. The faces of the damned had a grayish, ashen cast. Over their chests were hung large white placards giving their names in two or three Chinese characters.

Other passengers on the trucks raised a dreadful uproar behind them. They howled on, enumerating their crimes, while whistles, gongs, and tambourines intensified the racket. A car with a loudspeaker, all its windows covered over with posters, picked up and amplified the cacophony.

As the crowd made way for this sinister convoy, Loriot took Georges by the shoulder.

"Let's get out of here," he said.

As a matter of fact no one paid them any attention. All eyes were turned toward the official "ghosts and monsters" who were exposed to general opprobrium. As the two men stole between the first and second trucks, the engines started again.

"Look at the guy on the left, the guy with the tassel, the big yellow dunce cap," Loriot whispered to Georges.

There could be no mistake. That crucified face, those half-closed eyes belonged to Chen Wu-hsieh.

Georges felt like vomiting. He had seen with his own eyes, from Algeria to the Congo, a good number of atrocities, massacres, and even tortures. But the ceremonial of humiliation to which these men were subjected in this village-fair atmosphere, with an accompaniment of these sonorous and almost cheerful rhythms, as well as the total submissiveness shown by the victims turned his stomach. And the maotay he had downed with the Russian at the reception was still with him.

Totally calm again and at a brisk pace, Loriot guided his companion toward his hotel and pointed out the practical lessons to be got from the episode.

"They certainly are clever in Paris!" he exclaimed bitterly. "It'll really be easy to make contact with Chen Wu-hsieh now! Last week it wouldn't have been a problem. But now!"

"We've got to give up," Georges added quickly. "Chen is obviously done for. They probably have discovered what he's up to."

"Not so fast," Loriot checked him. "Things are never that simple or that clear in China. If we were in any other country I'd say the jig is up, let's clear out. Here that's not necessarily the case. You're right though, I don't see how we'll be able to set up the contact. Unless you put on a Red Guard outfit and got to the next accusation rally. Wait, that might not be as crazy as it sounds. Give it some thought."

Georges stared round-eyed at his companion.

"You must be kidding!"

But Loriot just went on with his monologue.

"The problem is," he said loftily, "that I have no way now to communicate with Paris and get new instructions. Ordi-

30

narily I go through channels at the French embassy. But the embassy has been practically under siege for four days by Red Guards from the Diplomatic Institute. There's no chance either for you the anticolonialist hero or for me, the expert in the service of People's China, inside. And the friend I have there who is usually in charge of messages—I won't tell you his name if they didn't tell you in Paris—"

Georges shook his head.

". . . has received express orders from the ambassador himself not to frequent any public places—no hotels or restaurants. The diplomats leave their place at San Li Tun in the new legation area only to go to the embassy fifty yards away. In any case, it'd be much too dangerous, the way things are, for that approach. And what's more, Paris is even less capable of judging the situation than we are here. And that's not much!"

At the intersection of Wang Fu-chin and Chang An, a long people's parade stopped them. Thousands of women, young and old, puffy and fleshless, some with their cotton dresses swollen by advanced pregnancy, others dragging small children, but all uniformly ugly, inched forward at a slow pace. The young women acting as squad leaders, more resolute in their expression, read a series of slogans from photostats. The flock repeated them faithfully, each time raising their knotty and chapped hands to the sky, clutching the inevitable Little Red Book.

"Here they are, knitting commandos on their way to the Central Committee!" said Loriot. "It's one of the daily demonstrations demanding that Liu Shao-chi be handed over to the crowd. Just routine. . . . But to get back to our problem, I'm going to think about it and I'll call you up in the morning, about nine, to tell you if I've found a solution."

"Is that wise?"

"What is wise here nowadays? We happened to meet this afternoon at the reception. Stick to that. I offered to show you the House of Friendship (that's where the foreign experts

31

live) so you could meet some people from North Africa. All of which is pretty believable. You know, things are so disorganized, it's no use looking for too complicated or too coherent an explanation. The only thing is not to attract attention with any kind of extravagant behavior."

They were in front of the Hsin Chao Hotel. Without saying goodby, Loriot turned on his heels. His tall figure melted into the bluish crowd roaming the Hatamen sidewalks.

3 ● ABOVE THE DOOR of the "European" dining room on the seventh floor of the Hsin Chao Hotel, the staff Revolutionary Committee had carefully calligraphed in Chinese, Russian, and English (so that no client could plead ignorance) the vengeful warning "Dog heads of Soviet revisionists forbidden."

In front of the sign, a graphic symbol of China's ingratitude toward the great Moscow ally, Zagachvili had taken his place to wait for Georges. The meeting with Loriot had made him forget his date with the Georgian. He is pushing the provocation a little far, Georges thought when he saw Zagachvili standing there. He foresaw the dreadful scene: the waiters refusing to serve the diplomat, by the same token he himself manhandled, the Chinese press getting hold of the incident, the authorities demanding his expulsion from the African delegation.

But Zagachvili pretended not to see him. With a discreet wink he indicated the elevator and then dived into it.

The prospect of sharing Abdouldawe's table, with his secretary who specialized in currency trading, with his wife and the official interpreters assigned to them, to listen for the fifth time to a recitation of all the speeches the champion of Somalia expected to make until the end of his stay, his comments on the political importance he had in his hosts' minds and on the honors prepared for him—so much greater and

32

more merited than those conceded to that idiot from Zimbabwe, that imposter, and the one from Angola, that crook! —all this settled it for Georges. Without doubt the Soviet's conversation would be more instructive. And he ought to find out what he had up his sleeve.

It was not hard to find him in a black Volga with diplomatic plates parked on the terrace in front of the hotel. As soon as Georges got in beside him, the Georgian started off, his foot to the floor.

"You look like you had five hundred thousand Red Guards on your heels," Georges observed.

"There might be something to that," answered Zagachvili. "You saw the sign inside. These people are crazy, damn crazy!"

Obviously his blood was up. Without letup he honked at the cyclists, at the hand-drawn two-wheeled carts, at the trucks and trolleys crawling along the street, as if these clamorous warnings were meant to express the full force of his rage.

"When I think that you were the ones to forbid 'dogs and Chinese' access to public parks in Shanghai and that it's up to us now to take the rap!" he hurled at Georges.

"I'm not an 'imperialist'; I proved it in Algeria and a lot of other places," Georges bridled. "I've no responsibility whatever for all the wrongs heaped on the Chinese in the past, which is more than you Russians can say."

The other laughed.

"First, I'm not a Russian, but a Georgian. Maybe you do work for the Algerians—but certainly not only for them. Anyway, you're French, and when all is said and done, in the eyes of our Chinese friends, an out-and-out imperialist. In any case, we are both—how would you say it?—in the same boat, which is beginning to look like Gericault's raft from the *Medusa*. Let's not argue."

The car had left the main arteries and swept into a narrow street, with blind walls on both sides and very few doors.

33

Children of all sizes were playing in the middle of what was a standard Pekingese "hutung." They stepped back grudgingly, after repeated blasts from the horn, to make way for the Volga. Small fists were brandished at the foreigners. On Zagachvili's advice, Georges closed his window. But he could see on the children's lips the usual curses: "Down with the Soviet revisionists!" The windshield soon became starry with spit. A small group immobilized them for some time: two urchins marched in the first rank, their heads low under miniature "big caps." They were the "enemies of the people." Behind them, a whole crowd of budding avengers recited a list of make-believe crimes.

"It's amazing to see how their political consciences develop at such an early age," Zagachvili commented.

Georges resisted the temptation to remind him of a certain illustrious Georgian who, in his time, in his country, had succeeded in laying down the same kind of public morals, and to ask him if he had then made as much of a fuss.

The car stopped in front of a large red wooden door with copper handles. The two men entered a courtyard where about thirty Chinese, settled around small tables, were merrily gorging themselves. A fat, sweaty man, almost completely bald, wearing a filthy apron, came running to meet them.

He bowed and scraped, smiling and greeting them lavishly. Once again Georges began to feel like "a distinguished foreigner" in traditional China, the China of politeness, gaiety, and sumptuous fare. The guests, busy knitting with their chopsticks, paid them no attention. At the end of their meal perhaps they would rejoin the great stream of the Cultural Revolution and enthusiastically beat up any revisionists or imperialists pointed out to them. Georges savored this brief respite.

They were installed in a private room ornamented with a large portrait of Mao and some of his quotations. A few minutes later, about ten dishes were piled up simultaneously on the table: crisp Mandarin fish under its own sweet gravy, dried jellyfish with cucumbers, fried crusty ducklings, slices of beef highly spiced and peppered à la Szechwanese, sweet and sour pork, chicken diced in small squares, in little balls, in strips, and the specialty of the house, a sort of cake of noodles, fried and caramelized, covered by a meringue sauce. As giddy as ever, the manager himself poured lukewarm rice wine into tiny cups and then retired quietly.

"This is the Four Tables, one the oldest restaurants of the capital," explained Zagachvili, who liked to show off his familiarity with everything Pekingese. "Szechwanese specialties. As a matter of fact it's what almost ruined them. Last summer, at the beginning of the Cultural Revolution, the Red Guards decided to turn it, like almost all the big restaurants, into a soup kitchen. Only steamed rice, noodles, and spareribs were served, the whole thing for five maos, a little more than a dollar. To have a real meal at that time was considered a disgraceful vestige of the bourgeois and feudal past. Customers were often beaten up. That at least didn't last. The good nature of the Chinese got the upper hand—which should give us some hope for the future of the country," he added with a boring insistence, going to any length to establish that Georges was indeed on the same anti-Chinese side as he was.

In the same fluent tone, with his vibrant and melodious voice, the r's slightly rolled, he went on.

"But it was at this time that they began to be really in trouble, because as you know, the Szechwan province has a very bad political reputation. It happens that the man who just served us—as the beef you're enjoying proves so abundantly—comes from Chengtu, the capital of Szechwan, a region more or less under the 'revisionists.' The Maoists had a hell of a time setting up a Revolutionary Committee. Blood flowed there for months. To top it off, old Chu Teh, a Szechwanese, was a regular here himself. Think of it, a really disgusting type—Mao's companion in arms from the early

35

days, a founder of the Red Army, and an organizer of the Long March, who pretends to have played a part in the history of the Chinese Revolution! Someone who went so far in his blackness as to sing the praises of his dead mother! . . . It was intolerable. So they closed the restaurant. It reopened a few months later after Chu Teh was seen again on the official podium on May Day. But I'm sure this won't last and it won't be long before it's closed again. Especially once my visit has been recorded!"

Gravy trickled down his chin and dripped on his shirt. Fibers of pork clung to his mustache. Around his bowl were chicken bones, fish bones, gluey noodles, and the accumulated seepage of various sauces. Between oratorical flights, he gobbled enormous chunks of food picked up with his chopsticks from the bowl which he held higher than his chin. One can see he is an "old China hand," noted Georges, who was well read. But he wondered what was the point of this lecture on the tormented history of a Pekingese restaurant during the Cultural Revolution. The yellow wine, the abundance and the succulence of the food, the purring delivery of the Georgian, added to the emotions of the day, began to have a soporific effect. But a name, dropped into the monologue, took him out of his torpor.

"I've seen Chen Wu-hsieh many times these last few days," Zagachvili proclaimed after having sucked up with a revolting slurp a spoonful of chicken broth just put on the table by way of dessert. "A charming man, very easy to take. But that's not news to you."

"What makes you think I'm especially interested in Chen?" Georges said. Zagachvili looked at him with a half-smile. He poured himself a glass of yellow wine and gulped it down. Then, very much the peasant, he wiped his mustache with the back of his hand. Obviously the alcohol had begun to work.

"Let's say that my—" by now he was stammering slightly—

36

"my superiors have told me the real reason you're here. As you know, the positions of Paris and Moscow nowadays are very close on many key points, on China in particular. I'm sure you too have been told to cooperate with us."

Georges shook his head, but the other persisted.

"We've known Chen's real feelings for a long time. In fact, they are shared by quite a number of highly placed individuals in the ruling bodies. Chen was in touch with us before he was with your bosses. But, for the moment, we're too closely watched to be able to attempt anything. That's why my superiors and yours—I don't have to name them, do I?— had decided between them to set up his departure and his resettlement in Cambodia."

"I don't understand a word you're saying," Georges interrupted. "Even if, which isn't the case, I was interested in Chen more than in any other leader, since he is chairman of the Afro-Asian Committee, I haven't been given any kind of secret mission concerning him. And believe me, it has never been planned that we work in connection with the Soviets in any such business. More than that, you're certainly better aware than I am of the situation Chen is in at the present time. I saw him this afternoon, with my own eyes, wearing the big paper cap, right in Wang Fu-chin."

Zagachvili winced.

"You're sure it was he? . . . You saw him close?"

"Just as I see you. The truck he was in passed three yards away."

"Well now . . . So, he's still in Peking. Perhaps it's not all lost. Now we must work hand in hand more than ever!" exclaimed the diplomat who seemed under the stress of extreme agitation. "It's urgent, very urgent. Because we're literally at the brink of war. And a man like Chen can play an essential part in preventing it."

In vain Georges tried to dampen the diplomat's ardor, but he got louder and louder, disregarding the manager who had

37

entered unobtrusively. There was no stopping Zagachvili; he didn't listen. He talked to himself, apparently a prey to an obsession.

"The Americans and the Chinese (we now have irrefutable proof of it) agree on the essentials. They agree to let the Vietnam war go on, intensified more and more every day. It's in the interest of the Americans because they need a victory at any price. And the Chinese—let's say more simply the Maoist clique—wants to demonstrate "Soviet impotency" in helping a people of the socialist camp. Believe me, they had very definite contacts to work this out, under the cover of purely verbal outbursts on either side. And not only between the American and Chinese ambassadors in Warsaw. In Hong Kong, too, and in various African capitals like Cairo and Algiers. Certain representatives of the National Liberation Front of South Vietnam were approached. That was when the Western press talked about contacts between America and the North Vietnamese. It was true, these contacts did exist, but they were under Chinese patronage. Their only concern was to eliminate all Soviet influence. American military circles and the CIA in Saigon had a full hand in the operation; they played Mao Tse-tung's card to the end. And Chen Wu-hsieh, because of his trips to Africa and Asia, because of his relationship with Arab leaders in particular, was in a better spot than anyone else to know all about it. Maybe you haven't been told, but this is the reason France is so interested in him, and why we are too. For the first time perhaps since the October Revolution, French and Soviet intelligence cooperated directly on a definite matter and against Washington."

He slavered with enthusiasm and good will. Faced with the yellow peril and American barbarity, "the good old Franco-Russian alliance" was reemerging. "Here we are—a Georgian gumshoe, a compatriot and doubtlessly an admirer of Stalin, formed without doubt in the Beria school, and I, the 'red foot' who doesn't know any more whom he's working for in

38

Algiers, in Tunis, or in Paris—here we both are in Peking, raised to the rank of united defenders of Western civilization!" Georges ruminated under the effect of a sweet digestive cheerfulness. The irony seemed delectable to him, and especially his own capacity to appreciate it at such a moment. He wondered, too, if Zagachvili had purposely failed to mention, in this exhibition of cooperativeness, the role played by Chen on the Atomic Research Committee.

"In short, what, concretely"—one of the favorite adverbs in discussions among left-wing intellectuals—"do you expect from me?" he asked after a long pause.

The other burped loudly.

"You'll know when the time comes. I'll let you know. Don't worry. And please don't make any move before we get in touch. I think I'll have accurate information on Chen within a day or two. He's really the key figure, and the others know it very well."

"Which others?" Georges asked.

But the Georgian had put his head on the table among all the leftovers, the dirty bowls, and the miniature ossuary he had piled up before him. He had fallen asleep, his mouth open—the candid sleep of a drunkard. Georges wondered, in dismay, what he was going to do with him. To abandon a Soviet diplomat in a Pekingese restaurant, in the present predicament, would be to expose him to the bloody violence of the Red Guards or at best to provoke an international scandal in which he himself would be entangled. He began to shake him insistently and emptied a whole bottle of mineral water over his head without the least effect.

The manager appeared, shook his head in disapproval, and left. He returned accompanied by all the members of his staff and some Chinese customers who exchanged delighted winks and what sounded like sarcasm to Georges, who paid the check and tried, in English and without success, to have someone call a taxi for him. At this point the altogether grotesque and dangerous aspect of the scene irked him. Really secret agents, whatever their nationality, impressed him less and less.

Forcing his way through the smirking audience, a little bucktoothed bespectacled Oriental in Chinese dress came up to him. From the pocket of his quilted jacket he removed a card and, with neat precision, held it out to Georges. He took it mechanically and read: "TAKEO YOSHIWARA, Special Correspondent, *Hokkaido Shimbun*." An address in Tokyo had been crossed out and replaced by Hsin Chao Hotel.

Georges groped in his pocket in search of a nonexistent card to give the Japanese in exchange. The latter addressed him in English.

"The manager told me you were in trouble. Colleagues must help one another out. Mr. Zagachvili doesn't hold his wine too well!" He accompanied this with a sort of happy whinny. "I'll call his embassy from the hotel to have someone pick him up. If it's all right with you I'll take you home. I think it's better not to linger here."

Very grateful, Georges left the restaurant with the little Japanese. Three of his compatriots, among them a woman, waited for him in a car surrounded by a pack of children.

"My wife and colleagues," Yoshiwara said with a vague wave of the arm toward them.

They emitted whistlings of Nipponese politeness and bowed. Georges took his place in front beside his host at the wheel. Three hundred yards further on the car stopped at the intersection of the main street. The two men got out and, with the narrow beams from pencil flashlights, began to decipher the panels of an endless poster. Mrs. Yoshiwara put a portable typewriter on her knees and, at their dictation, typed directly in Latin characters the Japanese translation of the text. Georges recognized certain names in passing: Liu Shao-chi, Chen Yi, the Minister of Foreign Affairs, and other high officials.

"It's for my paper," the Japanese explained with his ner-

40

vous whinny. "They accuse Liu Shao-chi of attempting an assassination against Mao Tse-tung in 1950 in order to re-install the capitalistic regime. Nothing very new, just routine. They also write about Chen Wu-hsieh. You know, the chairman of the Afro-Asian Committee. A very interesting personage, don't you think?"

Georges shuddered. Chen's name was starting to seem like some sort of password.

"I have," the Japanese said after a brief silence, "a rather complete file in my room on various personalities and particularly on Chen. If you wish to consult it, it's at your disposal. This evening even, if you're not too tired. As a matter of fact, I think you're next door to us; you're number 572 and I'm 574. It's very convenient. The bellboys in this hotel are, to say the least, inquisitive!"

He whinnied again at length. Georges didn't quite see what was so funny in these remarks. He wondered how he could find a way to put off giving Yoshiwara an answer. If only he could reach Loriot. But he had no way to do it. "You really won't have to take any initiative," Mr. Marcel had said in the café on the Batignolles. Mr. Marcel. There was somebody he'd really like to see right now, in this car, listening to that nasal voice dictating a telegram in Japanese, the crackling of Mrs. Yoshiwara's typewriter, and the short sentences of the husband, apparently insignificant but which seemed to wrap him in a cocoon of unavowed complicities and near confidences. His silence, he was aware, could not but implicate him even more.

His passivity in the face of events and the contradictory solicitations he had received surprised him. He found himself in front of Yoshiwara's desk, a glass of scotch in his hand. The young woman and the two other journalists had disappeared. They had to take the cable to the post office, the Japanese had vaguely explained. He made no move to look for the file he had mentioned. He could just as well have lured me here with talk about Japanese prints; it would have been even more appropriate, Georges thought, still very detached.

"Keep your eye on Zagachvili," Yoshiwara burst out without preamble. "He's not only an agent of the Soviet secret service, but above all an idiot. In fact, all the Soviet diplomats in Peking are spies, intelligence maniacs obsessed by hatred of everything Chinese. I'm surprised that a man like you associates with them. It's incautious, very incautious."

He spoke quite loud, his mouth almost glued to the telephone on the night table. It was clear he wanted to be heard.

"But what a bad host I am," he said. "I promised to let you listen to some of my records of Japanese music. I'm sure you'll like them."

With this, he winked collusively and turned on the record player. Sour music filled the room.

"It's because of the bugs," he said in a half-voice. "There's one in the telephone of course and probably one or two in the walls."

"That I understood," Georges said quite drily. It was becoming a bore being taken for an amateur by people who didn't seem any more professional than he.

But as soon as the record began, Yoshiwara changed his tack.

"You've put yourself in a very bad position. The Chinese certainly know all about the goal of your mission and the interest you have in Chen Wu-hsieh. First because you have accumulated mistakes since you arrived. Second because you are eminently suspect yourself. I'm astonished they haven't arrested you yet. Maybe they want to see how far you will go, and especially whether you have access to an organized network here. That's why I talked so loud in front of the telephone about Zagachvili. I tried to divert their suspicions. But it's probably too late."

Very agitated, he paced the room. He spoke in a jerky, barking way. Like the officers of the Imperial Japanese army

42

in old American movies, thought Georges, who was fond of cinematic comparisons.

He tried to stem the flow of words.

"You're pretty badly informed," he broke in. "I met the Soviet diplomat for the first time this afternoon at the reception for the African delegation. You were there too, I should imagine. He invited me to dinner. I had nothing better to do so I accepted. All of which is no concern of yours. As for Chen Wu-hsieh, I heard his name mentioned as chairman of the Afro-Asian Committee and learned after I got here that he's been having trouble with the Red Guards, like a lot of other people right now. That's all. Thanks for bringing me back to the hotel. But these melodramatic insinuations about a mission I'm supposed to be assigned to are perfectly ridiculous—in fact, totally incomprehensible. So now if you'll excuse me, I'm going to bed."

He stood up, attempting an air of dignity, and made his way to the door. At just that moment, there was a shuddering clap.

A bellboy barged in, carrying a tray with a water carafe and a glass. He grabbed a glass from the night table, replaced it with the one on the tray, filled it with water, turned back the bedspread, fluffed the pillow and left the room without a glance at either of the two occupants.

A little surprised, they looked at each other. The unexpected intrusion, seemingly fortuitous, eased the tension somewhat.

"Wait a minute. Don't leave, for your own sake," insisted Yoshiwara. "This is more serious than you seem to think. A long time ago Chen himself made a report of your conversation with him in Algiers. Since then you've been a marked man. The problem is to know whether or not they judge the time ripe for accusing you. Their only risk is that by doing so they might antagonize the 'progressive' elements in the Arab countries and in Black Africa."

"You ought to write spy stories; you'd probably do better

43

in that than in journalism, where a certain amount of truth is necessary," Georges tossed out without too much conviction.

Taking him by the arm to turn him around, Yoshiwara was plainly exasperated. His round face was flushed and shiny with sweat.

"We don't need amateurs around here to make the job more complicated! You're done for, completely done for, do you understand what that means?"

Someone knocked, this time not so abruptly. The door opened. A young Chinese girl came into the room. The two men froze where they were: Yoshiwara up against the table, his face red, pointing an accusatory finger at Georges, who was seated in a chair of ugly red velvet with a fake white lace on its back, his fists clenched, his mouth wide, ready to answer.

Relieved by the sudden appearance of his interpreter, Georges stood up politely. He had been surprised not to have seen her at the reception in the afternoon.

"Good evening, Miss Wang," he said extending his hand.

The previous days, she had irritated him with her sententiousness, her endless explanations of the simplest matters ("This is a railroad; here we have a public park," she would announce going over a grade crossing or passing a garden). But just then he could have kissed her. She had saved him momentarily from a very embarrassing discussion and from the disquieting specifics that the Japanese was getting ready to hit him with—the veracity of which he would be hard put to comment on, let alone react to.

As for the Japanese, he seemed a trifle embarrassed, as if they had been caught together in a compromising position. He looks like he's morally zipping his fly, Georges thought, resenting the unpleasant moments he had just passed in his company.

"If you're finished with this gentleman—" she said, contemptuously pointing toward the Japanese to underline what

44

was already pejorative in this title coming from a Chinese "—would you mind following me so that we can prepare tomorrow's program?"

He followed her without a word. To his astonishment, instead of going toward the elevator to hold their "work conference" in the main lobby, as on previous evenings, she stopped at the door of his room and quietly waited for him to take out his key and open it. The bellboy in charge of renewing the carafes did not turn his head.

"May I sit down?" she asked.

Without waiting for an answer she made herself comfortable on the bed, took a Shanghai cigarette from the pocket of her beige gabardine tunic, and lighted it. Then she offered him one. He shook his head and remained standing, slightly puzzled. Until now she had always refused his cigarettes ("We have better things to do than smoke, we young Chinese. We are building socialism").

She slowly inhaled, then artfully exhaled the smoke through her nostrils. She obviously had seen "decadent" films. Then she smiled frankly, sweetly, looking Georges straight in the eye. It was the first time she had smiled, and the first time since he had arrived in China five days ago that someone had made a gratuitous gesture.

But it is certainly a facade, he thought. More than ever, I'd better be on guard. He noticed that she was pretty, very pretty, even with her straight hanks of hair tied into pigtails by two little red ribbons, her fairly thick lips (Cantonese descent?), and her girlish round cheeks and chin.

"Why don't you sit down?" she said, fluffing the bed around her.

Events were taking a decidedly singular turn. Georges obeyed without a word. Throughout this long day, he realized, he had been playing the part of the watchful and astonished observer—he, Georges Benachen, whom his friends from Saint-Germain-des-Prés had nicknamed "the operator."

From the other pocket over her breast, which seemed to

45

Georges suddenly much more rounded than before, she took a note pad with a quote from Lin Piao calligraphed in gold on its cover, and a pencil, which she sucked at nonchalantly.

"Tomorrow," she began in her most official tone, "I suggest that you accompany the delegation on a visit to the Revolutionary Museum."

Talking and still smiling, she unhooked the upper button of her tunic. Perhaps she was too warm. She stood up then and casually went over to Georges' small transistor and turned it on. The manly strains of *The Great Helmsman* filled the room. She came back and sat down, closer this time. She took Georges' hand and squeezed it with force. Then, with the choirs still celebrating the Thought of Mao, she said: "You're horribly reckless in the company you keep. You begin with this Georgian, known by everyone as the principal representative of KGB at the USSR embassy, and you finish the evening in the room of one of the most notorious American agents in Peking. What are you up to? Do you want to be arrested? And have *me* arrested in the bargain?"

Georges noted with relief that she had not mentioned Loriot. "It doesn't take much to make me feel better," he said to himself. "I'll go merrily to the gallows thinking that they don't know everything. I'll be an intellectual to the end, able to analyze my emotions at the foot of the scaffold!"

This aspect of his nature always irritated him. He'd have liked to be a man of action, but he always found himself much too inclined to savor the pleasures of introspection.

As for Miss Wang, she seemed to prefer shared joys.

"Kiss me," the girl implored.

She drew him toward her. Georges had not been mistaken: She was well rounded. The rather rough cotton of her outfit was in no way feminine, but that was certainly not true of her body, which began to reveal itself. With her right hand she turned off the ceiling light, leaving only the bed lamp to light the scene of seduction in which the man was without doubt the prey. Her lips searched for Georges' without much

46

success. She covered him with clumsy kisses. "This is a provocation," he repeated to himself. The hotel room, the young interpreter, the bellboy. He'll surely appear any minute and open the door without knocking first. Every member of the staff has keys. He vaguely recalled a story told him in Paris before he left, about two Italian engineers assigned to the building of a factory who were caught in the same circumstances in a Chinese provincial town. Charged with rape, they were sentenced to a long jail term. The sentence was suspended a few months later only to allow the firm to carry out its contract, and under the strict condition that the Western Press never publish a word of the incident. "In my case who would bother?" But already fear had made room for curiosity, then for desire. Who among everyone he knew could brag that they had had a Red Guard? The pin of Miss Wang's scarlet brassard pricked his finger. His hand went on its way. One by one, he unhooked the buttons. She stood up to help him get rid of her tunic. She appeared frail and lithe in a flowered silk shirt, very feminine but tucked into an unfortunate pair of oversized slacks, with an enormous seat in which her pretty buttocks were lost.

Georges only had to untighten the belt and the slacks fell to the floor in a heap. She was wearing some sort of cheap cotton panties. She pushed them down very quickly. It was obvious that she was ashamed of her unattractive lingerie. But she was proud of her shirt, certainly an import from Hong Kong trimmed with a small round collar and shell buttons—frivolous adornments rejected with disgust by People's China.

He felt the young girl's nipples harden. She wore no brassiere, but not because she had no breasts. As they rolled together over the bed she bit his ear playfully, and arched her body so he could get into her more easily. There was no doubt about it, she was a virgin. He took her with a voracity he had thought himself no longer capable of after having been cuckolded so many times by Simone, his ex-wife.

("After all, if you're going to be shot . . .") It was then that the door half-opened. The bellboy stuck in his head, watched for an instant without a change in his expression, and closed the door.

"I'm done for," Georges said in a loud voice.

"Not at all," she whispered. "On the contrary; I just saved you."

He did not try to understand. Exhausted, he fell asleep, his head on the damp shoulder of the girl. Her skin was very soft.

The silence woke him up. The little Chinese girl had huddled against him, all curled up. Asleep, with her mouth half-open and her pigtails around her face, she again looked like a child. Her small, round breasts swelled gently.

From the wall Mao, the great educator, the great guide, the great commander-in-chief, and the great helmsman contemplated the couple benignly.

Georges rose up on his elbow: 2:30 in the morning. His move awakened his companion. She opened her eyes and smiled. Then she kissed him softly on the lips. She already aimed much better than before. She had benefited from the lesson. After that she put her finger to her nose to impose silence and ran naked to the transistor, which crackled miserably. She took it to the bed and, turning the dials, declared in her most "Cultural Revolution" tone, as if she was pursuing a conversation already in process, "Yes, you must understand me, Comrade Benachen. We young Chinese, hardened by the teaching of Chairman Mao and by the revolutionary fight, we definitively turn our backs"—matching action to words she playfully showed him her buttocks—"on the errors of the bourgeois past."

She put her mouth close to the telephone and gestured for Georges to try to find a program on his transistor. Then, in a thunderous voice: "In this great proletarian Cultural Revolution, we the children of the workers, of the peasants, of the soldiers and the martyrs, and of the revolutionary cadres, we

48

declare to all the beautiful people, to the out-and-out imperialists and revisionists: you are nothing but rotten eggs. We'll break your dirty dog legs! We'll oppose you to the end and crush all the plots, the counterrevo . . ."

Georges had finally got the Voice of America program, which at this late hour broadcast a jazz program. She stopped abruptly and closed her eyes with satisfaction. She turned the transistor to full volume and snuggled against Georges. Her lips on the pillow, she whispered: "Comrade, you're the victim of a provocation. I'm here under orders."

"I never had any doubt about it. I even expected to be arrested as soon as the bellboy closed the door. What will happen to me now? A public trial with accusation in due form in the *People's Daily*? The firing squad or what? Please note," he added with more gallantry than sincerity, "that I don't regret a thing."

"Nothing is going to happen to you, dummy!"

She savagely bit his ear.

"No," she went on, "it's far more complicated than that. See, we Chinese have known the real purpose of your trip from the day your application for a visa was deposited at the embassy in Algiers. We knew you would collaborate with comrade Chen Wu-hsieh and other turtle eggs to organize groups of opposition to the great proletarian Cultural Revolution."

Georges had expected that the girl, like every protagonist yesterday, would throw the name of Chen into the conversation. Apparently all Peking had this one name on its lips. Still, the precision of her talk was chilling. If I were James Bond, he thought, I would strangle this cutie right now, have her body disposed of, and go back to Washington in an atomic helicopter. Just for fun, he clutched lightly at the throat of comrade Wang, but the gesture turned to a caress; his hands moved along her breasts and rested on the hard little nipples.

"Go on," he said. "And tell me who made up this extraordinary thriller."

"Chen himself mentioned the conversation you had in Algiers, just after he got back to Peking."

For her it was that simple. She hated to have to spell out the obvious.

"You mean that Chen himself has set up this provocation?"

She went on again patiently, after remarking on his having slipped into the familiar *thou* and *thee*.

"One cannot imagine one of our leaders keeping a matter of this importance to himself. Or getting involved in it without a collective decision arrived at in advance."

"So Chen is hand in glove with Mao Tse-tung and his group?"

She smiled indulgently.

"With Chairman Mao certainly. Comrade Mao Tse-tung is our great educator, our great guide, our commander-in-chief, our . . ."

". . . great helmsman," Georges completed.

"Yes, great helmsman. And don't be sarcastic, it's an insult to the Chinese masses!"

"Forgive me," he whispered. "Let me kiss the Chinese masses to be forgiven."

She stiffened under his kiss: the time was no longer right for playing around. Then, like a teacher who doesn't let herself be upset by the childish interruptions of her pupils, she continued.

"Of course Comrade Chen works for Chairman Mao, for the great cause of the Chinese masses. Not for the clique that takes the advantage of his old age, of his fatigue after a whole life devoted to the service of socialism, and has grabbed the reins of power. It is in intimate agreement"—she lowered her voice again, her youthful lips buried in the pillow—"with the Thought of Mao that Chen decided to act, that he contacted you"—she corrected herself and used the familiar form again—"whom he considered an honest foreign comrade who sincerely keeps in mind the interest of the world revolution."

50

"And it's on Chen's orders that you're here with me . . ." —he hesitated a little—". . . dressed like this?"

"Oh no!" she objected. "Of course not. This is a collective decision of the Revolutionary Committee of the Institute of Foreign Languages. We held a meeting last week. And the comrades decided that the female interpreters assigned to foreign visitors should do everything possible to frustrate the counterrevolutionary plots they might hatch. Everything including . . ."—it was her turn to hesitate—"relationships like ours. Oh! everybody didn't agree! I said myself that it was a holdover of the detestable methods of the Kuomintang spies and the feudal era, that Soviet revisionists and American imperialists used the same methods. But then the comrades accused me of subjectivism and individualism. They told me that I attached too much importance to my own affairs, that I should proceed with my own reeducation by absorbing the teachings of my heroic comrades who sacrified ther lives for the people and for the triumph of the Thought of Mao Tse-tung. I was lucky though!" she added pensively. "My comrade Kuo, she is the personal interpreter for that fat African comrade, the one who sweats so much, and who always goes this way . . ." She puffed her cheeks and sputtered in a revolting way, a childish imitation of the honorable Diego Tombalou-wou, the hero of South Angola. "With him it must not be fun."

Georges considered himself flattered by this subtle tribute to his amorous talents.

"Let's get back to Chen," he said. "Apparently you think that he has been accused unjustly of bourgeois revisionist tendencies. But since you seem to know so many things, why don't you tell me what my part in all this is. Because, quite frankly, I don't understand a thing anymore. Except," he added, pulling her to him, "I do hope that, if I have to go to prison, you'll be in the same cell."

Annoyed, she pulled herself away from him.

51

"You say frivolous, stupid, typically bourgeois things," she proclaimed. "We have good reason to reject the decadent thoughts of the West that sap the revolutionary ardor of the peace-loving peoples."

She had abandoned all modesty; she had thrown the pillow which until now she had held against her mouth far to the side. Sitting up in bed, her breasts thrust out, hammering her words with her fist clenched, she resembled an oriental version of Rude's *La Marseillaise*.

She saw her reflection in the mirror. Astonished, she stopped abruptly and laughed.

"You know what," she confessed, "it's the first time since I was a kid that I've seen myself completely nude."

Georges was now totally confused.

"You know what," he replied, "it's the first time I ever talked high politics with a ravishing Red Guard completely nude. My mother always warned me to be careful with women. She was certainly right."

"Let's be serious," she said, holding the pillow tightly against her, tenderly, like a baby. "We haven't much time. It's Chen himself who chose me to be your interpreter. Besides, it has not been easy, because I was supposed to take part in the Cultural Revolution in Hupei this month with the comrades from the Institute of Foreign Languages."

Insistently Georges tried to resume his questioning. Too many threads continued to elude him.

"How can Chen be sure that you won't denounce him, that you won't be the leading witness against him?"

"He can't be sure. But I am his niece. He raised me. This I have hidden from the comrades, I haven't mentioned it in any of my applications for the university or for the Institute of Foreign Languages. What's more, he confided all his feelings and intentions to me when he returned from Algiers last spring. So my case would be at least as serious as his. Whatever you say, individual destinies are of no importance, Chen's, mine, yours—of no interest at all."

52

Georges felt that she was selling him pretty short. But it would not have been gallant of him, in this bed, to hold it against her. He sighed and tried to show his approval with a solemn nodding of the head and an expression he hoped was heroic enough. Ignoring all this, she went on.

"It's absolutely necessary for you to talk to Chen. You're our last hope. It won't be easy, especially now. But so much depends on it, for all of us! After all, you're a journalist. Here's what you must do: In a little while, when I come to pick you up at eight o'clock for the visit to the Revolutionary Museum, create a terrible scene in the lobby of the hotel. Claim that you haven't come here to play tourist, that you want to know the Cultural Revolution, not museums, that the past doesn't interest you, etc. You'd be acting like Edgar Snow or K. S. Karol if someone asked them, at this juncture in Peking, to go and visit a museum."

"Go on," said Georges, interested.

"Then you'll insist that you want to see an accusation meeting. Chen is to appear tomorrow afternoon in the Workers' Stadium along with a lot of others. After the meeting, I'll try to arrange an interview for you, pointing out its significance to the peoples of Africa who have suffered so much from his pro-imperialist manipulations. Maybe he'll be able to tell us all he has to."

"But really, if he's now a prisoner under the gun, what can he do? And why do I have to get involved in this ugly mess?"

She smiled sweetly.

"But you already are—how do you say?—up to your nose."

"To my neck," he corrected.

"Thank you. They aren't so good on idioms at the Institute. Especially since we only work in French from the works of Chairman Mao, translated I think by one of your friends."

One more illusion gone. Miss Wang apparently was also up on his relationship with Michel Loriot. Maybe it was actually better this way. "As a secret agent," he thought, "I'm really doing very well! Everybody around here knows what

53

I'm doing except me, and I don't understand a thing. I let them lead me around like a kid, and I seduce a girl who knows herself that it's enough to call in the cops and who wants to have me gather subversive messages in front of a hundred thousand Red Guards with all hell breaking loose! It's as silly as writing ads for counterrevolution on posters in large characters in invisible ink."

She looked at her wristwatch, which was the only thing left to ornament her nudity.

"Good God!" she exclaimed. "Three in the morning. I hardly have time . . ."

"Time for what?" Georges asked mechanically.

"To write my report, silly, on what we've been doing this evening!" (Blushing slightly.) "I mean on what you've told me."

"And what are you going to tell?"

"Oh! I'll find something! Don't foget to turn off the radio when I leave."

She quickly put on her clothes, resuming her anonymous virtuous look—a Red Guard among tens of millions. She rose on tiptoe and gave him a long kiss on the lips, the way he had taught her.

"Tomorrow, you'll understand better," she breathed. "But I'd like you to give me a little present."

He started. Now she was acting like a pro on Saint-Denis! Plainly there were more surprises to come. Quickly she reassured him. More out of modesty than for fear of security mikes, she spoke into his ear:

"Could you get one of your diplomatic friends to get something we can't find in China, and something I really need now . . . now that you've made a real woman of me?"

And then, even lower: "What ladies from the west put . . . every month . . . oh, you know . . ."

SATURDAY ●

● ● ● LIKE THE DAY before, the noisy accents of *The Great*
● ● ● *Helmsman* threw him out of bed at seven in the
● ● ● morning. He had not slept much since the girl left.
Any moment he had expected the Red Guards, or the Security
Police, to burst in, tommy guns ready. He was very tempted
to call in sick and ask to leave Peking by the next plane for
reasons of health.

However, he found himself in the lobby an hour later, Mao
button on his lapel, the perfect image of the progressive
journalist, the "friendly foreigner" come to eat up the manna
from the precious teachings of the Cultural Revolution.

Miss Wang—serious, her mouth pursed, pens in a row, her
cap screwed to her head, her bangs combed back in proletarian style, minus the cute little pigtails and their frivolous
red bows—symbolized again the virtues of the regime. For the
first time she wore those hideous rimless glasses. Georges
thought that, like most women, she had no sense of balance.
Everything in her behavior expressed the restrained disapproval which she must have felt, after the frolicking of last
night, toward the partner the collective decision had imposed
on her. In this way she made it plain that, though she had
done the job, she found herself politically soiled and, what
was more, had derived no pleasure from it.

She refused the hand he extended and greeted him with a
stiff nod of the head.

"The car is waiting to take us to the Revolutionary Museum," she announced without preamble. "This museum has
been totally renovated. At one time under the revisionist direction of Chu Yang, that rotten egg animated by savage
hatred of the Thought of Mao Tse-tung, they used to have
would-be 'relics,' objects and documents meant to recall the
steps in the proletarian march to power. But it was all meant
to mask the challenge to the supremacy of Mao's Thought
leveled by Chu Yang and his black band of bourgeois counterrevolutionaries. That's why there were no more than thirty-

56

three portraits of Chairman Mao there, but a great number of pictures of proved counterrevolutionaries, like Liu Shao-chi, the Chinese Khrushchev, Peng Te-huai, the traitor who wanted to put the Chinese armed forces at the service of Soviet revisionism, and many others. Now, there's nothing but photos of Chairman Mao, our great educator, our great guide, our great commander in chief, and great helmsman, and copies of his works translated into every language in the world. It's most interesting," she concluded, her face crimson with revolutionary ardor. (She had a little of the same expression last night when Georges initiated her into the world of pleasure.)

Georges burst out, "I haven't come to the People's Republic of China to see museums! You people are making fun of me! If that's all you have to show me I'm ready for the first plane back to Algiers!" That was probably the best solution anyway, he thought. "I want to see the man in charge!"

He had spoken with great vehemence, and many guests of the hotel, drawn by this explosion, began to gather in the lobby, quite entertained by the diversion.

Miss Wang took this loftily.

"The program has been arranged by the comrades responsible. There can be no question of change. You're free to protest if you like, or to discontinue your tour."

She turned on her heels. She was playing her part too well. Georges could not know if the scenario was still as they had written it the night before or if, on the contrary, she was trying to warn him that the plans had had to be changed at the last minute. At any rate he thought it was a good idea to make at least some effort at persuasion.

"Don't forget," he cried out, "I'm a friend of the Cultural Revolution, invited to Peking by the Afro-Asian Committee. My newspaper faces wild attacks from the imperialists and revisionists on the African continent, they want my report to help them meet these attacks."

She turned around, still an iceberg.

"If you have constructive criticism to offer, it will be taken into consideration," she announced.

Was this the green light? He decided to plunge.

"Yesterday someone translated some posters for me that announced a big accusation rally at the Workers' Stadium. A number of counterrevolutionaries will appear there, and among them . . . Chen Wu—" pretending to hesitate on the name—"you know, the old chairman of the Afro-Asian Committee. It just so happens that this man is known in Africa. I met him there myself."

The girl pouted disapproval. She had taken out her notebook and jotted down what Georges had said. Open-mouthed, ten or twelve members of the staff, leaning on their brooms or holding their trays, and two Japanese journalists watched what was going on without understanding a word.

"I want," said Georges in a tone of assurance, "to be at this rally so I can rub their noses in all their lies, this bourgeois revisionist press, and to assert that the Chinese people truly render a revolutionary justice. And also, if it's possible," he raised his eyes toward her to see if he was going too far, but he couldn't discern a thing, "to interview Chen so that he can disown personally all the calumnies which are probably being published everywhere against him."

Miss Wang did not blink. She went to the telephone. The conversation lasted a good fifteen minutes.

"It seems all right," she said to Georges when she came back. "But, for now, let's go to the Historical Museum."

At fifteen feet by nine, it was the most gigantic portrait of Mao he had seen since his arrival in China. The wide and majestic face, the full lips slightly parted in a near smile, the famous mole, the penetrating eyes, the receding hairline above the high forehead—copies of this picture were everywhere, on the radiators of bouncing trucks, on the crossbars of bicycles, carried on high everywhere. The crowds converged from all over toward the big stadium in disciplined procession, already in a hush of reverence for this strange mass of both divination and execration.

At one of the gates, the marshals with their red armbands checked Georges' passport at great length—upside down— and talked with Miss Wang as she showed a paper covered by a multitude of stamps. But once inside, nobody seemed to pay him any attention as he followed his guide to the box reserved for the few foreigners admitted.

The arena was black with spectators. "More than one hundred and fifty thousand people, twice the seating capacity of the stadium," Miss Wang whispered. In the crowd the tan uniforms of the soldiers from the People's Army of Liberation, in separate sections or scattered among the blues and grays of the civilians, provided touches of light.

The multitude was extraordinarily disciplined. Nobody exchanged a word and all eyes converged toward the great oval stretch of grass where, in less troubled times, memorable games of soccer had been played. Georges thought the atmosphere was more like that of a bullfight before the entrance of the bull than of a friendly sports event. He tugged at his partner's sleeve and pointed to the big door, under the official box, through which he thought the "enemies of the people" for the day would enter. "When will it be our turn?" he said in a whisper. She shook her head furiously. It was obvious he lacked tact as sorely as prudence. One doesn't ask this kind of question, and above all one doesn't whisper at a public gathering in Peking. It was proof of a scandalous propensity for bourgeois individualism.

All of a sudden, from the military section, a kind of recitative rang out. At this signal, from one hundred and fifty thousand pockets, all at once sprang the Little Red Book. Miss Wang helped Georges to find the corresponding page in the French edition. He read: "A revolution is not a dinner party, or writing an essay, or painting a picture, or doing

59

embroidery; it cannot be so refined, so leisurely and gentle, so temperate, kind, courteous, restrained, and magnanimous. A revolution is an upheaval, an act of violence by which one class overthrows another."

As if in church, the faithful lowered their eyes to their texts. Miss Wang too read with conviction the warning directed forty years ago by Mao Tse-tung to the peasants of Hunan, the prophetic sense of which appeared so clearly today. Out of the corner of her eye, she watched Georges to be sure that he followed on page thirteen of the French edition the words of the Master. All around them voices raised in English, Spanish, Arabic, Portuguese testified to the universal value of the sacred text.

Suddenly a tall shape sprang from the big door, wearing a blue top hat on which white stars were crudely stenciled, and a blue and white tailcoat—the Uncle Sam of Chinese imagery. Long cotton sideburns, an enormous cigar, and a bag with a dollar sign completed the caricature. Behind him a dozen young boys and girls, all made up in vermillion, bounded and gamboled about. Like chorus girls from the 1917 Folies-Bergère, they masqueraded in fancy soldier costumes and carried wooden guns. They began to execute a whirling series of somersaults. Gongs and cymbals set the rhythm for their dance. Their leaps and entrechats brought them closer and closer to the hated scarecrow. He, panic stricken, raised his hands to the sky. He let his money bag drop and one of the girls put her foot on it in a gesture of conquest. An immense rhythmic roar burst from the crowd: "All reactionaries are paper tigers. In appearance they are terrifying, but in reality they are not so potent!"

The words of Mao Tse-tung provoked a holy terror in Uncle Sam. He began to tremble and crouched down. The gongs and cymbals redoubled their ardor. In the stands the spectators stood up and howled their hatred of imperialism.

Totally shaken, Uncle Sam grabbed a kind of box painted gray on which was inscribed the character for "rock." He

60

turned it around in the air over his head and then let it drop on his feet. He hopped on one foot and grimaced with pain. An outburst of laughter coursed through the stands. With derision the spectators yelled Mao's vengeful epitaph at Uncle Sam: "A Chinese proverb describes the behavior of certain fools in saying that 'they lift a rock only to let it drop on their feet.' " Georges threw a quick glance at his partner. She was convulsed with laughter. Chinese humor was visibly appreciated even by detractors of the regime.

In a graceful chain the dancers approached the form prostrate in the dust. He groaned and held his aching foot between his hands. The circle tightened. One of the dancers placed her foot on the belly of the beaten imperialist. A huge red Chinese flag with golden stars unfurled. The orchestra struck up *The Great Helmsman*.

Uncle Sam raised himself in an entrechat. He took off his top hat, doffed his tailcoat and high boots and stood revealed as a young girl looking very much like the ballerinas, Miss Wang, or fifty thousand other girls in the stands. Good had triumphed over evil. The crowd burst into rhythmic applause. This was the hour for heroism and victory. Hundreds of balloons, in crazy cat shapes, soared into the sky, and one after the other broke with the noise of wet firecrackers. The crowd yelled out in chorus: "American imperialism is nothing but a paper tiger!"

A flourish of trumpets. At the mike the voice of the narrator, the Vice-Chairman of the Revolutionary Committee of Peking, announced the next event. Georges understood only the name, an Anglo-Saxon one, of a certain Peter Garrison. Miss Wang, still shivering with enthusiasm, answered his questioning look with a gesture of ignorance.

In the official box, at the side of the wizened little man with glasses who was the Vice-Chairman of the Revolutionary Committee of Peking, an imposing brute, all black, stood up. Georges could distinguish well his profile because the box for "foreign friends" was only fifty feet away from and somewhat below the speakers' platform. Under the slightly kinky head of hair, he had rough hewn features, a wide mouth, an arrogant Mussolini jaw pointed by a little beard. He was dressed in a long, flowing, silver-fringed boubou. Like a rock singer, he grabbed the mike with both hands.

"*Tungiamen!* (comrades)," he began in Chinese. But he went on immediately, not in the sing-song English of the southern black musical comedies, but in crisp, staccato, rising phrases. His voice was generally covered by that of the interpreter but Georges could see he had copied the style of Chinese public speaking—that is, the style of Mao Tse-tung, the unique source of all eloquence. This black American actually expressed himself in the very tone of the Cultural Revolution.

" 'Political power grows out of the barrel of a gun!' This truth of comrade Mao Tse-tung is a universal truth!" shouted the black.

The public repeated him in chorus.

"We, the blacks of the so-called United States, we on the American continent, we are the vanguard of the revolutionary proletariat. We'll blow up this worm-eaten world. We'll kill without pity all the counterrevolutionaries, all those who oppose our triumphant march, that is to say the whites. We'll eliminate them without mercy. Because Mao Tse-tung said it: rebellion is legitimate, rebellion is legitimate, rebellion is legitimate!"

He shouted into the mike, his flowing sleeves waving above his head, like a lawyer pleading an important case in court. Up again, standing on the benches, brandishing their books, the crowd proclaimed their approbation. The orator painted the future of the Black Revolution as a picture of Apocalypse: cities destroyed to the ground, burned, factories exploding in stacks of flame, white exploiters begging in vain the pardon of the slaves in revolt. "The innumerable masses of the disinherited, from the Vietnamese to the Australian bushmen, from the subproletariat of Soviet Asia, the Kazakhs and the

62

Uzbeks, victims of the ferocious repression of the Russian colonialists, to the Arabs of Palestine, to the Eskimos, the Redskins, the Hottentots, all united by the ideological cement of the Thought of Mao Tse-tung, coming together behind the 750 million Chinese and the twenty million black Americans, vanguard of the proletariat, will launch a decisive and victorious assault against the world of the rich, the world of the whites, the world of the cities!"

"But we must first," Garrison went on, "purge our own ranks of the agents and accomplices of the class enemy. We too have our black Khrushchev, our Pen Chen, our Lo Jui-ching, who make their deals with the whites and who can say nothing but words like collaboration, gradual liberation, integration!" He spoke each word with a derisive laugh which the audience confidently echoed. "They bear names like Martin Luther King, the lackey-pastor who accepted the Nobel Prize, that award granted by American imperialism to its best servants . . ."

Blasts of whistling, shouts of indignation drowned out his voice for three full minutes.

"They have names like Stokely Carmichael who, under the cover of fighting for Black Power, made his deal with the bourgeois leaders, the Nassers, the Boumediennes, and other hidden stooges of the holy Moscow-Washington alliance . . ."

The audience, surprised for an instant by this denunciation of a man who had been presented till then as being in the vanguard of revolutionary intransigence, booed again with confidence.

"These snakes, these monsters, these evil spirits, there are some of them right here, in this circle. Their names are . . ."
—he pretended to hesitate in the face of the enormity of the revelation—"their names are," he repeated, and his big sleeve, his large black hand, his long black finger on which a blazing ruby sparkled, described an arc before coming to a stop in the direction of the very section where Georges and his partner sat.

63

For a minute the journalist thought he was lost, denounced before the whole world.

The black angel of vengeance was ready to nail him to the wall, to enumerate his crimes against Africa, against the peace-loving peoples, to condemn his complicity with the Russians, with the French, with bad Chinese. He astonished himself with a silent prayer: "Nevermore will I accept the smallest secret mission, I will serve faithfully the cause of Mao, I will sign up for Vietnam, I will quit smoking, I will not get laid except for reasons of health, but please, make it . . . make it not me." The pause must have been long. He had time to complete this invocation of a God in whom he had never believed before the orator put an end to the tension. It had become unbearable.

The name exploded at last, like the trumpet of doom. Dragging on the last syllable, Garrison roared with a fierce joy, "Fer-ang Syd-neeeeeeey." The interpreter repeated, hammering the consonants in a Chinese accent, "Fer-ang Syd-neeeeeeey," and to the four corners of the stadium the loudspeaker reverberated the name in an echoing crescendo.

Just below Georges, a little old man, also black, withered in his seat. He was between a young Chinese—his interpreter—and a fat black woman. One had the physical impression that the immense finger bore into him, that it stripped him of his elegant black alpaca suit, of his green and yellow flowered tie, of his rimless glasses, and of his blue cap, his only concession to Pekingese fashion, from which his grayish hair showed. His face itself turned gray. He sank down even more. All around him people stood up, climbed onto the benches and jostled each other to get a better look at this new enemy of the people. The movement transmitted itself, in fractions of a second, from one side of the gigantic stadium to the other with the spontaneity at work in a crowd during a soccer game, after a particularly brilliant goal.

And then all hell broke loose. From everywhere there were blasts of whistling, invective, imprecations: "Rotten egg,

64

traitor, imperialist agent, lackey of Johnson and Kosygin!"
Pale with indignation, her eyes aflame, Miss Wang yelled with
the crowd and shook her Little Red Book under the black
man's nose. Obviously this brought her great pleasure.
Georges himself, standing up like the others, bawled out with
rage. He poured onto the man—crucified, sacrificed, already
liquidated—all the fear he had felt a few moments ago when
he was thinking it was he whom the lightning would strike.

The young interpreter had moved away from the denounced man as though he were stricken with plague, his wife
looked on with bewilderment. Somehow or other, silence was
restored. From the left, from the right, from up, from down,
dozens of Red Guards converged on the man. He started rest-
lessly. He closed his eyes, like a child in fear of being hit, and
prepared to protect his face with his bent arm. It took a long
time, a very long time for the avengers to reach him. When
silence finally settled over the stadium, the orchestra once
more broke into *The Great Helmsman*. The spectators,
jostled by the advancing Red Guards, protested. They hated
to miss anything of the spectacle. At last the first blue arms
with red brassards shook the prostrate body, collared him, and
dragged him away. Perhaps he had passed out, perhaps he was
dead. Nobody cared. The political execution was already con-
summated. He disappeared by the first exit as into a hole. It
was only then that Georges thought of questioning Miss
Wang.

"He is Frank Sydney. He has lived in Peking for three
years," she explained quickly, bluntly. "I'm sure you've heard
of him. He was considered the most intrepid champion of the
black American cause. He used to be invited everywhere as a
'friend of China.' As a matter of fact, he attended the reception yesterday at the table of honor."

Georges remembered then that Frank Sydney, a few days
before his own departure for China, had addressed an open
letter to the President of the United States to announce his
intention of recruiting a legion of black Americans to fight in

65

South Vietnam beside the guerrillas of the NLF. After that he would go back to the United States in order to hold a great public trial against the crimes of imperialism.

The arena was prey to a feverish stir. Very young boys, at double-time to a whistling tempo, ran in carrying planks. They put up a platform on which they lettered, still in an accelerated staccato as in an old silent movie, some of Mao Tse-tung's thoughts. "Power grows out of the barrel of a gun." "If the imperialists insist on unleashing a new war, we must not be afraid of it," translated Miss Wang under her breath. Bored children were running through the rows of seats screaming. The loudspeakers ground out a scratched record of *The East is Red*.

And then, all of a sudden, there was absolute silence; the children went back to their seats, the youthful builders of the platform ran off and vanished. The center of the stadium was empty; only a few red flags rustled softly, stirred by the wind. Chinese words began to flicker across the electric scoreboard, normally used for soccer games, and the crowd murmured in admiration of this technological miracle. Miss Wang deciphered the text as it came on: " 'We must marshal our strength to strike the gang of bourgeois rightists and counterrevolutionary, ultra-reactionary revisionists. Their crimes of opposition to the Party and the Thought of Mao Tse-tung must be thoroughly criticized and denounced. They must be isolated to the fullest . . .' This is point five of the sixteen-point declaration of the Central Committee, August 8, 1966," she added by way of explanation.

From the military sections thousands of voices repeated in chorus the prophetic admonition.

"Now is the time," Miss Wang whispered in Georges' ear.

Slowly the two leaves of the large door facing the official box opened. Soldiers, youths, girls irrupted running, leaping, jumping into the center of the stadium. Some of them carried flags which they brandished in conquering, heroic poses. And then came once more the effigies of Mao Tse-tung and some

66

grimacing caricatures impossible to identify because of the distance. A young boy—about eleven or twelve years old—was perched on a platform in the center of the stadium. He began a speech which the loudspeakers turned into an almost unbearable whistle.

"We the little red soldiers of Chairman Mao of Elementary Boys' School of Peking Number Fourteen do solemnly condemn to death all the ghosts and monsters!" he exclaimed shrilly.

He looked more like a dwarf than a child, his style and attitudes totally modeled on the adults around him.

"The revolutionary situation," he resumed with assurance, "is excellent. Everywhere the victorious breath of Mao Tse-tung's Thought sweeps away the hideous miasmas of the past and throws them in the garbage bins of history. But"—he dragged out the "but" very skillfully to intensify even more the impatience of his audience, which awaited the public punishment promised the counterrevolutionaries—"but a small handful of men, even though they are members of the Party, follow the bourgeois reactionary road and become the zealous flunkies of the Chinese Khrushchev!" Howling and whistling, a cacophony of hate, greeted the words. "They never stop oppressing the people, they try to provoke division within the masses. Even worse, they actively conspire to waste the blood of the revolutionary heroes. Look at this!" he yelled, snatching a rag handed him by a companion and brandishing it before the crowd. "Look at this tunic, torn and bloody. It belongs to the revolutionary rebel Li Kuo-yang, savagely slaughtered two days ago by the ferocious partisans of the Chinese Khrushchev in front of the West Market, while he defended, weapons in hand, the Thought of Chairman Mao!"

A murmur of horror and indigation coursed through the crowd. Voices broke out from all sections of the stadium: "Who killed him? . . . We want names! . . . Death to the counterrevolutionary assassins!"

67

"We the little red soldiers of Chairman Mao of Elementary Boys' School of Peking Number Fourteen," answered the urchin, "we are going to unmask before your very eyes the hideous faces of these ghosts and monsters!"

He pressed his mouth to the microphone so the sound of his own words would smother the questions of the crowd; he literally deafened the enthralled masses with: "You want the monsters? Here they are!"

With a dramatic flourish, he pointed with his finger to the large door. A growing concert of gongs and cymbals welled from it.

Their heads lowered, their chins touching their chests, grotesque and multicolored cone-shaped paper caps at right angles to their bodies, their hands tied behind their backs, the designated victims made their appearance. They walked in twos, very slowly in short steps, their ankles hobbled by loose cords proudly held at one end by little boys. In keeping with tradition, big placards hung over the penitents' chests showing their names and the crimes they were charged with in handwritten characters.

At the head of the procession, Georges recognized the black man subjected only a few moments before to public contumely. He was already transformed into the perfect expiatory victim: his attitude, like that of his unfortunate companions, reflected opprobrium, humiliation, repentance. But his elegant Western suit contrasted sharply with the miserable overalls of the other monsters. Behind him was a woman grotesquely decked out in an old-fashioned Chinese dress, the skirt slit at half-thigh, her face outrageously made up in white ceruse. They proceeded to the middle of the stadium where their youthful guards pulled them to a stop by yanking their ankle straps. They were turned to face the official box. Behind the twelve wretches, lined up in a row, little Red Guards took their places and, pressing down on their necks, forced them to keep their heads low.

From the first rows of the stands, hundreds, then thousands

68

of spectators sprang forth. They crossed the railing which set the stands off from the grass of the soccer field. ("More like a Roman circus," Georges said to himself, following the scene with the fascination he would have felt if he had been comfortably installed in the coliseum at the time of Vespasian.) The marshals offered no opposition to this incursion, apparently programmed in advance, but formed around the counterrevolutionaries and their guards a circle which kept the vociferous crowd seven or so feet away, the point being not to protect them against the legitimate wrath of the mob but to give the spectators who remained in their seats, and especially those in the official box, a better chance to watch the course of events.

The loudspeaker dropped out twelve names. Georges recognized in passing that of Sydney and then, at the end ("Like the guest star," he said to himself), the now familiar three syllables: Chen Wu-hsieh. As his name was called, each of the prisoners had to kneel, his guard pressing down with all his might on his shoulders. This was done so well that from a distance it looked like a perfectly rehearsed ballet, or else the preparation for a firing squad. The confessions then began. Ladies first. The woman was dragged up to the official box. A microphone was placed before her. She was on her knees, head lowered. Her big headpiece shook with convulsive trembling; it ended by dropping to the ground, amid laughter, and a Red Guard put it back on her head. From her mouth, even over the loudspeaker, nothing but a miserably thin voice came out, high and fragile like the singing of the young boys who play the parts of virgins in traditional Pekingese operas. She was named, she announced, Chang Tao. Daughter of a landlord, an exploiter and bloodsucker of the people. She herself, from her tenderest years, had the habit of pinching and beating her servants, and feeding them with unspeakable leftovers in a dog's dish. At the time of the Kuomintang she denounced innumerable revolutionary heroes to Chiang Kai-shek's cops, and witnessed their torture

69

and executions with sadistic pleasure. She caroused night after night with American imperialists, compradors, and Japanese spies. In spite of this sinful past, however, she succeeded in infiltrating the ranks of the Chinese Communist Party where she usurped positions of high responsibility. To what purpose? Obviously so she could, at the very start of the People's regime in 1949, reestablish capitalism and prepare for the joint invasion of Chinese territory by American imperialists and Soviet revisionists.

"Why did I act this way?" she went on. "From my hatred of the Thought of Chairman Mao Tse-tung, whose brilliant ideological sun I feared. But above all from fidelity to the Chinese Khrushchev, for whom the miserable wretch I married was a henchman—Peng Tsu-chi, Secretary by way of intrigue of the Party Committee in Tsingtao."

At these words a big-bellied little man was dragged from the group of outcasts; wobbling drunkenly, he was forced to kneel at the side of his wife. In cadence two of the guards began to beat him on the face with their Little Red Books. They passed then to his wife and performed the same methodical exercise on her cheeks. The howls of the crowd led them on. Standing up on her seat, Miss Wang swept the air with her book, close enough to Georges' face to make him flinch.

The couple now lent themselves to an awful dialogue, outdoing each other in self-castigation.

"I tried to corrupt the masses by proffering the absurd ideas of the Chinese Khrushchev and his Soviet model, the so-called 'state of the people as a whole' and the pretense of 'peaceful coexistence,'" whimpered the husband between blows of the book.

"I kept a diary and noted my own revisionist, bourgeois, and pornographic ideas instead of Chairman Mao's thoughts," answered the woman between sobs. "I could no longer stand the face of Chairman Mao. I got rid of all his portraits in our home. I forbade my son to wear his button."

At these words the Red Guards could no longer contain

70

their indignation. They fell on the couple, who then disappeared under the attack and were dragged toward one of the exits. A few strains of *The East is Red* heralded their departure.

"What will happen to them?" Georges asked his partner.

She started as though jerked abruptly out of a trance. She shrugged her shoulders.

"Who cares!" she said.

Then she smiled and, like a child, made a hatchet of her hand against her throat.

"Those two," she affirmed, "are not reeducable. They have gone too far."

Georges looked at her. Astonishment mixed with anxiety. Was she really the same girl who the night before, naked in his arms, had talked, even if in rather vague terms, of a vast conspiracy against the regime?

His reflections were interrupted by renewed howling. The black American denounced a few moments before now received blow upon blow. Garrison's high silhouette towered over the other avengers, his black full-flowing sleeves tracing graceful curves over the head of his unhappy compatriot. The onslaught was brief. A sparkling smile lighting his face, his hands rubbing together in a show of satisfaction like an artisan gloating over his work, Garrison went back to his place on the dais. Deeply moved, the officials embraced him ceremoniously while the spectators, all standing, applauded at length in cadence. Sydney had disappeared.

"His embassy certainly won't reclaim him!" observed Miss Wang.

Georges' heart skipped a beat. Were he to be the victim of a "professional accident," which seemed more likely every hour, nobody would claim him, except maybe a handful of the regulars at the "Village" on Saint-Germain-des Prés. The African Solidarity group? IIc had believed in it when he first arrived, before the exact dimensions of the intrigue he was involved in with increasing detachment had been spelled out. Now he couldn't fool himself. He scrutinized the girl's beaming face. How far she was from him—just an anonymous unit in an overexcited and bloodthirsty crowd!

He himself realized a solidarity with this bunch of poor wretches who, one after the other, were used as the ball in a new kind of game. The supersensitive microphones transmitted to the whole stadium the thudding blows and kicks of fists and sneakers ("Fortunately leather is too expensive," Georges thought) against the faces of the martyrs. He noticed that many spectators, taken by the hypnotic, excruciating cadence, leaned their heads first right, then left to the rhythm of the blows, as if they were watching a game of ping-pong.

The scene dragged on: questions, answers, accusations, confessions, repenances, the thrashing, the removal of inert victims to some kind of cesspool, to be piled up, year after year, into immense heaps of fecund "human fertilizer" in a slow, nauseating climb toward the remission of political sins against some remote People's commune of Inner Mongolia or Sinkiang, or, in the most severe cases, toward executions imposed but indefinitely postponed through acts of abject repentance. All notion of time was lost.

The guards brought forth a university professor guilty of trying to corrupt his students by praising the vaunted "humanism" of Tolstoy and Shakespeare. Long derisive laughter in the crowd. "Whoever talks 'humanism,'" droned the loudspeakers, "denies the concept of the class struggle and praises culture for the whole people, not only for the proletariat; this is treason which benefits the Soviet revisionists and the American pilots who massacre Vietnamese. And this is made even more obvious by the fact that Tolstoy was Russian, let's say Khrushchevian, and Shakespeare English, maybe even American. The point of this tactic is clear enough: this so-called 'man of culture'"—the laughter redoubled—"what does he think? That we're kindergarten kids to be easily fooled by his coarse and transparent maneuvers?"

Then it was the turn of a shock cesspool trooper. His was

72

also a hanging case, maybe worse because he could not put forth any "extenuating circumstances." He did not belong to the intellectual class, already corrupted and corruptive in essence. His crimes were the blackest! Chosen as worker hero by his comrades of Cesspool Cleaners Brigade Number Four of Mukden, Manchuria ("His ex-comrades!" one of them protested. "Such an abject creature has no comrades any more"), he had the nerve since his nomination to consider himself of superior class. Had he not bought gloves—yes, gloves!—under the shameful pretext that the raw material he had the honor to cart soiled his hands! (New howlings of indignation.)

"I've done worse," sobbed the prostrate man. "I passionately admired the precepts of the Chinese Khrushchev. Every morning, when handing out assignments to my former comrades, who began to be slaves to me, I proclaimed like Liu Shao-chi, 'Exploitation is a good thing.' I hoped by so doing to restore capitalism in my unit of honey dippers. With a former comprador of the Kuomintang clique I organized an enormously profitable sale of human manure. And with these ill-gotten profits I bought sumptuous suits in order to seduce young girls."

The man was interrupted by vehement protests. "This confession is a lie, it's incomplete. He didn't tell the whole truth! He has not admitted a quarter of his real crimes!" someone yelled from the crowd. A girl (perhaps one he had tried to seduce with the gold from Manchurian defecations) came and spit in his face. She received vigorous applause for this herioc gesture. Vanquished, then, he confessed:

"I had my picture taken in an arrogant pose, wearing the medal I won as worker hero in the Cesspool Cleaners Brigade."

He was forced there and then to demonstrate the pose. He had to climb onto a crate brought in haste. He threw out his chest grotesquely, raised his chin, and folded his arms. "Smile! Why don't you smile the way you did that day, you disciple of the Chinese Khrushchev!" he was ordered. It took a long, painful time. In spite of great effort, he couldn't make it. A little kid stuck two fingers to the corners of his mouth and lifted his lips. Satisfied, he removed his hand and stepped back to contemplate the job. Hardly daring to move his mouth, in order not to upset the living picture of all the revolutionary sins he symbolized, the man completed his confession. "And what did I do with this photograph? I put it on the wall in the place of honor in the community house."

"Where, exactly where? Be precise!" they shouted.

In the same breath, he said, "I removed Chairman Mao's photo so I could put mine up instead!"

The long contained explosion burst out. There was a rush to him; the crate was knocked over. The microphone for the first time transmitted howlings of pain. And then nothing.

Night had fallen. Projectors lighted the center of the stadium with a pallid glow. But the tension, far from diminishing, continued to grow. Georges noticed that armed cordons of soldiers quickly took positions in front of the stands and held their weapons aimed at the public. The counter-revolutionaries had disappeared one by one as if through a trap door. Only one man remained, on his knees under his big cap, as immobile as a stone. At last the chairman of the rally threw out his name—Chen Wu-hsieh! It reverberated to the four corners of the stadium. Then the silhouette, tiny from a distance, unfolded slowly. The man straightened. Georges noticed that his gestures had a freedom and nonchalance almost obscene. He turned his head, quietly, to measure these anonymous adversaries, these hundred and fifty thousand spectators who had come to attend his humiliation and ideological if not physical execution. With a sacrilegious assurance, he took the ignominious mitre from his head and gave it to the closest Red Guard who, confused, put it on the ground. The crowd did not react.

In an awesome silence, Chen began to speak, carefully articulating every word.

74

"Our Central Committee has asserted, 'In a debate persuasion must be used, not repression or coercion. In the course of debate every revolutionary must develop the communist spirit, which is to dare to think, to dare to speak, and to dare to act.' Our Central Committee, imbued with the Thought of Mao Tse-tung, has also opposed the erroneous practice of attacking honest revolutionaries, of putting big caps on their heads, of branding them without proof as counterrevolutionaries."

A voice shot out from the Red Guards around him: "Crack the dog-head Chen who follows the capitalist road!" The cry was repeated but without conviction by hundreds of revolutionary rebels. Georges did not understand why the crowd, so eager a moment before to demand the ruthless chastisement of victims offered up to its rage, remained frozen now; why his neighbors had become suddenly such impartial observers. A woman from the official box shouted into the microphone: "Down with all those who hide themselves in the folds of the red flag only to tear up the red flag!" Chen, very relaxed, resumed almost didactically.

"Who then is hiding in the folds of the red flag? Our Leninist Central Committee, of which I'm still a member, invited us in its historical Resolution of August 8, 1966, to answer the question of primary importance: 'Who are our enemies? Who are our friends?' And I ask you to say if your friends, if Chairman Mao's friends, are recruited from the small clique hiding in the folds of the red flag or from among the hardened revolutionaries who have always been in the first rank in the struggle against the opportunists and careerists! . . . Here are your counterrevolutionaries!" he shouted.

And, in a dramatic gesture, he pointed his finger at the official box.

Once again the storm broke. In the box a man rushed to the microphone, followed by the woman who had just accused Chen. Both of them launched into a series of imprecations against him. Their voices overlapped. The shrill falsetto

75

of the woman cut short the resounding bass of the man, who had the oratorical flair of a real professional. But they were hardly heard. In the stands some held up their fists or their little books toward Chen, who remained completely at ease, his guards having given up keeping him in an attitude of humiliation. Others shouted at the occupants of the box with an equal virulence. Newspapers and leaflets rolled into balls, glasses with the tea or hot water dispensed in the aisles by the ushers were thrown about awkwardly in all directions. But these projectiles fell on other spectators and they, furious, rushed after those who had hit them, jostling their neighbors, who in turn protested with indignation. Many fist fights broke out. Some spectators came down into the arena to take Chen to task and fought there against the Red Guards. Other Red Guards tried to plow their way to the official box. After a few moments of this, someone—probably the stadium engineer—took it upon himself to cut the electricity. When the spotlights went out, the voices, which shrieked their lungs out through the mikes, and Chen's voice, which sought to calm his partisans, stopped abruptly.

In the shadows of the autumnal dusk, Georges could see the jumbled mass of opposing groups and the immobile form of Chen still protected by his guards—or bodyguards. Now the scene was not so much a bullfight as a rugby scrimmage with Chen the ball—but a thinking ball, Georges thought, not unhappy with the metaphor.

"Those defending Uncle Chen," explained Miss Wang, "are from the 916th Regiment, the September-Sixteenth of the Physics Institute, the soldiers of 'The East is Red' and the Police Academy, and I think, but I'm not quite sure, part of the 'Red Sun' Brigade of the Marxist-Leninist Institute. His adversaries are the youth of the Diplomatic Academy and the Aeronautics Institute and all of the Third Headquarters of the Red Guards."

The fight spread. Some women screamed. The spotlights came back on for a minute and revealed the jumbled mass

76

roaring and surging in long waves like the sea. Chen could not be seen anymore because the fight returned to the circle of guards where it had begun. Every time the light came on briefly the sound was also reestablished, and scraps of speech and exhortations to calm were heard. The fight had reached the row of foreign guests of honor, the very row occupied by Georges and his partner. Insults were hurled in English, French, Spanish, and Russian. Sydney's wife, who had impassively watched the political crucifixion of her husband, threw a fit and rolled over her bench. She tore her dress, revealing adipose chunks of graying flesh on which her nails had etched stark zippers of blood. But nobody paid her any attention. Georges saw a little American lifted by anonymous hands, thrown in the air, and hurled three rows below. He was a markedly Jewish type whom Georges had noticed before because of the vehemence of the insults he had hurled against the counterrevolutionaries. Whistles shrilled through the darkness. The power came on again. The spotlights followed the soldiers, tommy guns held out from their hips as for the October First Parade, falling into impeccable ranks, striding over the prostrate bodies to reach the exit and desert the field of battle.

The official box was empty. Below, a seething crowd broke into the arena, while the stands emptied slowly, arduously. Georges put his arm around the girl's shoulders; she was shivering, perhaps with fear, perhaps with political excitement. "Let's go," he said firmly, and he drew her with him. The crowd carried them along, literally crushed them. On the way, Georges came upon a screaming little lost girl and hoisted her to his shoulders. All around he could hear pantings, moanings, curses, and from time to time dry cracks that might have been bones being broken. At last they found themselves in the open air out of the stadium. A warm and viscous liquid dampened his shoulder. He thought he was wounded. He sniffed and made a face—the little girl was vomiting. He put her down and tenderly held her forehead. She was about

77

four or five years old, very pretty, neatly dressed as a Pioneer. She still held a crumpled paper flower which was supposed to be given at the end of the festival to the esteemed leaders of the Chinese proletariat in the official box. Soldiers stood guard at the doors, perhaps to arrest counterrevolutionaries—but which ones? Georges looked for the car assigned to him, but Miss Wang drew him toward a truck draped with red flags. She jumped in and gestured for him to follow. He hoisted the little girl, holding her up to Miss Wang. She made a sign of refusal but then smiled and accepted the child.

"We look like a happy family," Georges thought.

2 ● MICHEL LORIOT was waiting for them in front of the Hsin Chao. His eyebrows went up when he saw Georges, followed by Miss Wang, coming down out of the truck behind the jabbering Africans and their starchy interpreters. She carried the sleeping child in her arms. He stared at all three and said, "So soon? . . ."

The presence of the "expert" did not please Georges at all. He was exhausted. The only thing he longed for was his bed. "A young wife and a child," he thought fuzzily, "that wouldn't be such a bad idea." On the inclined head of the child, the black and shiny hair stuck out straight.

"Maybe I should try to find her parents," Miss Wang put in without much conviction.

The little girl opened her eyes. At the sight of the white faces she began to scream, and all the attendants of the hotel parking lot came running. Miss Wang explained her problem. There was a big burst of laughter. The idea that she had inherited a lost baby in the panic of the stadium seemed extremely funny to them. Miss Wang rocked the child, shushing her with words of comfort. The urchin became quiet and finally slipped to the ground. Plumping down firmly on her little legs, she cast a withering glance at the sniggering boors

78

and the puzzled white devils. With a thin but sententious little voice she ejected a phrase which stopped the gibes and laughter.

"What did she say?" asked Georges.

"She said," answered Miss Wang, " 'certain fools lift a rock to let it drop on their feet.' You know, Chairman Mao's famous proverb. See what happens!"

The parking lot attendants repeated the passage by rote and set about completing it. Georges searched his memory to find what the scene reminded him of, and came up with the colored picture that slipped out of his catechism when he was eleven: the child Jesus confounding the doctors of the Temple with His knowledge of holy scripture.

With the parking lot attendants reciting the sixth chapter of the Little Red Book, Miss Wang stole off to deliver the prodigy to the hotel desk.

Loriot took Georges' arm and drew him aside.

"Do you know the news? Chen has totally turned the tide. At the end of the stadium rally he had the name of Liu Shao-chi acclaimed. He's marching to the Central Committee with two hundred thousand of his partisans. The whole city is up-side down."

"That's nonsense," Georges replied. "Look, I just came back from the stadium. It's true, Chen did find some support, but there was no mention of Liu Shao-chi. And the march on the Central Committee is just pure fantasy."

"In any case," insisted Loriot, "the battle is on. Yesterday I was telling you that the timing was wrong, that Chen was not in a position to do anything. But today the situation is radically changed. Whether you like it or not, you'll be able to carry out your mission. Now we'll be able to reach Chen."

Miss Wang's return interrupted Loriot.

"You know Michel Loriot. He works on foreign language publications. Miss Wang, my interpreter."

Miss Wang threw a rather icy glance at the interloper.

"I've heard about Mr. Loriot," she said; "It seems he's a

very active man. This estimable gentleman," she explained to Georges, "wrote the great Ta Tzu Bao, that poster in big characters which calls on all foreign experts in Peking to submit themselves entirely to the Chinese system, to work for the same wages as their Chinese colleagues. Quite a meritorious proposal. By the way," flashing her most charming smile, "did you get many signatures?"

"Some," Loriot answered, and then went on, changing the subject. "I've come to ask our friend Benachen for some information on the rally at the Workers' Stadium. It looks like there were some surprises there, that the Chen Wu-hsieh line won."

"Yes, it was an especially interesting session," Georges said, practicing a tone he intended to use at Parisian dinners to describe China, if by any chance he got out of here. "Miss Wang was kind enough to translate the crucial parts of Chen's defense for me. It was fascinating."

"I've no doubt about that," said Loriot. "So maybe Miss Wang, who certainly seems to be a very efficient interpreter, could arrange a meeting with her uncle this evening. The honorable Mr. Chen *is* your uncle, isn't he?" he asked, bowing with feigned politeness.

"Wait for me at the hotel bar," the girl ordered.

At the seventh floor of the Hsin Chao, the "expert" insisted strongly that his friend taste the "Chinese whisky."

"The bottle certainly has the look of scotch," conceded Georges.

He swallowed a glassful, made a face, and rushed to the toilet, holding his belly. The bartender threw a knowing look at Loriot.

"He musn't have been in Peking very long," he said to Loriot in Chinese.

"You don't miss much, do you?" Loriot answered, and prudently poured the contents of his own glass into the ashtray.

When Georges came back to the bar, ten minutes later, a

trifle pale, he found Miss Wang waiting for him with Loriot.

"I've been able to get someone on the telephone. It's settled," she announced. "A truck will wait for us in an hour at the Hsien Pien Men intersection. We have just enough time to get there."

She seemed to consider it very natural now to organize this expedition.

"I suppose," she added studying Loriot's face, "that you want to come too?"

He bowed without a word.

3 ● INCONGRUOUS ON THE wall, an immense chart of Mendeleyev's periodic table of the chemical elements. Work benches cluttered with test tubes and dusty bottles, all pinkish, greenish, and purplish-blue. On the floor, rat-eaten manuals, covered with notes and chemical formulas. Also, as Georges was a little puzzled to discover, packages of Hong Kong condoms in cellophane wrappers.

"This is the laboratory of the Research Institute of the Third Ministry of the hemical Industry," explained Miss Wang in her most formal tone, upon entering the room. "It's quite dirty because, since the beginning of the great Cultural Revolution, students no longer work here. They have no time. Nor do the teachers—they've even less time. They have to perform their self-criticism, to go on with reconditioning. Ah! At last, here is the dean, Yang Po-lao in person."

She pointed to a very old man, an acacia broom in his hands. He was even dustier than the floor he was in charge of cleaning.

As soon as these foreign devils popped up before him, with their well-fed, prosperous look, the venerable university man opened a toothless mouth and retreated. He left behind him a scent of sweat and dried urine. Even Miss Wang condescended to smile.

Georges did not react. The fate of Dean Yang Po-lao, Nobel Prize Winner in chemistry in 1947, who returned to People's China in 1956 after having taught at Berkeley and MIT, had provoked endless speculaion in the Western press. This scientist, educated in the West, covered with honor and glory, friend to all the eminent men of the scientific world, who rallied to the communist regime with no little publicity and was welcomed by Mao Tse-tung and photographed at his side on his arrival, had been reduced in one day to the symbol of all that the Cultural Revolution had meant once and for all to sweep away. Denounced by his students as a revisionist, pro-capitalist, and cosmopolitan intellectual, accused of having put his own thought on a pedestal in the place of Chairman Mao's, he had dropped out of sight after a short walk through the streets of the capital, wearing the infamous headpiece. Some people had contended that his hands had been cut off and that he was hanged (they had apparently confused his case with that of a famous violinist); others said that he was working as cowherd in a people's commune in Inner Mongolia. And here he was, in his own Institute, reduced to the humblest role, but alive.

Georges was too exhausted to react. The ride had seemed interminable. On leaving the car, after some vague explanation to the chauffeur about this foreign comrade's wish to enjoy the beautiful evening like a simple tourist, they had to walk back and forth at the intersection, with a detached air, for almost an hour. Many times people came up to Miss Wang and, staring with curiosity at her companions, asked questions which she brushed aside with a discouraging loftiness. Finally, an old American pickup truck, a trophy of the Korean War, stopped before them. Out came a young man supplied with a roll of posters and assisted by a companion who carried a bucket and a brush, the basic tools of the Pekingese propagandist. They began to apply the latest news on top of previously posted murals, which were already some five inches thick. It was a report of the stadium rally in twelve superbly

82

calligraphed sheets. Miss Wang had no time to decipher it: she had just then recognized, on the red brassard of the crew chief, the number 916 she was looking for.

She went up to him and introduced herself. No mysterious patrol sign, no password. She merely extended her hand and said, "I'm Wang. I wish to go to your meeting with the foreign comrade." As though it were, here in Peking, in the midst of the Cultural Revolution, a perfectly normal request, the boy nodded approval. After parking his vehicle in a propitious shadow between two streetlights, he invited them aboard.

They drove for a long time through darker and darker streets, each more torn up and rutted than the last. After a violent jolt, a bucket overturned and a thick, stinking paste spread all over the floor, sticking to their pants and shoes. No one spoke. In the dark Georges took Miss Wang's hand and squeezed it gently. She turned her head and seemed to be smiling to him. This contact made him feel good. Because at thirty-five, for the very first time since his childhood, Georges was out of his depth, lost in unknown terrain. Up till now he had thought himself staunch, hardened, surprise-proof. Hadn't he broken with his family, his past, his homeland, even with the Communist Party, when he thought it was too timorous to rally to the cause of the Fellagahs at the height of the Algerian War? And then, out of that Algerian whirlpool, didn't he surface—and it hadn't been easy—among the little group of leftist expatriates he had joined for the ousting of Ben Bella and the manhunt for "red-feet" which followed?

"I'm scared, simply scared," he said to himself. Every moment he expected the fatal tap on the shoulder. The two escorts, here in blue overalls, would take him by the elbows, flashing incomprehensible plastic-covered cards from their pockets and muttering "Security Police" or something like that (in English or in French this time?). Then they would take him in a black car and speed up to a barracks behind a barbed wire fence. These images had pursued Georges for years, through the vicissitudes of an existence which had kept him almost everywhere at the edge of the blurred line of political legality. Now he found himself running insane risks he was not prepared for. It was no longer a matter of a few months in *La Santé* as a political prisoner with all the petitions on his behalf in *Les Temps Modernes* or *Le Nouvel Observateur.* "What does a Chinese jail look like?" he asked himself. "A Chink clink?" He recalled reading that two Americans from the CIA, captured during the Korean War, still rotted in a cell in Peking or Shanghai.

The pickup stopped with an awful screech of the brakes. Georges saw a courtyard cluttered with wooden planks, building materials, rolls of paper, debris of all sorts. Youngsters stood about talking in little groups, like spectators back home waiting for a show in front of the parochial school. A light rain began to fall. The only light in the court came from inside when the door opened.

Miss Wang drew Georges off to the side.

"Say as little as possible. I'll simply prsent you as a foreign comrade worthy of confidence. I think that'll be enough. . . . Are you sure you really want to come?" she asked, for the sake of conscience as much as anything else. "This could be dangerous. If someone should denounce you . . ."

Georges shrugged his shoulders.

"We're already at such a point . . ."

They went in. As it turned out, no one paid them any attention. There were only about ten chairs and some hundred people already packed into what was once a laboratory. Most of them squatted on their heels. Others leaned against the walls closely pressed against each other with the extraordinary ability of the Chinese to occupy a minimum of space for hours. At the other end of the room was a raised desk, the teacher's no doubt, now the platform for the presidium. Georges knew none of the men seated there and Miss Wang did not provide any explanations. Everyone talked at the same time. Georges had no idea if the meeting had actually begun.

84

A little man got up on a chair. He was a hunchback, all twisted. He tried vainly to make himself heard. From his gasping mouth came an incoherent gargling. Georges looked imploringly to Miss Wang.

"There's really no need to translate," she said. "He talks nonsense."

She pouted a little and Georges found her irresistible. Someone grabbed the feet of the speaker's chair and made it tip over. The hunchback collapsed in the midst of laughter, but got back up with some dignity and brushed himself off. An army man who looked like he meant business took his place. Relative silence was established. Miss Wang agreed to sum up the speech, which lasted about ten minutes. Sent here by the garrison of Wuhan, he spoke out against the "so-called triple alliance" of the military, the Red Guards, and the revolutionary cadres which the emissaries of Peking wanted to impose.

"It is we who express the aspirations of the masses, not the puppets of the Committee of the Cultural Revolution, those who usurp power and erect a wall between Chairman Mao and the people!" he clamored.

The name of Mao was applauded at length; references to the Committee of the Cultural Revolution were greeted by derisive whistling.

He lowered his tone. All eyes were on him.

Georges kept asking, "What's he saying? What's he saying?"

Miss Wang hesitated to transalte, as if the enormity of the ideas terrified her—a reaction which seemed to be shared by most of those present.

"He says that Chairman Mao can make a mistake. That he is a man after all, not a genius or an emperor of the legendary dynasties. That it's crazy for China to isolate itself from the USSR and the rest of the socialist world at a time when America wants to destroy us as they have tried to destroy our brothers in Vietnam. He also says"—she lowered her voice—"that the comrades from Wuhan are determined to reject the authority

85

of the 'Peking clique.' . . . That's what he said, the 'Peking clique.'"

The speaker got down from the chair. Enthusiastically hemmed in, he continued his peroration with a small group of fans. Some of the older cadres, with something of the cop in their manner, solemnly nodded their heads and compared notes. A few people went discreetly toward the door. The atmosphere became noticeably heavier, as if everyone, after this sacrilege, expected soldiers to burst in at any moment, fully armed. A boy came up to deliver a passionate defense of Chairman Mao. But Georges was unable to figure out whether he was condemning or defending current policies. Prolonged booing interrupted him. Someone tried to upset the chair again, but a few brutes protected the speaker and permitted him to finish his speech. At the door there was a great commotion. A young man, his head wrapped in some questionable linen, made his way through the crowd. Some comrades lifted him to their shoulders and there he harangued the crowd in a powerful voice. He waved a torn and bloody coat.

"Just this afternoon at the stadium the counterrevolutionaries shot at us! This coat belongs to Comrade An Hsi-kui, today's martyr. Chairman Mao has proclaimed that the rebellion is justified. And in spite of that, openly, in the middle of Red Peking, the revolutionary rebels of Technological Institute Number Three are oppressed! They are trampled under foot! And now some even try to defile the best of us, the veteran of the fight for liberation—I mean none other than comrade Chen Wu-hsieh!"

This time what parliamentary reporters refer to as "prolonged applause" occurred. Voices rose up demanding Chen's presence. But he remained out of sight. The army man intoned a long litany of the names of all the genuine revolutionaries who had been unjustly accused. Someone came up and whispered something to the speaker. He stopped abruptly in the middle of a phrase and without a word left the room.

A group of boys and girls with accordions, tambourines, and flutes began to sing and dance. The sound was at once traditional Chinese music, with all the dissonances and high-pitched miaowings of tortured cats; Russian military marches; and an apache number from a tavern on the banks of the Marne. Boys and girls hopped around, heavy and awkward, face to face without touching, without smiling. A couple came close to Georges. And then something happened that he would never have believed possible in People's China. A young man seized his partner and grabbed her round and fresh peasant girl face in his hands. They smiled sweetly to each other. They touched cheeks, his right to her left. They exchanged a little salute and then swapped their Mao buttons. They were applauded. Leaning their heads against each other, they left the room. The music resumed, hectically punctuating their departure as if it were a wedding march. Someone cut the electricity. What light there was came through the dirty panes of the window from a flickering lantern outside.

When the intensity of the music abated, one could hear whispering and muffled laughter. In the shadows Georges glimpsed couples embracing. Once he thought he recognized the tall silhouette of Michel Loriot, but too many dancers were between them and he gave up joining him. All fear had left him. He simply felt embarrassed, like an uninvited adult witnessing the frolics of a group of adolescents or a seance of hippies on LSD. He thought, by some kind of association, he could really use a scotch. The lack of alcohol, or of any stimulant other than ideological ones, made the unleashed eroticism of the situation all the more incongruous. He looked around for Miss Wang but she had disappeared.

Suddenly the lights came on. Caught in their gambols, some thirty couples sat down all at once on the stacks of posters which served them as couches. The girls put their hands up to hide their faces rather than their breasts or their still hairless groins. A boy grabbed one of his felt shoes and threw it, vainly, against the bulb. Encouraged, others imitated

87

him, still without result, and soon it became a kind of game. A boy hoisted his half-naked partner onto his shoulders so she could unscrew the bulb, but a harsh command from a rasping voice stopped them short. Someone came up to Georges. It was the army man who had acclaimed Chen Wu-hsieh during the meeting and whose imperative voice now quashed the attempted blackout. He shouted in English, "No photo, photos forbidden!"

Georges showed that he had no camera slung over his chest and offered his open palms.

"I have no camera," he tried to explain, "no camera, see!"

But the other went on shouting: "I said no photo! Give me your film!"

The fur was ready to fly. Someone called Georges counter-revolutionary, class enemy, revisionist. "For someone who wanted to go unnoticed, I'm some success!" he thought. And why had Miss Wang abandoned him?

Three Red Guards flanked him and escorted him to the door. The correctness of his dress, his shameful apartness gave him the feeling of being the one caught with his fly open and his tool ready for action at the main door of the Molière Lyée when the girls come out. The great politics and the doubtful conspiracy that had brought him here were totally forgotten. As soon as they were outside the light was cut off, bringing a long sigh of general relief from within.

They crossed the courtyard where other "masses" who had not found room inside listened through a loudspeaker to the scrappy, disconnected conversations taking place. Through another door they entered a long dark passageway and went up a staircase just as dark.

"Where we go?" he asked. "You no police?"

Instinctively he adopted the "pidgin English" from the colonial stories of his childhood. Nobody answered. The grip on his arm tightened.

A door opened and Georges was shoved rather brutally into

88

a small room. The lamp placed on the table was directed at the visitor. Behind the table a man was seated. "This is it. The arraigning judge!" But the man addressed him in good French.

"Good evening, Mr. Benachen. Welcome to Peking!"

It took Georges a good thirty seconds to realize that it was the man he had come here to find—Chen Wu-shieh.

Chen looked smaller and less imposing than a few hours ago at the stadium when he stood alone facing the frenzied crowd. Very calm, he was playing in a characteristic way with his shell-rimmed glasses. He had exchanged the stained dress he wore at the stadium for a well-cut tunic of lightweight navy blue gabardine. Above the left pocket was the inevitable Mao button.

Imperiously he sent the two guards away, took out a cigarette, and lighted it.

"American cigarettes, you see," he said, "but don't draw any conclusions. It would be premature, completely premature. You don't smoke, I believe."

"I was at the stadium this afternoon," interrupted Georges. He was eager to show right away that he had not come this far just for a chat. "I'm flabbergasted by the quick reversal of situation you accomplished. I'd never have thought it possible. And it's very encouraging, it seems to me, for"—he hesitated, weighing his words—"for the realization of the project we discussed in Algiers."

Chen stared at Georges. Two vertical wrinkles furrowed his smooth, slightly bulging forehead.

The pause went on uncomfortably. Chen was now playing with a pen he had taken from his pocket, unscrewing the cap, rescrewing it.

"You are very reckless," he said at last. "Intelligence must really be disorganized not to have arrested you long ago. There must be a . . . guardian angel"—he smiled, pleased at having found the right word—"for amateurs like you. The situation has noticeably worsened since our meeting in Algiers," he went on. "Today I escaped uninjured. It could well not always be the case. So now I must make a decision."

"Why are you telling me all this?" Georges asked. "Why do you take me into your confidence? What makes you think you can trust me?"

"Nothing, nothing at all. On the contrary, I have a hundred reasons to think that you work for a . . . specialized foreign service, and probably for more than one. And it may well be that we'll find ourselves standing side by side"—he smiled—"at the first great espionage trail in Peking."

He clapped his hands. Miss Wang appeared. She held a tray with three cups of steaming tea.

"You know my little niece, of course. She plays the young lady of the house, as you say in your country."

Georges threw a black look at Miss Wang. He was still annoyed with her for her desertion, but she pretended not to notice. "Our relationship," Georges thought with some satisfaction, "has become almost conjugal."

"Should I call Loriot?" she asked her uncle in French.

He shook his head no. She delicately put one buttock on a chair and from her pocket she took a ballpoint pen and her famous red and gold notebook, in which, like all the young Chinese, she noted reflections and thoughts as they occurred to her in the progress of the Cultural Revolution. She waited, the perfect interpreter, the perfect mistress, perfect Red Guard, perfect conspirator, and now perfect niece.

Chen stood up and went to make sure nobody was listening at either of the doors.

"Here we are fairly sure that there are no microphones," he declared, yet with a trace of uncertainty in his voice.

"You were talking about espionage," Georges threw in. "These are words you shouldn't use lightly, don't you agree? After all, I'm here"—he hesitated—"as a journalist. And I sincerely believe that within this function I can be useful in

90

telling what I've seen. As a matter of fact, I imagine it's for this very reason that you encouraged me to come."

Energetically the Chinese shook his head no. He shrugged his shoulders. He was obviously one of those who think it necessary to accentuate every word with a gesture or a bit of mimicry.

"Mr. Benachen, I'm a political man, a Chinese patriot, and a sincere revolutionary—not an adventurer. It happens that I traveled abroad more than most of my colleagues. That I am more conscious of realities and of the balance of powers, that I don't pay myself off with words—you believe this, don't you?"

Georges made a sign of agreement, putting the maximum show of conviction into it. But he didn't understand the other's point at all.

"Mr. Benachen, do you think that our leaders are crazy?"

"So I've been told by a certain number of people abroad. I haven't had the opportunity so far to find out for myself."

"Mr. Benachen, what is your opinion on Chairman Mao's essential principle—power grows out of the barrel of a gun?"

"It can apply, it seems to me, to certain revolutionary necessities. I don't take it for a universal principle able to replace all analysis in specific situations."

Chen seemed satisfied with the answers. He was wreathed in the smile of an examiner ready to give an "A" to a candidate for a degree. He looked to see whether Miss Wang was taking notes of everything that was said.

"Mr. Benachen, I think it's time now to explain the reason I had you come to China. Because I hope you understand that I, and I alone, had you come here, and placed beside you—not an easy thing to do at the time of your arrival—my charming niece." He nodded in her direction, a bad imitation of French gallantry as imagined by the students of the Alliance Française in foreign countries. "I tried to make your trip interesting, let's say, and I hope pleasant."

91

"If that's what you like to think," said Georges with little grace. He had had enough of being manipulated.

"Mr. Benachen, the Mandarin Wei Cheng in the seventh century of our era was not afraid to criticize the Emperor Tai Tsong. Do you think, in this age when the dangers of a bad reign are infinitely greater for China and all humanity than they were then, that we should show less audacity than this feudal dignitary?"

"If I remember well," Georges answered, pleased to show off the knowledge he had gleaned from French newspaper files before his departure, "the former propaganda chief, Lu Ting-yi, one of the principal members of the Black Band, used the same analogy when he advocated the right to criticize Chairman Mao. And he was seriously censured for it."

"You're perfectly right. It's a pleasure, Mr. Benachen, to talk with you."

"So then, what are you driving at?"

Chen stood up, went to the window, and leaned his forehead for a while against the glass. He turned around abruptly.

"Mr. Benachen," he said with visible effort, "it's not easy for a man my age, for a veteran of revolutionary battles, for a Yenan oldtimer to reveal a state secret to a foreigner, to appear—perhaps in his own eyes, certainly in the eyes of most of his compatriots—as a traitor. You understand . . ."

Georges also stood up.

"I asked nothing of you. I didn't solicit your confidence. And your crisis of conscience doesn't interest me. You're right—all this is of no concern to a foreigner, and I should never have come here. Miss Wang, would you be kind enough to take me back to my hotel? I wouldn't be able to find my way alone."

Was he sincere in this attempt at a dramatic exit? He asked himself this question long afterward. As it was, he was torn between a restlessness inspired by the anglings of Mao's old companion and the growing feeling that the adventure had gone too far, as well as by a more or less professional curiosity. The latter won out. Neither Chen nor his niece had to insist—he sat down, let the girl refill his cup, and waited for the end of the speech.

It came in one blow. Chen came up to him—perhaps he was not so convinced of the lack of microphones—and spoke in a low voice. "In a few weeks or a few months—I don't know exactly when, the date has not been determined—a Chinese nuclear bomb will be dropped on the Americans in Vietnam," he said carefully spacing out his words.

Then he stepped back to savor the effect on Georges of this revelation.

Georges didn't flinch. His training as a journalist, the constant dealing with political figures, had at least taught him to be suspicious of everything he heard. In this case particularly, he had all the reasons in the world to be skeptical, and most of all not to play the game prepared for him—the part of the good guy so terrified by extraordinary revelations that he decides to join up with his informant in order to help avert all dangers. A reverse cliché came to his mind—the famous inscrutability of the occident.

It was plain that Chen was extremely moved. Drops of sweat flowed like tears from the wings of his nose down the deep creases that furrowed his cheeks. And the hand carrying the cup to his mouth was perceptibly shaking. He unhooked the collar of his tunic. From a pocket he removed a paper fan and unfolded it in front of his face. A plump little Pioneer, very pink, was painted on it playing with a ball, in the style of the gift calendars that the artists of China have rediscovered and perfected for the edification of the working masses.

"What target have you decided on?" Georges asked at last, more out of politeness than true interest. He was really prepared not to believe a word of this confidence.

"We don't know exactly. It could be the base of Danang. Or Tan Son Nhut airport right outside Saigon. This would be settled at the last moment, according to the meteorology and

93

the winds—something to do with radioactive fallout, and many other factors."

The expression "radioactive fallout" released in Georges the trigger that the announcement of the operation had not. He began to take the affair seriously. Maybe it was pure mystification, more probably a provocation. But big enough. And its promoter was not just anyone—at least until these past days he was one of the most powerful figures in China, one of the men closest to Chairman Mao, and in fact the person in charge of projects of just this kind.

"Why are you telling me all this?" Georges asked. "What do you expect from me? And why should I believe you?"

"Three good questions," replied Chen, resuming his professorial tone. "We'll come to them when it's time. Let me tell you first the decision made by the people, of whom I am one, who participated in a joint meeting of the group of the Cultural Revolution in the army, and of the Military Commission of the Central Committee, which took place at Tsinan, in Shantung from the tenth to the fifteenth of May. Look here, Wang, would you translate please?"

He took from the pocket that had contained the fan a sheet of paper covered with Chinese characters. Miss Wang skimmed through it without changing her expression. Then, with the clear voice of a well-bred girl, she began to translate into French, stumbling at times on difficult words.

"Chairman Mao teaches us a tale from *The Three Wise Old Men,* 'How Yukong moved the mountains,' to 'take our resolution, not to shrink from any sacrifice, to overcome all difficulties for achieving victory.' This is the spirit that must inspire our heroic Red combatants in the mission entrusted to them by Chairman Mao, the Party, and the Chinese People.

"The objective is to hit at the very heart of his lair the arrogant enemy, the American imperialist, to show him that there is no refuge possible for him in Asia as long as our soldiers, our scientists, our whole people under the inspired direction of Chairman Mao combine their efforts to demon-

94

strate in a striking manner that, quoting the immortal words of Chairman Mao, 'all the reactionaries, all the imperialists, are paper tigers. In appearance they are terrifying, but in reality they are not so powerful.'

"We know that the enemy, stricken by fear and impotent rage, will not disarm all at once. As Chairman Mao has proclaimed, provocation, failure, new provocation, new failure, and so on to total ruin, is the logic of imperialists and they will never go against this logic.

"So it is certain that the American imperialists who possess powerful weapons will pour them down on our industrial installations and our air bases, that they will transform our smiling and fertile regions into deserts and cemeteries. Hundreds of thousands, maybe millions of our brothers, our wives, our sons will suddenly perish in the blinding lightning of atomic death or after a long and atrocious agony."

Miss Wang changed her voice. Standing to attention and raising her voice, she went on with her recitation.

"What will happen then? The Soviet revisionists who are, as Chairman Mao has demonstrated so well, the active partners of American imperialists, at first will rejoice. They will think in their limitless stupidity that the great Cultural Revolution, which inspires in them a deadly fear, is defeated. But it will not be long before they realize their mistake, for they are, as Chairman Mao has said so well, like flies batting themselves against the glass. And it will not be long before the peoples of the world, and first of all the Soviet people in the homeland of the great Lenin, will sweep away with indignation the despicable clique of the Brezhnevs, Kosygins, and other emulators of Khrushchev.

"Imperialism and revisionism would have dug their own graves. Chairman Mao has said, 'We stand firmly for peace and against war. But if the imperialists insist on unleashing another war, we must not be afraid of it' (*On the Correct Handling of Contradictions among the People*)."

The girl paused and then rose up on her toes. Changing

95

her voice to that of a primary school pupil in a recitation contest, she went on:

> *Red, orange, yellow, green, blue, indigo, and purple;*
> *Who dances in the sky and waves this multicolor*
>   *ribbon?*
> *After the rain, the setting sun comes out*
> *And row upon row, the hills are blue like the valley.*
> *Here, long ago, a terrible battle raged*
> *The bullets from the guns transfixed the walls of the*
>   *village*
> *Now they are an ornament, and the hills*
> *Today more beautiful.*

She went back to her natural tone.

"It is one of the most beautiful poems Chairman Mao has written. . . . That's it," she concluded.

She carefully folded the paper and gave it back to her uncle.

"That's it," he echoed.

"If you don't mind," Georges ventured, having summed up Mao's quotations to himself, "I think it's all pretty vague."

Miss Wang pouted disapprovingly, making her seem even younger. But Chen smiled. And Georges noticed for the first time that he could also look mean.

"Of course," he admitted, "the document my niece just read shows only the political and ideological aspects of the operation planned. Not the technical details. Don't forget that Chairman Mao has declared 'politics must be at the command post.' "

Without a word Miss Wang stood up and left, carefully closing the door behind her.

Chen gave himself up to a strange series of exercises involving long, stretching movements of his arms and legs as he counted rythmically. He resembled a boxer, training alone, filmed in slow motion. Then he sat down and cleared his throat with a sound from the depths that reverberated thunderously through his windpipe. And a superb hawker, all round and yellow, arched ten feet through the room directly into a spittoon of blue and white enamel. The success of this typically Chinese performance seemed to reassure Mao's old companion.

"Be suspicious of my little niece," he cautioned in a small voice. "Be suspicious of everybody, even yourself."

"Of you too?"

"Oh yes."

The door opened. Miss Wang entered soundlessly on her blue sneakers, followed by the young army officer who had upbraided Georges—how long ago? Ten minutes, an hour? —about his phantom camera.

"A comrade from the People's Army of Liberation," said Chen. "It's not essential that you know his name. I can only tell you that he played an important role in perfecting the plan of attack we've been discussing."

The newcomer didn't bother to look at Georges. In a monotone, totally unlike the passionate flow that earlier had marked his speech, he began his recitation. From Miss Wang's uncertain resumé—she was out of her element, but no more so than Georges—it appeared that the operation called "East Wind" would be carried out by ten or so Ilyushin-28 attack planes from a base in Yunan, only twenty-five miles from the border of North Vietnam. They would make a large detour so they could come in over the sea from the South, whence they would be least expected; they would hedgehop, perhaps their only way to elude enemy radar. At best, one or two of them would arrive over the target. The crews were almost certainly doomed, either by enemy action or by the atomic explosion itself, for the bombs would be launched at little more than one hundred feet without any delaying mechanism provided for the explosion. The hope was that at least one bomb would explode in South Vietnamese territory, although

97

not necessarily near an important American base. The inevitable American reprisal and not the Chinese raid itself was the essential political result they looked for.

"Recruited from among the best sons of our fatherland, our hand-picked crews have now been in training for three months," the staff officer boasted. "They are proud to have been chosen by Chairman Mao to carry out this harsh blow against the imperialist enemy. They have been imbued with the rightness of Chairman Mao's precept, 'Never engage in combat without preparation, nor in combat whose outcome is uncertain. Strive to wipe out the enemy by adopting a war of mobility."

He said something in Chinese to Chen, took his hand, then Miss Wang's, and left, nodding with visible antipathy to the foreigner to whom these secrets had been disclosed. Georges asked himself once more why these people kept invoking Mao while trying to sabotage the goals he pursued by open treason.

"All right now," said Chen, "are you satisfied?"

"Why should I be satisfied?" said Georges. "This plan seems monstrous to me. I'm neither Chinese nor American. As a progressive I disapprove of the atom bomb, no matter who uses it. And besides, so do your leaders if I remember correctly; they've said more than once they would not be the first to use it. In short, there doesn't seem to be any proof of the reality of this project. And as I asked you before, what would you want from me, even if all this information you've given me were beyond question?"

It was the longest speech Georges had made since he had arrived that evening. He soon realized that it made little impression on Chen, who waited patiently for Georges to finish in order to resume the lesson on nuclear strategy. He sought a pretext to get away, to take time for reflection, so he said awkwardly, "I have to go to the toilet."

The request hardly sparkled with invention. But it had the advantage of simplicity and truth.

"My niece," Chen said amiably, "will accompany you. To the door, that is."

The john was not too squalid, no worse than those in a French school. There were some graffiti on the eight wooden doors which were raised about a foot from the floor. A single oil lamp lighted the foul-smelling area. The noises of defecation and of the inevitable hawking were added to the panting dialogue of an amorous couple closeted in one of the cubicles. The first two doors were locked. The third opened, but Georges bumped into a squatting form. He suppresssed a "pardon me" in French and moved to get out. But an aged voice whispered in French, "No, wait. Aren't you the foreigner I saw a while ago?"

Georges fumbled in his pocket, found the box of matches Miss Wang had provided just in case. Quitting the "Turkish" toilet he had been busy cleaning, Dean Yang Po-lao turned. He studied Georges over the rimless glasses that the Red Guards, indulging in censurable generosity, had allowed him to keep. In his astonishment, Georges let the match burn down to the end; it scorched the tips of his fingers and he dropped it with a ringing "Shit!"

"That's the right word," the Nobel laureate approved. "I don't know who you are, young man, and it's not important. But when you leave this madhouse that China has become, if someone asks you what the Cultural Revolution is, tell them 'It's shit.' And tell them, too, that you got this from Professor Yang Po-lao, Nobel Prize winner in Chemistry, Gold Medal from the Paris Academy of Science, and, as you see, great specialist of chemistry—organic, that is."

He bleated like a goat and went back to scrubbing the toilet with ardor.

Georges backed out. In the next cubicle he relieved himself. He was to reproach himself afterward for not having had a word of sympathy, of human warmth, for this desperate old man exiled to this excremental purgatory. But too many images popped into his head: Chen, Miss Wang, the "East

Wind" operation, the Georgian doubled-up dead drunk on the restaurant table ("What had become of him, anyway?"), the neat little Japanese with his flashlight, the black giant Garrison pointing his compatriot out for the execration of the masses with that vengeful finger, he himself undoubtedly destined soon to a like fate. The young girl was waiting for him, immobile as a governess who has sent a child to piddle alone for the first time, like a big boy, but is concerned that he not stay too long and that he not talk to strangers.

He followed his interpreter docilely and found himself back in the little office. Michel Loriot had taken the place facing Chen on the chair Georges had left. His endless legs were propped up on the table. As a sign of welcome he waved his cigarette in Georges' direction. The staff officer stood by with two sidekicks. Their backs to the wall, they seemed to stand at attention. A true council of war.

Chen led the attack. "What does it take to convince your . . . friends that the affair we're discussing is serious, that it's not just a newsman's hoax or—how do you say?—"

"A big put on," Loriot said.

"I don't know that expression," said Chen. "What does it mean really?"

"The problem is not so much to convince my . . . friends, as you put it," Georges replied, "as to convince myself. And we're far from that! Very far!"

Miss Wang went on translating what had been said into Chinese for the benefit of the silent military triumvirate.

The three heads with their red-starred khaki caps huddled together. There was whispering and hawking up of phlegm, familiar signs of concentration. Chen joined them. The two Europeans looked at each other, both prey to the same perplexity, the same disquiet.

"It's a trap!" Loriot said in a low voice.

"Of course it is! But so what? What are you going to do about it? Call the police?"

At this instant trucks stopped with a grinding of brakes in

front of the building. Muffled shouts, insults, sounds of feet in felt-soled shoes. About twenty seconds later there was the crepitation of machine guns followed by the shrieks of women. All the lights went out.

Georges recognized Miss Wang's hand in his. She tugged at him without a word. He never would have thought he'd be able to go down a stairway in the dark so fast. In the courtyard shadows moved about in all directions. Sacks of pamphlets and posters were heaved over the six foot wall. Sporadic firing continued to crackle in the street where the 916th Regiment was apparently making a stand against its attackers. Chen and Loriot had disappeared. The girl jumped onto a bale of posters, grabbed the top of the wall, pulled herself up, and disappeared on the other side. Though somewhat rusty, Georges followed her without too much effort. They found themselves in a vacant lot with empty crates here and there and mountains of stinking garbage. Shadowy forms, taking the same escape, ran along at full speed. Georges thought for an instant he had lost Miss Wang, but with relief he recognized her silhouette, bent in two, outstripping her competitors. Nobody was in pursuit yet. All traces of fear left the journalist. Instead he felt rejuvenated, as if he were taking part in a totally absurd game whose rules he did not know but which presented no danger to him. The empty lot was almost a half mile wide and ended in a row of brick buildings now plunged in darkness.

The girl was waiting at the corner of the first building, fresh and smiling. Georges thought his lungs would explode. Miss Wang came up close, rose up on her toes, and lowered his face to hers. Her lips were very soft. For a while he forgot everything.

"Where to now? I certainly can't go back to the hotel."

In an uncertain voice she said, "Well, I can't take you to my place."

"Why? Your reputation?"

"I don't think they're after you," she said, ignoring the

absurdity of his remark. "But there is a risk. Anyway, you have no choice. You'll have to go back to the Hsin Chao. There's nobody who could take you in. Not even me."

There was no discussing it. Not one single Chinese out of 750 million could shelter a foreigner, even someone the authorities considered OK. A gigantic web choked every household—committees in every street, every neighborhood; ever-vigilant old matrons assigned to check the cleanliness of every house, the placement, the size, and the number of Chairman Mao's pictures in every room; numberless kids playing in the hutungs awaiting the problematic reopening of the schools; neighbors; for that matter, the whole implacable system of assurance and counterassurance which makes every one the guarantor of ideological purity in the neighborhood as well as the guarantor of his own.

Again he gave in to discouragement.

"Someone certainly must have put the finger on me, turned me in! I'm done for. You too! We're finished!"

She did not answer but slipped her arm under his, something she must have learned from the movies. She shivered a bit, perhaps from the cold, because the autumn wind had come up, or from fear, or just because she felt good. They went along the deserted street. Under a lamppost Georges looked at his watch. It was only a little after midnight. They walked in silence for half an hour. Now and again they would stop to kiss until they came into less deserted areas behind the covered market. There she hailed a pedicab, ushered him in, and gave the address of the hotel.

"I'll come to pick you up tomorrow at eight. We have a tour organized to the tombs of the Mings," she threw out in her official voice. The man got quickly onto his seat and began to pedal swaying from side to side. He had a bony back, the dark neck of a man from the south, and a shock of gray hair. He panted. He would have to be more than sixty.

Georges must have fallen asleep. The man was shaking him, shouting into his ears incomprehensible words which

102

obviously meant that they had arrived. But Miss Wang must have given the driver instructions, for he stopped the pedicab some distance from the hotel, in Hatamen, in front of what was formerly the Marco Polo antique shop. Georges stumbled to his feet. He wondered what he would do with the printed receipts for twenty and thirty maos that the old man had given him for his crumpled bills. Put it on his expense account? And give it to whom? The director of *African Will Power*? Mr. Marcel?

4 ● HANDS IN HIS pockets, the honest journalist coming nonchalantly from a dinner at the ambassador's, he walked the two hundred yards to the Hsin Chao. In front of the Mongolian restaurant, closed at this hour, which took up the eastern side of the hotel, stood a big black car. When he got up to it, the front doors opened simultaneously and two men in dark suits barred his way and pushed him silently into the car. "So, Chinese security hires Europeans!" he said to himself.

In the back seat between two men, as the Volga he already knew sped away from the curb, he heard a familiar voice ask, "Well, how is the honorable comrade Chen?" It was the voice of Zagachvili.

Which is better in Peking—to be kidnapped by the Russians or arrested by the Chinese? Unhappily, the first doesn't exclude the second. On the contrary, it makes it more inevitable. Settled into the cushions of the Volga, not very well upholstered but less battered than the pedicab, Georges gave himself up to perfectly futile reflection. He was not listening to the buzzing voice of the Soviet diplomat. Trying to be sociable, he apologized for his behavior at the Four Tables. ("You know how it is, my friend, in this town, with all the tension we have to cope with . . .") He thanked him for having told the embassy to come and get him ("The chargé d'affaires really worked me over! What a reaming!"), he offered cigarettes ("Papiruski or American?"). The driver and the man next to Georges, both of them silent, had the silhouettes of the perfect flatfoot—massive shoulders, round felt hat pulled down square over the head, the face—at least that of his neighbor, because what Georges could see of the driver was just the back of the neck crossed by two horizontal folds à la Eric von Stronheim, but they must have been of the same type—fat and blondish, flaccid, jutting (but double or triple) Roman chins, enormous mitts without rings. They surely were armed. Noncommittally, like a beginner homosexual, Georges edged against the hip of the mute beside him but found nothing.

Zagachvili talked on and on. He persisted in excusing himself.

"I hope you won't hold it against me, this . . . cavalier invitation? But we doubtless have a lot to talk over. And, my friend, you've made yourself rather scarce. Is it your little interpreter, the one I saw with you yesterday at the Hsin Chao, who keeps you so busy night and day?" He had a dirty laugh. This is the last straw, Georges said to himself—first the complicity, and now a dirty mind. "Let me give you some advice." Big brother, the learned Pekinologist! thought Georges, vaguely enraged in spite of the sleepiness that this flow of words sank him into more and more. "Be careful! They're all informers. They have no choice, poor things; if not they're sent back to the country. Understand? A cigarette? Ah no, of course not, you don't smoke."

The car rolled along down wide deserted streets. They encountered here and there the first poster-hangers of the night with pails suspended from the handlebars of their bikes, a girl sometimes perched on the crossbar, her braids hanging out from a cap. After turning a corner, the avenue narrowed. "Anti-revisionism Street," Zagachvili sighed. As they passed, some kids who should have been asleep at that hour waved their fists and shouted insults. The car's right window was ornamented, after the current fashion, by a superb star of spittle. After signaling with the headlights, a big door opened in front of them. The car wound past an ugly white mansion with a fake-classical colonnade, and penetrated a thicket of low trees. A stone bridge arched over a little brook. At last the driver stopped in front of a three-story brick building. There was the sound of frogs croaking.

"I'll show you the way," Zagachvili said.

He opened a door and tried with no success to switch on the light. The cop followed close behind Georges; on his neck he could feel the strong breath of onion and cheap tobacco. Georges stumbled in the dark against a metallic object, sharply nicking his calf, at which he let out a ringing "shit." Zagachvili came back; his cigarette lighter disclosed a child's bicycle.

"It's Volodya's. When he left with his mother and all the other Soviet families—you know, during the big demonstrations—he was not even allowed to take it. I'm sure he misses it in Moscow. Judging from the size of the bicycle, Volodya would be seven or eight. "He's a good boy," pursued the fond father. "If you like, I'll show you his picture."

By the trembling flame from the lighter they climbed three stories. They entered a petit-bourgeois home. A full-color picture of the Kremlin faced a view of the snowy peaks of Georgia. Georges sat down in a far from comfortable chair in the living room. "What do they call Henri II furniture in Russia? 'Ivan the Terrible'?" he asked himself. The cop busied himself in the kitchen and brought an almost full bottle of Georgian "koniak" and three glasses.

"Make yourself at home," the Soviet said undoing his tie. "But maybe you're hungry?"

Georges nodded. As a matter of fact, how long had it been since he had eaten?

"You'll have to excuse us. Since Galia left . . . you know how it is . . . a bachelor's place . . ."

The flatfoot went back to the kitchen. Zagachvili pulled

105

his chair up close to his guest's. He no longer acted the good guy.

"You didn't answer me before about Chen. Don't you think it's time you put your cards on the table?"

In one gulp Georges downed the smelly glass the flatfoot had put before him. The alcohol burned his throat and his face reddened. He got up and went to help himself to another.

"I'm in no mood for games. You brought me here. Thanks for the invitation. And for the brandy. Now be kind enough to have me taken back to my hotel. I had a very rough day. The other members of the delegation, my friends, will be looking for me. We're supposed to go on a tour to the tombs of the Mings very early tomorrow and I don't want to miss it. So goodnight!"

He directed himself to the door with what dignity he could muster. It was his second false exit of the evening.

The other did not move. In an even voice he said, "I'm not keeping you. We have no cellar here and no torture chamber. Don't believe everything you read in spy novels. But we are very far from the hotel. My driver has put the car in the garage. And you won't find a taxi around here. Not even a pedicab. You Westerners, you really go for pedicabs, don't you? It's so picturesque, so much local color, so much old China! . . . No, all you'll find outside the embassy are Chinese, and Chinese very badly disposed toward anyone coming from here. But what would you expect—they take everyone for Russian!" He affected a bitter laugh, which did nothing but increase the exasperation of his guest. "Come on, please sit down. And let's talk, like reasonable, civilized people. You can't accuse a Soviet citizen of being a racist. But all the same, we're all in the same . . ."—he hesitated—"in the same boat here."

"Sure," Georges interrupted, "a boat that floats on a yellow sea. Don't talk to me, old boy, I know all the clichés. They don't interest me. You guys in Peking, you play your own game. Believe it or not, I don't give a damn. Count me out,

106

I'm not playing. So we have nothing more to say to each other."

The cop put some very appetizing "zakuski" on the table—smoked salmon, herring, salmon roe, cucumbers, chopped liver, pickled tomatoes, rye bread. Georges went mechanically back to his chair and helped himself to a large portion of Russian herring. His mouth full, and extracting bones all the while, he concluded, "As for Chen, I saw him at the stadium along with a hundred and fifty thousand other people. I admired his mastery, his art of turning the crowd. That's all. Now, since you won't let me return to my hotel, at least let me eat in peace. Georgians have a reputation for their hospitality. Here's your chance to prove it."

This little speech made no impression on his host, who also helped himself generously; one after the other he gulped two large brimming glasses of brandy. Then he sat back in his chair, belched and began again in an even voice.

"The situation is far more serious than you seem to think, for you personally, for us, for the USSR, and for anyone interested in peace. We know—no use telling you how—that Chen had you come to Peking only to let you in on China's present atomic projects. You seemed a curious choice to us. But in light of the fact that you are, or give the impression of being, politically uncommitted, vis-à-vis France as well as the United States and the Soviet Union, and also given the fact that Chen knew you, that your series of articles in *African Will Power* had done him some good without lousing yourself up at the same time in the eyes of the ruling clique, you offered him certain advantages, certain guarantees. At least it must be so, because you're here."

He heaved a sigh and Georges broke in. "You have some imagination. It's you, apparently, who gets high on spy novels."

Zagachvili looked at him sharply.

"Let's not waste time. I assure you that we're aware of many things. You're just an amateur in this area, you know.
107

Which is not the case . . ."—he hesitated at the edge of a formal admission—"with everybody. Where did you come from a little while ago in your ridiculous pedicab?"

"None of your business. But if you must know, I was at the Algerian Embassy."

Georges received two terrific slaps across the face. He whirled around to see the cop standing behind his chair. He had not heard him approach. He felt surprised even more than indignation at the show of violence, the first so far in the whole adventure.

The henchman looked to Zagachvili for what to do next. The Georgian was turning the glass of brandy distractedly in his closed hand. He affected not to have noticed the incident. At last, with a negligent gesture he ordered his man to leave the room.

"We have no intention at all of torturing you, or using drugs, or giving you the third degree"—Georges admiringly noted his mastery of the language—"to make you talk. We only use such methods as a last resort, and never in our embassies. But I thought it necessary to bring you back to certain . . . realities. Don't you see, Mr. Benachen, you're in this thing a lot more deeply than you seem to think?"

He continued in a professional tone but very low, as if, even in the heart of the Russian enclave, he was afraid of being heard by his own compatriots as much no doubt as by the Chinese.

"Beyond his official function on the Committee of Solidarity, Chen had been assigned until a few weeks ago to the political supervision of the 'special arms' program. But the ouster of Chen, at least until the meeting at the stadium this afternoon, fitted in with, according to our . . ."—he stumbled on the word—"sources, the decision to place ballistic missiles with nuclear warheads at Lop Nor—that is say, pointing right at our Siberian bases."

He lowered his voice even more.

"We have every reason to believe that with the expulsion
108

of Chen, if it's confirmed, Peking's ruling clique plans to go on the attack against us, and with the direct complicity of America. That's why it's vital that we know, through Chen, whom we consider a reasonable man, where we stand on this matter. This is where you come in. Do you begin to understand?"

What Georges really understood was that Zagachvili was mistaken or pretended to be, because Operation "East Wind" was directed against the Americans in South Vietnam and not against the Russians. Unless . . . unless of course Chen had deliberately misled him in order to hoodwink the Soviets. These near confidences, the flow of which he seemed unable to stop voluntarily, furnished no clue as to reliability. It must be that he was altogether intoxicated and intoxicating.

"Apart from the couple of slaps and the Georgian brandy, which is hardly great I might add, what do you offer in exchange for the . . . intelligence you seem to think, and you're wrong, I have access to?" Georges asked.

The man stood up—pale, romantic, with the lock of black hair pasted to his forehead, his slender hands showing dirty nails. A kind of Slavic Malraux with Proust's mustache, Georges thought; a secret agent who really liked his job and also the China he had been assigned to.

"One doesn't offer money to a man like you," Zagachvili answered. "At least not essentially as a stimulus. No, we offer you something else—our files. Something to feed a sensational book from behind the scenes of the Cultural Revolution." ("And also," Georges said to himself, "a good way to get a certain number of Chinese cadres fired by letting it be known that the Soviets were their friends for the sole purpose of having them put out of circulation.")

"I'll think about it," Georges promised without conviction. "But I haven't the slightest idea whether I'll see Chen before I leave. I have no way to reach him. He is the one who can reach me. And it's highly unlikely that he will."

The other continued unperturbed.

"Above everything, I'm convinced that your . . . superiors would approve your decision to work with us. I already told you that the relations between our governments—and also, for some time between the specialized services—have become very close. I'm really astonished that no one told you about this in Paris. We have very good friends in the "pool." Do you want me to tell you some names, though of course that would be highly irregular?"

"Useless," Georges put in. "I'll say it again: I'll think about your proposition. In the meantime let me go back to my hotel If not I'll certainly have everyone on my heels by tomorrow morning—all of Intourist, the Wai Shao Pu,* the Afro-Asian Committee, my interpreter, not to mention your Chinese colleagues."

He stressed the "your" in order to emphasize how much he dissociated himself from such a vile species.

"Boris will take you back."

The cop named Boris, the ape with slapstick mitts, silently entered the room and took his place behind his boss's chair, dreamily studying the onion spires of the Kremlin in the big full-color lithograph.

"I'll go with you to the gate and come back on foot, for a little walk," Zagachvili said.

He was again the friend, the man of the world, the diplomat anxious to please his guest. In the car which moved through the miniature Siberian forest of birch and pine around the embassy, he felt the need to give Georges one more piece of advice.

"I'll be informed the instant you have your next meeting with Chen. Believe me, it's no use your trying to keep little secrets. So that we understand each other, all we want from you is a bit of information: what is the significance and most of all the target of the next live firing of Chinese atomic weapons? It's all to our advantage, I repeat, that we cooperate.

* Ministry of Foreign Affairs of People's China.

110

No need to mention—and this isn't a threat, simply a statement of fact—that any allusion in any paper to the friendly arrangements you've made with French intelligence would certainly have the most disastrous effects on your literary and political career in North Africa or any place else. Don't you agree?"

Georges felt as though he were listening to Mr. Marcel.

As the car stopped in front of the gate a muffled roar came to them from beyond the iron grill. It was like wild animals waking up in the zoo as fat little kids approach their cages. At that moment a spotlight shot out, clean and bright, and whipped pitilessly against the three men. A loudspeaker spelled out in Russian, then in Chinese, a litany of imprecations. Georges could see, under the grotesque effigies of Brezhnev and Kosygin, clusters of agitated humans pressed against the iron work of the gate and savagely swaying back and forth to express their loathing of revisionism.

"Here they are," Zagachvili sighed with resignation. "Now the demonstrations begin again. True, they've left us alone since Tuesday. Now we're in for it all night and all day tomorrow."

"Isn't there some way to get out?" Georges asked.

"Be my guest," said the Georgian.

Georges tiptoed to the gate. The howling amplified itself until it reached a degree of intensity far exceeding what he had heard at the Workers' Stadium.

When the woman at the microphone stopped to take her breath, Georges could hear an immense tramping of feet from the masses who had come to swell the ranks of the troops stationed in front of the gate. Pushed forward by the newcomers, the pressure increased. The gate ground on its hinges. Suddenly, with a metallic crash, it crumpled to the ground. Some hundreds of demonstrators found themselves on the embassy lawn. Uncertain for a minute, they rushed toward the pavilion to the right of the entrance which sheltered the consulate staff. The three men got into their

111

car in a rush and sped toward the chancellery buildings a few hundred yards away. Some boys ran after the car shouting and bombarding it with clots of dirt.

Boris made a sharp turn and two Red Guards who had got onto the roof were thrown to the ground to be greeted by their comrades' laughter. The chase ended and the pursued were able to reach the main entrance of the chancellery without any more trouble. About twenty Soviet functionaries stood about, massive in their dark suits, their arms folded, contemplating the scene. Some wild and gesticulating nuts had got into the consulate pavilion and back out with their arms loaded with files which they threw down in piles in front of the gate torn from its hinges, gaping.

With a detachment born of long habit the Russians asked themselves what had caused this new outburst.

"I think," risked a reddish tub of a man, "it's the affair of the fishing boats our coast guard has intercepted in the Amur."

"Oh no, it's Comrade Brezhnev's speech last week calling for an international conference of communist parties."

Putting an end to the discussion, a technician came to set up an intricate camera with a telescopic lens as long as a bazooka.

"It works on infra-red," Zagachvili proudly explained to his guest. "With it we won't have to excite them with flashes and can analyze their slogans with a calm head."

Some Chinese militia finally came on the scene and, with little effort, drove the demonstrators to the other side of the wall. The loudspeaker sounded an appeal for calm. "Comrades, Chairman Mao has said, 'Revisionism is even more dangerous than dogmatism.' That is why we must fight it on all fronts without tiring, with all our means, as if it were a mad dog. But if we must pursue the heroic battle on the diplomatic front, we must treat these mad dogs more with contempt than with violence—these representatives in Peking of the revisionist clique these successors of Khrushchev who

112

cynically betray the heroic people of the great Soviet Union, fatherland of the great Lenin and the great Stalin. Let's express with dignity our indignation for the derisory provocations of these vain ideologues, the Brezhnevs, the Kosygins and associates, who have ordered their valets in the Amur river to intercept the ships of our heroic fishermen armed with the Thought of Mao Tse-tung, and who have renewed their monstrous appeal for a would-be conference of fellow parties, a meeting that, as Chairman Mao has proclaimed, would solemnize their own descent into the grave. . . . Comrades, follow the orders of responsible comrades of the Revolutionary Committee of Peking! Demonstrate outside the gate without soiling your feet on earth stolen from the Chinese people by the Soviet revisionists!"

While the demonstrators slowly fell back, the spotlight went out. Upon the return of darkness the shouts of the unchained masses took on a new consistency. It was no longer the zoo, but the virgin forest that seemed to take over beyond the limits of the Russian compound. Suddenly a flame shot up; a bonfire raged, fed by the consulate archives. Cries of joy and applause welled up. The purifying fire had just reached the straw effigies of Brezhnev and Kosygin hanging from the end of a rope.

"The Chinese people have won a new victory," murmured Zagachvili, mimicking the style of a Radio Peking broadcast.

One by one, almost regretfully, the Soviet diplomats went back inside. Zagachvili invited Georges to go with them.

"Let's have a drink," he said. "If the demonstration doesn't break up and you can't get back to your hotel—this time you can't blame me—we'd be very pleased to have you spend the night. There is no lack of empty rooms since all the families left."

In the immense reception hall under portraits of Lenin, Podgorny, Kosygin, and Brezhnev an atmosphere of siege

113

prevailed. Men sat around morose, smoking, with glasses of vodka or Armenian brady in front of them; they went without letup for refills from a centrally located table loaded with bottles. From time to time tall fellows in black leather coats and the usual dark felt hats arrived from outside to report on the progress of the demonstration. One could still hear, even through the closed windows, muffled echoes of anti-Soviet recitals and quotations from Chairman Mao interspersed with music. *The East is Red, The Great Helmsman,* songs from the Long March, the unvaried repertory. Finally, beyond irritation, one of the Soviets went over to the phonograph and soon the Red Army Choir filled the room. At this three or four of them let loose their nostalgia. One of them wept. The big tears of the Russian patriot, the drunkard, the deceived lover of China coursed slowly down his flaccid cheeks. The example was followed by many others around Georges.

"What on earth have we done to them for them to hate us so!" a stocky towhead exploded.

He smashed his fist down on a little table full of glasses; everything clattered to the floor.

"We've never brought them anything but good, and that's just what they resent," put in the sententious Zagachvili. "Take, for instance, the day our families left; at the airport they spit in my wife's face. And then they bent down so they could spit into my son's face more easily, poor little Volodya. I'm sure the air traffic controller who arranged the thing—you know, the regimental chief, 'Red Hero of the Aeronautical Institute'—was really determined to pay back old debts—the years of study we'd given him at the Sverdlovsk Institute of Aeronautics, flight training in the IL-18, radar duty in Leningrad. The Chinese are like that. What can you do?"

"It's certain that they don't have the normal human reactions," the little fat man agreed—a consul named Vassily, he was considered one of the best sinologists at the embassy. "For instance, I recognized among the mob looting the con-

114

sulate premises an old secretary of mine, a Manchu from Harbin who had worked at the embassy since 1949, who bounced my children on his knee. My little Tania called him Uncle Li. He saw me and spat in my direction. Luckily he was too far away."

"These people understand nothing but force," put in a junior with an air of importance. "We were wrong to treat them like Westerners, to build their factories and dams, and especially the nuclear reactors."

This last phrase was pronounced in a strangled voice as if he were pierced by the enormity of the political error.

Georges grew nervous.

"It seems to me you talk exactly like colonialists deceived by their former subjects!" he threw out in Russian.

Zagachvili started. Clearly he hadn't suspected that the journalist had the slightest notion of the language. As for the others, who had forgotten the foreigner's presence, they stared at Georges with disapproval colored by astonishment.

Zagachvili thought it best to protest.

"You are comparing what is not comparable. The relations between the Soviet Union and People's China have never been, as you well know, relations of a colonial nature. It was a matter of the older, more developed socialist country aiding a newcomer in our camp. Only the big-power chauvinism of some deviant Chinese leaders, drunk with pride or watered by American gold, has succeeded in changing China's course, steering her temporarily outside the great socialist family. In reality, the Chinese people love the Soviet people and tolerate ever more grudgingly the evil counselors who now surround Chairman Mao. In any case, this is just a simple family quarrel which a socialist foreigner such as you couldn't possibly understand!"

This orthodox outpouring made Georges smile. "That's exactly the opposite of what you told me just ten minutes ago."

But what he had said made the other functionaries fall

back on their reserve. Zagachvili would certainly be repri-
manded for the lapse in security he had committed in introducing a foreigner onto Soviet territory without being aware
that he spoke Russian.

"You haven't introduced us to the . . . citizen," Vassily
challenged Zagachvili.

He insisted on the term *grazhdanin* used in the USSR to
mark the distance of someone who is not, or has ceased being,
for moral or penal reasons, a "comrade."

Fortunately the general uneasiness was dissipated by the
noisy entrance of two young men, quite free and relaxed,
obviously also strangers to the embassy.

Zagachvili went to greet them and spoke to them in French.

"Welcome to the embassy!" he exclaimed. "But how did
you get in?"

"We ran the blockade," the smaller of them answered
cheerfully. Dark-haired, with the short beard of a student, he
wore a parka and was strapped with a bandoleer of sophisti-
cated cameras.

His hand extended, he went all around the room, introducing himself to everyone in a kind of jabberwocky: "Mo-
ricemokegirar of Agence Europe-Reportage."

He came up to Georges and looked him up and down.

"You're not Russian. And not a diplomat either, for which
I congratulate you by the way. Don't I know you?" he asked.

"That might be," Georges answered, "but I don't know
you. We're colleagues, however. Georges Benachen from
African Will Power."

"Ah yes, you've come with the colored delegation. I'm a
Belgian myself. But I'm not a racist," he hastened to add. "I
goofed again. Never mind though. I spend my time doing
that. That's why someone from the press service of the Wai
Shao Pu had me in to tell me that 750 million Chinese were
positively outraged over my prose that, he said, brought
grist"—he raised his voice so everyone in the room could
hear—"to the mill of the Soviet revisionists. Doesn't this de-

116

serve a glass of vodka?" he asked Zagachvili directly, who was listening to him, brow screwed up, not too happy with this affectation of lightness in circumstances so serious.

The second of the two, much at ease, had engaged in an animated dialogue in Russian with the other diplomats. With a lot of gesturing he narrated the heroic epic of how they were able to get to the embassy by a secret route, foiling the vigilance of the masses.

"Look what we've brought you."

From a musette bag he took a pack of Red Guard news-letters. The Russians fell on them voraciously.

"We got them at the risk of our lives!" bragged the other. "It happened at the Tien Men intersection. I spied a queue—which always attracts me irresistibly. I infiltrated it. Fifteen minutes later, here I am in front of this newsboy, a kid twelve years old, covered by Chairman Mao buttons from head to toe. On his sheets, *The East is Red* and *Red Guards of the Capital,* I can see cartoons that make my mouth water. Right there, see, I'm pretty sure it's Chen Wu-hsieh as a hyena, chased by the angel of the proletariat with a pitchfork. And on the other page, Chen again, this time as a snake whose head is crushed by big blows from the little red book. He's been promoted, our friend Chen—it's the first time he's been honored with the front page!"

Zagachvili had a wan smile. "Go on, this is very interest-ing. . . . Don't you think so, Mr. Benachen?"

"Wait and see, it gets juicier," Mocquet-Girard promised. "I throw my two five-mao pieces—naturally I had them ready, I know the ropes—I grab up my sheets, the people around shooting daggers and black looks. But I don't pay much atten-tion to that—nowadays one doesn't draw many white looks, I must say, from our Chinese friends."

He stopped, expecting some laughs which he didn't get.

"And here I am, going back to the jalopy. Vladimir's there" he said pointing to his Polish companion. "But then, my dear friends, everything breaks loose! I no sooner turn around

117

than the kid hollers all kinds of things at me: 'You a big nose, you a big nose!' is what he yells. What's so special about my snoot? Nothing at all. . . . Never mind. Vladimir, who knows their *lingo,* like the Americans say, assured me that that's exactly what this little punk called me. A revisionist bastard! A stooge of the American imperialists! Slaughterer of the Vietnamese! Someone who laughs at the Thought of whatsisname! OK, it's all there. But, you ain't seen nothing yet. The best is still to come. The punk yells again, this time that the cartoons were not supposed to be out before he got new instructions. And just then, a higher cadre walks up. I can see from his bike that he's an important type; it has a double portrait of Chairman Mao mounted on it, a super-pennant coming out of the handlebars, chromium springs on the mudguards—everything but a footman in the basket to help the boss get off and watch the equipment while he talks to us. And this minister—he must have been sixteen years old—he's really arrived, nobody could be more serious, not at all like these little shits who are sent out once in a while to spank an ambassador or burn the British Embassy. He begins to check up on all the Red Guard newsboys in the neighbor-hood; there were twelve of them—you know how it is—and to pick up one-two-three all the sheets that the attacks against Chen appeared in. 'The line has changed,' he says, 'Comrade Chen has been the victim of horrible calumnies from the rotten opponents of the Thought of whatsisname. In fact, he's the best pal the everloving chief ever had. Without him China would fall apart. Rockefeller would already be Chairman of the Revolutionary Committee of Peking, and Westmoreland would have replaced Lin Piao.' Well he praises this character to the skies. At least that is what Vladimir here understood, the shrewdy. He already puts his own papers, these right here, safe in the trunk of his '67 Warshawa parked in a dis-creet hutung in the neighborhood, before coming back to lend a no less discreet ear to the lively discussion about Com-

118

rade Chen, who might well become the future new companion in arms."

He struggled to catch his breath and threw a satisfied look at the people around him. He took two big glasses of vodka one after the other and wiped his mouth with a boyish gesture—"in keeping with the character he has created for himself!" thought Georges, who abhorred this kind of lower-class eloquence, fake Céline for foreigners.

"And there you are! Now I'm going to go back to my place and try to put this all in a telegram, none of which, as usual, my readers will understand, and that will bring down the wrath of not only 750 million Chinese—which I'm used to, in fact I'd feel bad if it didn't happen two days in a row—but also the ambassador and my editor in chief. His honorable Flemish excellency will call me to his office, under the portrait of that other whatsisname, you know His Four-eyed Majesty, and will tell me something like this (turning it on ultra-suave): 'My dear chap, I've read your article about . . . how is he called, this gentleman? Tchan, Tchin, please refresh my memory. Ah! yes, Chen, of course! Thank you, my good man. Very interesting, truly quite interesting. But don't you think, look here, I've underlined it in red pencil, yes here, that the hypothesis you advance on the so-called ostracism of this gentleman followed by a so-called rehabilitation, is, to say the least . . . hazardous? That's precisely the opinion of the Department where the role of this personage is, I must say, considered entirely secondary. In any case, my dear boy, when you have information of this kind, be it ever so doubtful, it's better that you let us know here, where we have at our disposal, you can be sure, all the means of investigation we need, rather than . . . how do you fellows put it? Oh yes! . . . plant fake items in the press. That will be all, my good man. So good to have seen you. We'll get in touch with you for the next reception. . . . And all this, of course, is between you and me. You understand, don't you?'"

119

He stopped to down another shot of vodka and went on, delighted to have such an attentive audience.

"As for my editor in chief, he'll send me a wire tomorrow, something like this. Quote: Can't use your telegram such a number, comma, Chinese names too complicated will bore readers, stop. Please specify briefly if central character considered promaoist or antimaoist and send us exclusive interview Chairman Mao on treated subject, stop. Still awaiting expense voucher May to August. Close quote. . . . Well boys," he added, "it sure is interesting being a newsman in Peking! The whole world envies us, the whole world is watching! Right, Mr. Benachen? By the way, if you want a lift I can take you to your hotel."

Georges stood up and said goodby to Zagachvili.

"I'll call you or stop by to see you in the morning," the Georgian said, shaking his hand at some length.

And then he checked himself and brushed his mouth against Georges' lips. "He's playing the Slav a bit much!" Georges thought, embarrassed. But the diplomat used the opportunity to whisper, "Don't forget about Chen, as we agreed. It would be . . . even more dangerous for you!"

It was the first time he had used the familiar thou-thee— obviously a sign of their supposed complicity.

"And now, fasten your seat belts!" warned Mocquet-Girard as he took his place beside Georges in the rear seat of the car. "Prepare terry-cloth diapers, our special spitproof variety! Arm yourself with the Thought of Boumedienne, or Sékou Touré, or General de Gaulle, or whichever superman you follow ideologically. We'll try to get through. Ready? Good! . . . To the club, James!" he barked at Vladimir, who chortled and, with a play of fake deference, raised an astonishing cap with pompoms and earmuffs that must have come right out of a Polish drugstore.

The car wound through the Embassy grounds into the silent driveway of the park and, for about a quarter of a mile, along an outside wall which was very high with broken bottles

120

planted on top. Vladimir stopped the vehicle, with its lights turned off, in front of the sheet-iron gate. He turned around and put his finger to his lips to tell the two passengers to be quiet; then he tiptoed toward a sentry box where a feeble light glowed. Two fat Soviet goons in leather jackets came out, nodded their heads in recognition, and unlocked the chain, trying like burglars to work as silently as possible. A bumpy road, following the outside of the wall, gave onto an empty lot.

"I think we're OK now," Mocquet-Girard sighed.

"Don't relax yet!" his partner threw back at him.

He drove along very slowly in almost total darkness. Suddenly, at an intersection of their road and a more important street, demonstrators surged from all sides and surrounded the car. In seconds they ornamented the windows with the ritual stars of proletarian spit. The side windows and the rear windows were thus sanctified. Faces came up to press against them. The three inside could hardly distinguish the flattened noses and mouths open in mute imprecations.

"Just what I expected," Mocquet-Girard whispered.

From under the front seat he took a big cardboard sign calligraphed in Chinese and waved it before the crowd. A hail of fists shook the body of the car.

"I don't understand," grumbled the Belgian.

"Let's see it!" ordered his partner.

Mocquet-Girard showed him the poster. The other struck a match and swore in Polish. But it was in French that he said, "You smartass! Do you know what that says? Embassy of the United States, Taipei, Republic of China. What jerk gave you that?"

"It's that little bitch of a Swedish secretary-interpreter, Helga or something like that," the other answered without losing his composure. "I asked her to make it Swiss Embassy, Peking. The Swiss are neutral everywhere, everybody knows that. She wanted to make a little joke. Some joke!"

But he seemed more amused than angered.

121

The mob outside tried the locked doors. The shaking, more and more violent, made the car rock dangerously.

"If someone had told me I'd be seasick in the middle of Peking, I'd never have believed it!" the Belgian joked.

A blinding light pierced the night. A spotlight had just been focused on them from a truck parked thirty feet away. The sight of the three Europeans brought the fury of the masses to a climax. The car seemed to be carried away on human waves. Suddenly a window shattered under the well-aimed slap of a blackjack.

"Now," Georges thought, "this is really an absurd development, right in line with my mission—to be pulled apart by a Chinese mob because the girlfriend of a Belgian journalist decided to have a little fun!" He imagined for an instant the bold headlines:

RED GUARDS FOR FIRST TIME MASSACRE FOREIGNERS. THREE JOURNALISTS LYNCHED IN PEKING DURING DEMONSTRATION IN FRONT OF USSR EMBASSY. ALGERIAN GOVERNMENT PROTESTS TO CHINESE GOVERNMENT OVER DEATH OF WRITER GEORGES BENACHEN . . .
FOLLOWED BY LEARNED COMMENTARIES SADLY RECALLING THE SIEGE OF THE EMBASSIES DURING THE BOXER REBELLION.

"I think it's time you did something," Mocquet-Girard advised the Pole.

He sweated profusely. His hands trembled clenching the steering wheel. He took a deep breath like a trapeze artist ready to leave the platform and, without further hesitation, lowered the window. A ball of crumpled pamphlets hit him full in the face, drawing cheers from the crowd. Hands came through the window and opened the door. Vladimir was pulled from his seat and dragged unceremoniously out of the car. His two passengers chose to follow him before the car

122

was turned over or set on fire. They found themselves in the usual circle. The Red Guards passed the infamous sign from hand to hand venting their indignation. Georges thought he was reliving with multiplied intensity the scene with Loriot at Wang Fu-chin, which had been his real initiation into Peking.

Vladimir took his Little Red Book gravely from his pocket. Perhaps he expected his assailants to recoil before the sacred volume, like a vampire before a crucifix or a consecrated host. But the Chinese began shaking their own copies, setting a rhythm for the antirevisionist litanies they sang out in full voice.

The leader, a pimply ape of a man with bulging eyes, hesitated a moment. He had come to the end of the list headquarters had given him before the demonstration, and he wondered if he was supposed to start again from the beginning or to go and get new instructions, considering the obvious importance of the provocateurs they now had in their hands.

Vladimir took advantage of this pause. In halting Pekingese, carefully articulated, he began a speech which was greeted at first by howling and wild animal cries, even by "Yankee go home!" which did honor to the teaching of English as dispensed by the schools before they were closed for reform and before the teachers were purged.

Maintaining his composure, Vladimir continued his speech, his head lowered as a sign of repentance. Mocquet-Girard and Georges followed his example. Silence settled on the crowd.

When at last, after fifteen minutes, the speaker paused, chin down to his chest, his peroration was saluted with applause. And it was almost as heroes that the three men, their sins washed away, went back to their car. It was hidden under layer on layer of calligraphed strips of paper which the propagandists had stuck all over the body and windows. Their new friends helped to scrape part of the windshield clean and the pimply cadre cleared a way for them through the demonstrators. They started off under a bower of honor formed by Little Red Books, like a second lieutenant and his new bride leaving Saint-Louis-des-Invalides under the crossed sabers of his comrades.

"What did you tell them?" Mocquet-Girard asked.

"I told them we were East Germans," the Pole answered with a wry smile for having compromised his good allies from beyond the Oder. "That we had been warped by the sinister propaganda of Walter Ulbricht, the Khrushchev of the German Democratic Republic, into considering the Soviets our ideological guides and best support. But that the spectacle laid before our eyes at the USSR Embassy, where the diplomats licked their chops over an erotic film, a Russo-American coproduction with Brigitte Bardot, Frank Sinatra, and Mme. Furtseva in the leading roles, brought us to such a point of disgust that we began to understand that only Chairman Mao showed us the right way."

"But how was that enough? They seemed entranced."

"I told them the movie in detail. Frank Sinatra played the role of an American missionary, Brigitte Bardot was his wife, and Mme. Furtseva, USSR Minister of Culture who was, according to certain evil gossips, Khrushchev's mistress, had the role of the Empress Tzu-Hsi. The action took place in Peking in 1900 at the time of the Boxer Rebellion—just right for the fix we're in—and little Chinese orphans were cheerfully laced on a skewer!"

"That might be an idea for Hollywood to dig into," Mocquet-Girard said. "What a cast!"

They arrived in front of the Hsin Chao. Georges said goodby. As in the hymn to Mao, the red sun rose in the east. It had been a rough day.

Sunday ●

● ● ● THAT SAME TUNE again. The trumpets woke him
● ● ● with a start. At the same time someone knocked at
● ● ● the door. He expected to see the little round face,
the pretty pink cheeks of Miss Wang. What was her first name,
anyway? He would have to ask her. It was ridiculous to always think of her as "Miss Wang."

Like the Three Wise Men they appeared in the doorway,
the dark and shining faces of Diego Tombalouwou, John
Seymour, and Ahmed Abdouldawe, the heroic combatants of
the anti-imperialist struggle. Georges had almost forgotten
their existence, which was still the reason for his presence in
Peking.

"Get up, lazybones!" Abdouldawe droned in his beautiful
bass.

The two others imitated him in English and in Portuguese.
In the corridor, their wives in chorus echoed these morning
incitements. With their bandoleers of Leicas over their
boubous, respectively cream white, lilac, and sky blue, they
were superb.

"You have forgotten," insisted Abdouldawe. "It's Sunday!
We have a big excursion to the Ming tombs on the program.
Maybe, if we have time, we'll get to the Great Wall."

"And we're going to have a picnic!" shouted his wife,
bursting into the room.

Her bright boubou was red with yellow flowers, and on her
head she wore a blue Madras kerchief, a reminder of her
Martinique origins, something she was particularly proud of.
She was a tall, majestic woman, still quite beautiful in spite
of her fifty years (ten more than her husband, whom she had
met at La Pitié hospital where she worked as a nurse's aid).

Georges had to fold his legs as she put an enormous basket
on the bed. Hard-boiled eggs, tomatoes, sandwiches carefully
wrapped, a thermos, bottles of Tsin Tao beer (a leftover of
the German colonization of the beginning of the century), all
of which made an appetizing still life.

This morning Georges did not feel in a traveling mood.

126

The prospect of this happy Sunday trip filled him with abhorrence. He took on a vague, defensive tone. "I think I have the flu. And then I have this article to finish. Do you realize I haven't sent anything to Algiers yet? I'd really better stay."

"There is no question of your staying here," Abdouldawe protested. "What would we do without our newspaperman? And you know the Chinese—they're very touchy. Your absence would upset them terribly."

"They might even find this odd," Tombalouwou put in. "You must be aware of how suspicious our friends from Peking are at this moment. And well they might be," he was quick to add, "if you consider what provocations the imperialists and revisionists of all kinds are guilty of!"

A very light-skinned mulatto, he pretended to have learned French from the Franciscan Fathers of Saint Paul de Loanda, and spoke it almost without accent. His talk always demonstrated a sound, pro-Chinese conformism. Since he left Algiers a week ago, he had been asking insidious questions about Georges' past and present political orientation. The journalist wondered if he suspected something or more probably if he had not been commissioned by the information services of Algiers or Cairo (where he usually lived) to detect the "pawns" who had undoubtedly infiltrated the group. Anyhow, Georges had the strong feeling that the Angolese's allusion to "provocations" was aimed at him.

"If the ladies would agree to leave, I'll get out of bed!" he said with a light tone.

Miss Wang was not waiting for him downstairs. Georges felt disappointment and some anxiety. Perhaps she was busy right now unwinding in a security office the threads of the conspiracy, which all led to him—unless this conspiracy were a myth invented to discredit through him his real or supposed employers.

In this dark mood Georges got on the bus. Apart from the members of the delegation, diverse people, dark-skinned, black, yellow, copper-colored, even white, were already seated.

In the rear, a long arm went up. Michel Loriot waved for him to come and sit beside him. But still no Miss Wang.

At first the two men kept an embarrassed silence. All around them people were jabbering in French and in English. Extreme caution was essential. Among the passengers the journalist recognized some of the occupants of the "foreign dignitaries box" the day before at the Workers' Stadium rally. Most of them wore Chinese outfits and gave evidence of their loyalty toward the Great Helmsman by the number of Chairman Mao buttons sported on their chests. A fat woman sat alone, bravely smiling—Mrs. Sydney, the wife of the denounced and condemned black American leader. Her companions avoided her. She absorbed herself in reading the Little Red Book. She seemed to find great comfort there, like a widow of a Grand Banks fisherman immersed in her missal.

Loriot folded his long legs beneath him. The circles under his eyes were deeper than ever, his breath fetid. "Signs of tension," Georges thought.

"I think," Loriot burst out for everybody to hear, "that we met yesterday at the Peking Hotel reception. Can I be of any assistance for your better understanding of the great attainment of the Chinese people under the leadership of its great educator, great guide, and great commander in chief?"

"No thank you," Georges said. "I've already received enough information from Chinese comrades, better aware of realities than foreigners can be, even if they have the chance of living permanently in Peking."

"Still," the other persisted, "certain projects you hear of in this country are absolutely fascinating! Sometimes they seem a little . . . fanciful, or too . . . optimistic maybe. But nothing is impossible to the Chinese, armed as they are with the Thought of Mao Tse-tung. They are capable of undertaking anything, or of attacking anyone. They have adopted the few precepts of the bourgeois French Revolution of 1789 that still have something to teach: 'Audacity, more audacity, always audacity!'"

128

Georges answered ungraciously. "As a journalist I want you to know, I believe just in what I see for myself. I'm an adept of 'live' reportage, if you get what I mean."

Loriot went on. "You haven't seen . . . our friend since last evening, I suppose?"

"No," Georges cut him off.

The conversation seemed to him useless and dangerous. Besides, he disliked this "resident" of the French service more and more and trusted him less and less. He pretended to be absorbed in the landscape.

The bus ran along Pei Hai Park, then through streets congested by cyclists and the Pei Sheng Men gate, one of the relics of old Peking looking like a fairy castle.

Almost without transition, a flat and quite arid country succeeded the suburbs. Along the straight road, edged with pale gold willows, signs in English, in Russian, and in Chinese reminded the foreigners at every intersection that it was forbidden to venture beyond the prescribed route. Far away on the left, the bluish line of the western hills was drawn, topped by conic temples.

After crossing a small bridge the bus pulled over to the side of the road. Escorted by many jeeps, their roofs decorated by big portraits of Mao Tse-tung, an army convoy of covered trucks sped by. It entered a lateral road to the west which led, a little more than a mile farther on, to a group of metal-roofed barracks half-hidden by a small stand of trees.

Seated beside the driver, like the guide in the usual sight-seeing tour, the chief of the expedition, a prosperous-looking civil servant, explained, "The trucks that just passed us carry hateful creatures who, though leaders of the Party, follow the capitalist way. Those who are still capable will be reeducated, through the teaching of Chairman Mao, under the principle of 'unity-criticism-unity.' Those who follow to the end the line of the Chinese Khrushchev and his masters, the chiefs of the Soviet revisionist clique, the most poisonous weeds, will be presented to the masses during rallies organized by the revolutionary headquarters. They constitute negative examples and can still play a useful role by virtue of that. These buildings were used in the old days as recreation and entertainment centers"—he let out a contemptuous whistle—"for the turtle eggs of the ancient clique of the Peking Committee, the Peng Chens, the Wu Hans, and other personages. They find themselves there again but under slightly different conditions."

He was rudely interrupted. A young interpreter, seated at the rear of the bus, had made his way up to the orator and tapped him on the shoulder. Surprised, irritated, he made it plain that he wanted to finish, but the intruder persisted. He pointed energetically to certain phrases in the little book which he placed right under the nose of his superior. For four or five minutes the guide submitted to the whispered insistence of the young man. Then, his head low, he stood up, got off the bus, and ran toward the reeducation camp.

"This comrade," the interpreter declared, "lacked vigilance and political conscience. He gave way to subjectivism and exposed nonverified facts that foreign comrades were not to be informed of without the authorization of his superiors. He will be justly punished."

In tense silence the bus started out. The interpreter took the place just abandoned by his careless boss and absorbed himself in chapter XI ("The Mass Line") of the little book.

Soon, the vehicle stopped in front of a massive wood construction, painted red, with three vaults. Stone lions, camels, elephants with their front legs oddly bent forward, chimeras, and horses offered themselves. It was the famous Alley of Statues.

With some difficulty, Mrs. Abdouldawe lifted her imposing hulk over a horned chimera, its body covered with scales of stone. Her companions applauded the exploit; the cameras clicked, fixing forever this symbol of militant Africa crushing the hydra of feudalism.

The interpreter smiled with unexpected indulgence but pressed his clients onward on their tour.

130

"Let's not waste our time here," he advised passing over twelve statues of military, civil, and "emeritus" mandarins who succeeded the animals. "They are the ghosts of monsters of the past. Not so long ago a handful of leaders, who, though members of the Party, followed the capitalist road, invited us to admire these things blindly in order to divert intellectuals from revolutionary action, to encourage them to consider themselves superior to the masses, to become 'experts' in bourgeois professions. Thanks to the teachings of Chairman Mao, all these illusions have forever been extirpated from the sacred soil of our fatherland, as these 'works of art' soon will be too."

At just this moment, as in a well-performed opera, a small group of youngsters appeared, singing in full voice "to sail the open seas, one depends on the helmsman." The interpreter went immediately to meet the chief of these Red Guards. Without shaking hands, the two men waved their little books together, each opened to the first page where the handwritten message of Lin Piao recommends a careful reading of the text.

"Let's follow them," he said.

They left in a procession. Gongs and cymbals marked time for the march. The Africans, delighted by this interlude, joined arms with the young Chinese.

On a path through the woods they began to climb a low hill. After a graceful stone bridge, they soon came to a big red door with gold fittings. In the first inner court tufts of grass, already yellowed by fall, grew between flagstones. Then a flight of stairs, another courtyard, a terrace between two one-story stone pavilions.

With an air of importance the interpreter announced, "We are now in front of the tomb of Emperor Chuang Lieh-ti, the last issue of the ghost-and-monster dynasty of the Mings. The legend says"—this with an embarrassed laugh for the manifestly absurd idea he was about to put into words—"that this individual had committed suicide after foreign conquerors entered Peking more than three hundred years ago! But it is,

131

of course, the so-called 'experts,' the bourgeois revisionists, who spread such legends. As if, at that remote age, the great feudal masters could have had any notion of 'patriotism'! Such a story in times like this, when the red sun of Chairman Mao's Thought covers all China with its benign rays! It cannot be of any interest. And so I invite you to have something to eat while enjoying this beautiful sun."

Was this an allusion to the ideological sun or to the celestial one which warmed the old stones of the Si Lung mausoleum? The famous autumnal sun of North China had never seemed purer. Never had the refined civilization of the Ming court, of which this suicide had marked the end, seemed farther off.

Mrs. Abdouldawe called Georges over, had him sit between her and her husband, and like a good mother buttered egg sandwiches for him, of which she compelled him to eat every last bite.

The young Red Guards, this time perfectly friendly, formed a circle around the exotic visitors. Wide-eyed, they watched them eat this bizarre food, the pieces of bread, the meat not cut in advance, the suspiciously fresh eggs. They commented among themselves on the doings of these Martians with their whitish or tanned skins, their too sharp or too flat noses, all marked by the so regrettable characteristic of not being Chinese.

Suddenly, at a whistle from their chief, the boys and girls— the oldest of them hardly more than fourteen—turned back and entered the sanctuary. Intrigued, Georges and the Abdouldawes fell into step with them, their mouths still full. Most of the other tourists, deaf to the scolding of the interpreter who urged them to finish their meal and enjoy the fresh air, the beautiful sun, and the Sunday's rest, also went along.

In the shadowy light, Georges did not at first see very clearly what the adolescents were busy doing. He barely saw their backs in a scene of apparently confused agitation. There were muffled shocks, the noise of broken dishes and of stones being thrown back and forth. As his eyes grew accustomed to the near darkness, he understood. With hammers, mallets, and picks they were systematically demolishing the wooden funeral figurines, the small idols in ornamented dress, and the stylized Ming horses placed on the museum's shelves. With a crisp rustling sound a sumptuous imperial dress of gold brocade was torn to shreds. Two little girls, their cheeks glowing excitedly, hammered with rage at a stone basin adorned with dragons and overturned the two enormous candlesticks that had been stuck into its top.

Urchins jostled one another to get into the principal vault where the coffins of the emperor, the empress, and the imperial concubine, Lady Tian, rested on a platform covered with silk drapes. From a musette the young man in charge pulled out some tire irons and made a sign for the strongest to begin opening the coffins. They panted in the same rhythm as the workers harnessed to the demolition of the ancient wall outside the windows of the Hsin Chao Hotel. Finally, the lid of the first coffin opened a crack. The chief played his flashlight around inside and made a face—the box was empty. The excitement stopped suddenly. Stamping over the debris of exquisitely colored cups, the tatters of silk, the broken marble, the young vandals returned to the inner court. Their hands were empty. The idea of looting had not crossed their minds. Their punitive action was purely ideological.

Back in the open air the youngsters, paying no attention to the foreigners, intoned a passage in unison: "The world is progressing, the future is bright, and no one can change this general trend of history."

"All the same," Abdouldawe ventured, "it's still vandalism!"

He was gray with emotion. He pointed a vengeful finger at the interpreter.

"A great people has no right to attack its own cultural treasures, to destroy its past this way!"

The Chinese began to stammer before such a blast and

feverishly went through his Little Red Book in search of an appropriate answer. Then, like a jack-in-the-box, a gigantic form sprang to the center of the circle. It was Peter Garrison, the public prosecutor at the Workers' Stadium.

Georges had noticed his presence in the bus—the blue Chinese tunic strictly buttoned, the cap of the same color that made him look like a Fifth Avenue chauffeur. But his style was more that of a Baptist preacher promising the flames of hell to all sinners.

"Here we have zealous servants of imperialism and colonialism. But we shall not tolerate their provocations!"

Caught unaware by this sudden attack, Abdouldawe retreated. "Our intention is not," he said weakly, "to interfere in the affairs of the great Chinese people, but . . ."

"Shut up!" Garrison howled in English. "To us the scene we just witnessed is exemplary! The oppressed masses, wherever they are, must step forward and radically destroy the so-called 'cultural treasures' of their oppressors! And where would that be? Well, in North America—I don't say 'in our country' because black Americans don't have a fatherland—and in Washington, at the very heart of the American imperialist system which is a hundred times worse than the rule of Hitler or Louis XIV, the black fighters must begin by destroying the Lincoln Memorial, the monument to that arch-hypocrite who pretended to free the slaves only the better to enslave them, and the tomb of Kennedy, that champion of an exploitation more vicious than any humanity ever knew! We must burn down the Museum of Modern Art in New York, that receptable of all the ignominies fabricated by depraved artists who perpetuate the system by turning the attention of the masses away from combat! And, on top of that, we must at the first opportunity get rid of all the Uncle Toms who preach submission for the greater profit of their masters! These Uncle Toms, some of them are black, but some are white"—he stopped to take a breath and turned openly

134

to face Georges and Michel Loriot—"these so-called 'friends of the colored people' make me puke!" Like a real Chinese he spat out a long jet of brownish saliva which spattered the interpreter's sneakers.

"You are radishes," he added, "all radishes! Red—or black, or yellow—on the outside, but white, hopelessly white on the inside!"

After this bold metaphor he turned toward the group of young Chinese who followed the events, mouths agape. More inspired than ever, Garrison fired at them. "Go ahead, my brothers! Burn these remnants of the past cheerfully! Let the flame of the revolution consume this garbage to the very end! And so much the better if you bring crocodile tears to the eyes of these imbecile bourgeois as they watch you! . . . Translate!" he ordered the interpreter, who obeyed.

Abdouldawe had now recovered from the first shock. He was not ready to be called an "Uncle Tom," which was all he had extracted from the indictment. The little Francophile intellectual raised in the cult of Victor Hugo and Michelet rose to face the Black Power fanatic formed by lynch law and the Bible.

"My dear friend," he began in English, "I'm afraid you have no clear notion of negritude, of what it represents for us revolutionaries of Black Africa, vigorously attached to the profound values of our civilization, which the colonialists tried in vain to uproot. I must say besides that this difference of views is perfectly normal because you are, contrary to us luckier ones, transplanted into foreign soil. Fanon has demonstrated this quite well, in *The Wretched of the Earth*, which you have certainly read . . ."

"I don't understand what you're talking about, and I don't want to understand!" interrupted the other, who added somewhat illogically to the unhappy interpreter, "Translate!"

This done, he exploded. "Fanon! Fanon! . . . You talk revolution to them and they quote books! That's all they

135

know how to do! If you would read a little more Mao Tse-
tung and a little less from the comic books of the colo-
nizers . . ."

Having summarily executed Fanon, who deserved a better
fate, he turned on Georges Benachen.

"And you, the fake Frenchman, fake Algerian, I've heard a
lot about you! I know quite a few white liberals in the States,
the so-called 'friends of the blacks.' Nine out of ten are FBI
informers, spies on the payroll of the imperialists. Yes, really,
if I were the Chinese, I'd be pretty leery. You too, even! Remember what happened to your friend—and he was your
friend, Sydney, wasn't he?"

He smiled with satisfaction at the mention of the people's
justice that had thanks to him, leveled his unhappy compatriot.

Georges returned the attack. "Hasn't Chairman Mao
warned us against ultraleftists who hide themselves in the
folds of the red flag only to tear up the red flag? Hasn't he
praised in his article *To the Memory of Norman Bethune*
a foreigner who, without being pushed by any personal interest, adopted the cause of Chinese people's liberation and of
all colonial peoples as his own?"

Approving murmurs greeted this display of erudition.
Georges was gaining ground. But his opponent was not disposed to be outdistanced. He turned toward his audience and,
demanding a phrase-by-phrase translation of his speech, declared with passionate ardor, "I know you, *Mister* Benachen!"
He emphasized the "mister", a symbol of opprobrium and
insubordination. "You and others like you, reactionaries,
birds of a feather, all of the same stripe! You must think we'll
be as naive as they were yesterday at the Workers' Stadium,
those who were taken in by the pretty speech of Chen Wu-
hsieh! I saw you there at the Stadium, *Mister* Benachen! You
were full of admiration for this personage. By the way, I wonder if it's not he who inspires you, you and your ilk. This
Chinese Khrushchev and his partisans turn your head."

136

Georges was beginning to relish this man-to-man combat without forgetting, however, the dangerous implications in the words of the black.

"Why," he asked, "don't we let the Chinese comrades settle their own affairs? Don't you think they're capable? Do you really think that Chairman Mao needs you to make his ideas prevail over these miserable dwarfs who dare to oppose them?"

"Brothers," the black retorted, his voice vibrating with indignation, "listen to him! Listen to that sweet talk! He preaches ideological disarmament. He tells you: leave the revolution to the professionals and in particular to all those like him, like his friend Chen Wu-hsieh, who have an intense desire to sabotage it. Is this how the great purifying breath of the Cultural Revolution will be able, after China, to sweep the whole world? Already this revolution is beginning to emerge on the North American continent. Next summer we'll see a series of uprisings without precedent against white tyranny there, and it's the mottoes, the thoughts of Mao Tse-tung which, thanks to our work here, will inspire the black fighters of Harlem, Detroit, Alabama, and, yes, even Washington, that citadel of imperialism where the black majority is preparing right now for a real fight. . . . I'll tell you something, my friends, you'll be very surprised soon, and then you'll understand what I myself and others have been doing here in Peking, so far away from the front. . . . But before anything else, we must liquidate the white *agents provocateurs* and their Chinese accomplices who have infiltrated our ranks! We must clean our own house!"

This time his words took effect. Tombalouwou, the hero of Angola, who had followed the speech with rapt attention, went up to the speaker and effusively grasped both of his hands. His example was followed by the other occupants of the bus, except Abdouldawe, who was still under the shock of the rebuff he had just shaken off. Now the Somalian found himself, with Georges and Loriot who tried not to be noticed,

137

the object of angry looks and increasingly menacing gestures from the young Chinese as well as the Africans.

The head of a Ming horse crashed at their feet. Projectiles, fragments of statues, amber Buddhist prayer beads, funeral tablets were piled up at the feet of the young assailants. They only awaited a command from Garrison. One of his admirers, a little girl with neat braids, outraged by the horrors that had just been revealed to her, red-faced from the effort of holding onto an object far too heavy for her frail wrists, held out an admirable marble Buddha, his eyes lowered in the classical attitude of contemplation.

"Let me have it," cried Garrison. "Here's the best use one can make of these relics of imperialism and superstition!"

With a formidable toss, worthy of an Olympic champion, he let the statue fly in the direction of the three enemies of the people who had begun a cautious retreat. Hit on the cheek, Abdouldawe fell down whimpering. Blood flowed down his face and stained his lilac boubou deep purple.

Excitement subsided at once. For the Chinese the affair was becoming serious, taking on proportions no one had foreseen. The youth leader went up to the interpreter who had remained dumb since the dispute had left the oratorical ground, and told him with much energy to take these troublesome foreigners who were assigned to him back as soon as possible.

"During a debate," he reminded, citing an August 1966 decision of the Central Committee, "one must have recourse to reason and not to coercion or repression."

This time it was Garrison who had become the dangerous provocateur.

"After all who put him in charge of this purge?" murmured the Africans, suddenly full of sympathy for the wounded one.

Neither Loriot nor Georges opened their mouths during the trip back from the Valley of the Mings all the way to Peking. From time to time Abdouldawe let out a low whimper. He held against his forehead a white handkerchief which was slowly staining red. The interpreter, seated behind him, made an effort to comfort him. He offered heartfelt exhortations in a not quite adequate French on the necessary sacrifices that must be endured in the cause of the oppressed peoples' liberation. All the while, at the martyr's side his wife vigorously imposed silence. "Can't you leave him in peace, after you'd have let him be killed!"

Peter Garrison, tight-mouthed and scowling, pretended to ignore all this ridiculous agitation. He had taken a red notebook from his pocket, one with the golden ideograms of Lin Piao, and composedly scribbled some notes, apparently as indifferent to the bumps that shook the bus as to the disapproval that the Africans now showed him.

Loriot asked the driver to stop in front of a whitish building in a suburb west of the city. "The Hotel of Friendship," he whispered. "I live here. I'll call you up tomorrow morning. Don't make a move until then. And above all, no reckless decisions." With a detached wave he saluted the group and stepped to the ground. These exhortations to prudence— they came a little late—made Georges smile inwardly. He had hardly smiled otherwise since his arrival in Peking.

That's what Miss Wang made him realize. Because this time she waited for him in the lobby of the hotel, the rendezvous for Peking's elite.

The survivors from the Valley of the Mings effected a dramatic entrance. Abdouldawe was supported on one side by the interpreter and on the other by his wife. His whole face had swollen and turned gray. Dried blood was all over his lilac boubou. He trembled from head to toe, from sorrow, from emotion, from retrospective fear. Everybody rushed up to him. The manager of the hotel, waiters in white jackets, the young lady from the stamp collection shop, the elevator man who had abandoned his car, Albanian basketball players, two West German businessmen. The victim was laid out on a sofa and two chambermaids began to fan him with towels.

139

The manager launched an interminable conversation on the telephone, punctuated with "Hai hai" and "Wei wei." Garrison had vanished. Taking advantage of the hubbub, Miss Wang drew Georges into the main floor dining room, which was deserted at this hour.

"Give me your passport. I have to get you a new visa right away. We're taking a train tomorrow morning at 6:15," she declared point blank.

"A train? . . . but where to?"

"To Canton and Hong Kong of course! Where else would you want us to go? To Tibet? And please, don't look so dumb!"

"But why the train? Why not fly?"

"We have a meeting on the way. A meeting in Wuhan. You'll see. It's a . . . very interesting city. And we'll probably meet some people there who'll be able to answer some of the questions you asked yesterday. You haven't forgotten I hope?"

"You mean 'Operation East Wind'?"

"Why use names? I'm simply referring to . . . the subject we're all involved in."

Never before had the girl addressed him in a tone both so peremptory and so protective—almost wifely. Georges, consciously or not, took real pleasure in this, especially because in venturing upon this unknown and dangerous terrain, he preferred to let himself be guided. He couldn't help teasing her.

"In three days we have become a real couple."

"Do you think so?" she asked, visibly pleased. Then she corrected herself, using the familiar form.

Monday •

● ● ● THE SQUARE WAS nothing but a vast dormitory. From
● ● ● Chang An Avenue up to the station, which could be
● ● ● seen vaguely through the darkness, its two towers like
two small pagodas (the architect, a servile imitator of the
style of the past, paid for his errors in a distant province),
hundreds of thousands of people, perhaps a half-million,
camped out with their baggage. After much leaning on the
horn and switching off and on of the lights, the chauffeur
abandoned them at the corner of Pei Ching Chan. It took
them a good hour to walk the quarter mile which separated
them from the entrance to the station. They had to step over
bodies stretched out on the street; they stumbled over bundles, children, and the aged who did not even stir. It looked
like a refugee camp in the worst days of a civil war.

"It's normal," commented Miss Wang. "They have to wait
sometimes four or five days, maybe more, to get a train which
will take them back home. But they are happy. Almost all of
them have seen Chairman Mao. Or they expect to see him
soon."

The young interpreter had him wakened at four in the
morning because their train was to leave at 6:15. "The station
is only a half mile from the hotel but, you'll see, we won't
have much time," she had said the day before.

He had rather hoped that she would come with him to his
room. "As long as we leave so early, you might as well spend
the night here," he had said with the tone of one who knows
what he's talking about, and reverting himself to the thou-
thee, more loving than proletarian. But she had shaken her
head. "I've a lot to do before we leave. You'd better rest!
You'll need it." She had said goodby without shaking hands.
He found himself alone, before an enormous dish of sweet
pork he had not ordered. He returned to the lobby just in
time to see the unfortunate Somali combatant carried out on
a stretcher, surrounded by attendants in white, their faces
covered by surgical masks. They took him to a hospital across
from the hotel.

142

Back in his room, Georges put a telegram blank in his typewriter. With two fingers, he typed:

PRESS COLLECT AFRICAN WILLPOWER TUNIS
PEKING EXSPECIAL CORRESPONDENT GEORGES BEN-
ACHEN STOP WITNESSED DURING LAST 48 HOURS DE-
CISIVE TURN CULTURAL REVOLUTION BISTOP TRUE
DEMOCRACY INSTALLED IN PEKING WHERE PURGE
VICTIMS BEFORE CROWD HUNDRED THOUSANDS RED
GUARDS FREELY PRESENT DEFENSE AND MAKE VOICES
HEARD AND RALLY TO THEIR CAUSE WILDLY ENTHU-
SIASTIC CROWD . . .

He typed for three straight hours, describing with ardor the scene at the stadium and Chen's performance, without giving his name. He presented Chen as the most faithful disciple of Chairman Mao, vilely calumniated by the counter-revolutionaries. He refrained, of course, from mentioning anything related to the scene at the Institute, but he made a point of demolishing Garrison.

AMERICAN AGITATORS SO FAR UNKNOWN WHO TRY
TO ACHIEVE CELEBRITY BY HARASSING MOST RE-
SPECTED LEADERS OF AFRICAN INSURRECTION LIKE
AHMED ABDOULDAWE CHAIRMAN OF SOMALIA PEO-
PLES MOVEMENT VICTIM OF UNSPEAKABLE AGGRES-
SION WHILE DEFENDING CHINESE CULTURAL VALUES
STOP DO SUCH EXCESSES SERVE CAUSE CHINESE REV-
OLUTION WHICH MUST REMAIN EXAMPLE FOR OUR
LIBERATION QUESTIONMARK WE DONT TIIINK SO
STOP MORE THAN EVER AS GREAT LENIN SAYS LEFT-
ISM IS THE INFANTILE SICKNESS OF COMMUNISM

143

AND ALSO ONE OF PRINCIPAL DANGERS THREAT-
ENING IT STOP THIS NOWHERE SO OBVIOUS AS IN
PEKING STOP AND WHEN ONE KNOWS IMPORTANCE
OF INFILTRATION FBI AND OTHER DEGRADING AMERI-
CAN POLICE SUCCEEDING INSIDE BLACK POWER
MOVEMENT IN UNITED STATES ONE WONDERS HOW
WISE TO LET CERTAIN NONMANDATED INDIVIDUALS
SET FASHION IN PEKING STOP GREAT CHINESE PEOPLE
DO NOT HAVE TO TAKE LESSONS FROM UNKNOWN IM-
MIGRANTS WITH DUBIOUS PAST STOP IT IS FROM
THEM WE EXPECT LESSONS THE END

Quite satisfied with himself he went down to mail his five
pages at the hotel post office. It did not cross his mind that
the character of the double agent he had just described suited
himself more than the black. Georges was an experienced
journalist. It was not in his makeup to put himself personally
in the center of his articles. All things considered, he had a
clear conscience most of the time. Even more now, because he
had done his duty toward his magazine, toward the poor
Abdouldawe, toward Chen. He almost forgot his mission, this
mysterious stop at Wuhan which was now before him.

A friend of his, who had traveled all over People's China in
less dramatic times, had often repeated to Georges, "You'll see
the new station in Peking. It's clean enough to eat off the
floor." He personally had never felt the need to eat off the
floor in any public place. Anyway, he was struck by the image
of a population of 750 million trying hard, wielding fly-
swatters, anti-sparrow campaigns, enamel spittoons, to take
from the Swiss the award for hygienics—it all seemed an
enchanting idea.

That morning Peking central station did not remind him a
bit of a Zurich bank. As in the square, crowds of travelers
waited their turn, lying on newspapers, surrounded by bun-

dles, blankets, portraits of Chairman Mao, and bicycles. Rice was cooking on twenty thousand portable stoves. Mothers were suckling their babies. The loudspeaker did not broadcast any departures or arrivals; only the reading of Mao's quotations and the morning editorial of the *People's Daily*, interspersed with more prosaic announcements: "Comrade Chi Wen-fu has lost her little Wei-san. He is four years old and wears a quilted red jacket and a yellow bonnet. He is barefoot and he will certainly catch a cold. Comrades, bring back Wei-san if you find him to the office of the Revolutionary Committee of the station, to the right of the clock. As Chairman Mao has taught us in *Serving the People*, 'We must reduce to the minimum useless sacrifices.'"

Nobody seemed to know where the train for Wuhan and Canton was to leave from, nor even if it still existed. Finally, succumbing to Miss Wang's insistence, a young employee suggested platform twelve and offered to accompany them. She went on ahead, continually blowing on a whistle with evident pleasure but with modest success. Nobody made way for them. She had introduced herself as a student of the Coal Mining Institute of Mukden, Manchuria. She had come to Peking by foot a few months ago to participate in the Cultural Revolution and see Chairman Mao and had been able to make this double dream come true. Reluctant to make her long march again in reverse—from the north to the capital had taken her two-and-a-half months—she decided to ensure herself faster and less exhausting transportation in the future by becoming a railroad worker. She was presently employed as "agitator" in "the 517 Regiment of the Revolutionary Rebels of the Thought of Mao Tse-tung of the capital railroad system." She seemed to be about the same age as Miss Wang.

They became friends right away; arm in arm, whispering confidences interspersed with bursts of laughter, they walked ahead of Georges who, loaded with his partner's luggage and his own, played the part of the gallant American father shepherding his teenage daughters.

145

Nobody checked the tickets, the passports, the visas. But climbing into the second-class car itself proved laborious. "Comrade Li," Miss Wang explained pointing at her new friend, "is terribly sorry but there are no first-class cars reserved for foreign comrades on this train. Most of the foreign comrades travel by air now."

Georges felt he was transported back twenty years. Lyon-Perrache under the occupation: "The passengers for Valence, Montélimar, Avignon, Tarascon, Marseille-Saint-Charles, all aboard please, platform number four!" The smart guys, unpacking their lunches in the WC which they had commandeered hours before departure. The peculiar gymnastics of keeping one's balance in the vestibules, swinging to the rhythm of the switches. The look, both satisfied and apprehensive, worn by the occupants of the compartments, all of them fearful of seeing someone privileged, provided with a travel permit, with a mission, a uniform (in order of priority: a German soldier, a militiaman, a Vichy high official, a black-market racketeer) come and pick up the seats they themselves had fought for tooth and nail. . . . That same scent of urine-soaked diapers, of sweat, of soiled clothes, maybe here a bit more sour.

Miss Wang waved goodby, from above three rows of heads, to the little Manchurian worker who remained on the platform. Then without hesitation she knocked at the window of the first compartment, began an animated conversation with its twelve occupants, and showed her brassard, with no success. Nobody moved or showed the slightest interest in her little speech. She repeated it at least fifty times through the length of four cars. Same effect. "Let's stay in the aisle," Georges proposed several times over. But she preferred not to hear him.

The fifth car was apparently reserved for a tight-knit group of Red Guards. These young Peking students, thirteen to sixteen years old, had volunteered to spread the word among the political minority in Kiangsi. "Who knows how

146

long we'll be on this train?" said one of them, a big guy with a good build who mouthed a few words of English. "We'd have much preferred to go there by foot, following the glorious example of Chairman Mao's Long March. But the Cultural Revolution doesn't work according to what we want. We must display discipline." All the youths seemed healthy and happy to be alive. Their farewells to their families, perhaps for good, did not seem to have affected them.

Miss Wang excitedly introduced the foreigner she was assigned to: "A revolutionary comrade from Algeria, here in Peking at the invitation of a group for the Cultural Revolution from the Central Committee, who is aching to get back home so that the African masses, fighting against revisionism, imperialism, colonialism, and neo-colonialism, can profit from his experiences.

"He'll need all his strength for this exalted task. He must travel under the most comfortable conditions possible. More than that, he's not, as we are, used to long marches and keeping his balance in the aisles of a train. What impression would we give if we made him suffer all our ordeals? Remember what comrade Mao wrote in his famous article *In Memory of Norman Bethune:* 'a foreigner who, without being pushed by any personal interest, adopted the cause of Chinese people's liberation.' "

The boys could not resist this reminder of the Canadian Communist Party hero immortalized by Mao Tse-tung. In spite of Georges' protests, somewhat hypocritical, not only two seats but a whole compartment was surrendered. Miss Wang was very pleased with herself; Georges took a dim view of her cynicism.

It was almost noon when the train jerked out of the station. Georges threw a last look at the walls of Peking and the three-tiered tower of the Temple of Heaven. After a few minutes they left the suburbs behind; the bare plains of North China spread out infinitely. In the aisle and in neighboring compartments the young people sang. A girl from the

147

group, smiling broadly, brought a thermos of hot tea. She scrutinized the foreigner with a frank curiosity, whispered something into Miss Wang's ear, and stifled a laugh behind her hand. The trip had begun. Neither Loriot nor Zagachvili had shown up. Georges had not told any of the members of the African delegation of his departure. He suddenly realized that he was really in flight. On Miss Wang's insistence the girl with the thermos agreed to take a seat across from them. She fell asleep immediately.

Georges opened his eyes. The train was rumbling through the night. As in a Western, the whistle of the locomotive sent out long ululations. The young girl had quietly gone away. Miss Wang studied him from the opposite seat. She was wearing the shadow of a smile. She had pulled down the shades on both the window and the aisle sides.

"It's almost like a honeymoon," Georges said.

"What's that, a honeymoon?" she asked.

She seemed bothered to be caught short in her knowledge of French language and customs. Georges thought it best to attack this candid ignorance on a practical rather than on a theoretical level. He came and sat beside her, took her round little chin in his hands, and raised the face she offered. She quickly pulled herself away and went to lock the door.

"These are old cars from before the Liberation. That's why we can lock ourselves in," she explained.

"You have to admit that, for once, something from the past is all right."

Before sitting down again she went to put out the light, leaving just the blue night light which was hardly enough to show Chairman Mao's face in its frame and, across from that, a photograph of his birthplace at Shaoshan.

It was she, laughing lightly, who undressed him. The tie gave her some trouble. "It's not exactly the same as the knot of the Pioneers' red scarves," she said to excuse her clumsiness. Georges refrained from asking how many Pioneers she had undressed.

148

They made love endlessly, precisely, ravenously. He taught her some of the techniques the French are justly renowned for and which allow the partners to taste symmetrical pleasures simultaneously and top to bottom. He explained the symbolic number. With the Chinese love of numbers she was an apt pupil. He rediscovered her firm, fresh body, smelling of cheap soap, her slight, round and nicely parted breasts, the light aureoles, the thighs of a gymnast, and the touching callouses on the soles of her feet. "My little long marcher," he murmured to himself. He could see himself going into the Lipp restaurant with her on his arm and introducing her to his friends. And then he imagined the face on Mr. Marcel were he to bring her into the Batignolles café. But he banished this inopportune image. He was not inclined to think of his mission. He could not help saying, "I'd like to take you with me."

"Where to?"

She had placed her head on her lover's knees, breathing deeply, her eyes closed.

"I don't know. Does it matter? To Paris or Algiers. Or, yes, to Djerba. It's a very small island. Plenty of sun. The Mediterranean there is as blue as your tunic. Early in the morning the fishermen come down to lay out their nets. Everybody knows everybody. It's full of pederastic American painters. I'm sure they'd be crazy about you."

"What does that mean, pederastic?"

"They are fools," he answered and gave her a long kiss on the lips.

Almost out of breath she nudged him away.

"I've never seen the ocean," she said. "The summer I was supposed to go to Peitaho, on the Gulf of Pohai with . . . with my uncle, we made the Cultural Revolution. So, you understand! . . . Up to now I had never thought of going abroad," she went on. "But now that I know you . . . Of course I won't go. It's not possible. But . . . Oh! let's not talk about it."

149

For the first time he felt she was vacillating, uncertain.

"Maybe there is a way," he said. "If you could get yourself into Hong Kong . . ."

"Hong Kong," she protested, "that's not abroad. Hong Kong belongs to us, even if the British imperialists still occupy it for a few years until we consider it necessary to drive them out."

Georges persisted. "Will you come to me in Hong Kong . . . after? I'm sure that we could be happy away from all this mess."

As if to reinforce his position, a metal object, maybe a key, banged against the compartment door. Women's voices screamed something in Chinese. Miss Wang sat up startled, covering her breasts with her hands, and quickly put on her clothes. In twenty seconds she became again the anonymous little Chinese in blue overalls, her tunic docorated by the inevitable button. Even her face was transformed; she took on the serious, concentrated, somewhat hostile look of a person assigned to escort a foreigner who goes about the job without the satisfaction she would find in working on a higher ideological level, such as digging an irrigation ditch or public latrines, or attending a meeting.

Georges too leaped into his pants, adjusted his tie and grabbed an issue of *L'Humanité Nouvelle,* organ of the "Marxist-Leninist" communist movement in France that he had picked up at a kiosk in Algiers.

She made a sign for him to open the door. Immediately, like so many characters in a Mack Sennett movie, about a dozen people, who were squeezed together in the aisle, found themselves thrust into the compartment and forced to sit on the benches, on the knees of the two occupants, between their legs. Everyone bounced with the rhythm of the bumpy car. Someone turned on the ceiling light. The invaders, both boys and girls, were young—again the seeming rarity of adults in China. Two or three among them had musical instruments, a guitar and tambourines. They talked among themselves and

150

to Miss Wang in very loud, high-pitched voices. She answered in the same tone. Everything went on in good humor, even joyfully.

"The comrades," said Miss Wang, "want to put on a show for the foreign comrade."

With some difficulty they cleared a space in the center of the compartment. The little books sprang out. Three girls stood up on their toes, pursing their lips in a mannered way. The musicians squeezed onto the benches, the tambourine player onto Georges' knees. Two of the girls gave themselves up to a complicated two-step while the third stood immobile, looking wrathful, then joined the others in a kind of farandole. The choir accompanied them with a passage they read in the recitative manner of traditional Chinese theater. When the number was over Miss Wang asked amid the applause, "Guess what it is?" Without waiting, she answered triumphantly, "But of course! 'The correct handling of contradictions among the people'!"

The artists ran out of breath. They squeezed together again, panting, onto the benches, not without asking Georges' permission. The journalist found himself with half a male buttock on one knee, and half a female one on the other, and all around young, open, intense faces. A girl across from him started the conversation.

"What do you think of our country and of the great proletarian Cultural Revolution?" she asked witlessly.

"All progressive foreigners, me among them, admire most of your accomplishments and consider Chairman Mao Tsetung one of the greatest of Marxist-Leninist thinkers. His influence continues to spread all over the world. Already a number of Western youth take him as a guide."

After Miss Wang had translated the answer, which Georges thought at once conformist, true, and sincere, a glacial silence settled over the compartment. One of the boys finally pointed an accusing finger at him.

"Ah . . . so you adopt the revisionist line."

151

"Why, there is nothing in what I just said . . ."

"You said that Chairman Mao was *one* of the greatest Marxist-Leninists."

"That means that to you there are others!" shot out the girl. "Liu Shao-chi, the Chinese Khrushchev maybe?"

Miss Wang interposed, trying to defend her client. Apparently without success. The air thickened.

"How do you explain," asked the boy while his companions took notes feverishly in their red pads, "your revisionist friends making common cause with the imperialists for the annihilation of China?"

"Yes," said one who had not spoken before, "we know very well that Ko-sy-gin, Johnson, and the Chinese Khrushchev held a secret meeting last month in Taiwan. They were settling the final details of their plan for invading our fatherland. Five hundred thousand mercenaries from the Chiang Kai-shek clique will be the first to attack. The great Chinese people like an ocean whipped to fury will of course engulf them to the last man. Not one will escape. But then American bombers out of Vietnam, and Soviet bombers out of stolen Chinese territories of Northeast Asia, around Irkutsk and Khabarovsk, will try to launch atom bombs over our country."

"We know this too well, because the day before yesterday, at the meeting of Textile Institute Number Four, it was comrade . . ."

"Imperialists, revisionists, and all their atom bombs are nothing but paper tigers," the oldest of the group interrupted passionately. He had remained silent up to now. "It's pointless to brag about secrets in front of strangers. It's putting on airs and proof of conceit. Chairman Mao disapproves of conceit, and rightly so."

Ramrod straight in righteousness, he stood up and made a sign for the rest of the group, including Miss Wang, to follow him. She disappeared for a few minutes into the aisle and then came back, thoughtfully. She sat down beside Georges.

152

"What did he say?"

"He told me to be suspicious of you. That you talked like a revisionist. I explained that, as a foreigner, you couldn't have a class consciousness and level of ideology as developed as ours. I certainly didn't convince him but I don't think he'll do anything."

"Why?"

"Because he himself is at fault. He should never have allowed the boys and girls to open a discussion with a foreigner, and most of all to divulge the secrets of our friends."

"You don't mean to tell me that you believe this tale. It's enough to make you sleep standing up."

"I believe," she said, "that our pilots would be right to act first against the American aggressors. Ah! I just don't know any more! I should never have listened to Uncle Chen, and strayed from the right road, the mass line of my comrades. Do you think I'm a traitor?" she asked anxiously.

After locking the door, Georges tried hard to reassure her. Their anxiety, their bad consciences, created an additional tie between them. They fell asleep in each other's arms.

TUESDAY ●

●●● THE COMPARTMENT SMELLED stale and stuffy from
●●● the sweat of their bodies and the sperm. Miss Wang,
●●● her forehead pressed against the window, watched
the lights as they swung slowly by. Night had fallen. He
looked at his watch. One in the morning. He went over to her
and opened the window. A draft of fresh air and smoke
entered in a rush. New sounds came from the train as it
trundled along at low speed on a steel bridge, thumping
rhythmically over the ties. Someone was shouting incomprehensible orders. A bent silhouette ran past on the catwalk
between the tracks and the bridge railing. The train creeped
so slowly that the man passed their window. Images from
the occupation, the resistance, an aborted assault he had taken
part in, when very young, against a railroad trestle in south-
west France, came to his mind with extreme accuracy. Maybe
it was because he had the same fear of arrest, torture, or
execution he had felt that first time.

He leaned his head outside. The train came to a stop with
creaking agony right in the middle of the Wuhan Bridge, one
of the grandiose achievements of the regime, which links, over
the Yangtze Kiang, the north and the south of China, Hankow
and Hanyang on the north bank, and Wuchang on the south.

"European travelers," Georges recited in his mind, following a 1911 Baedeker that one of his friends had given him as
a joke before his departure, "must take the ferry to cross the
muddy waters of the Yangtze. It is recommended that one
settle the price with the ferrymen, who are in the habit of
robbing their passengers, and of arming oneself with in-
secticides, because of the extreme filth that prevails on these
embarkations. It is also preferable to put currency and jewels
in a safe place; brigands sometimes do not hesitate to lay
hands on ladies to satisfy their greed. The consuls in Hankow
are frequently besieged by complaints, even though it is quite
rare for Europeans actually to be molested."

In the car itself, he heard the sound of tramping feet and
muffled exclamations. There was rapping on the doors of
156

nearby compartments; people came out grumbling. Miss Wang threw Georges a little smile intending some reassurance. Was this the Wuhan rendezvous? It was hard for him to believe that the conspirators had enough power to stage such a thing in advance.

At the other end of the car a woman let out a high, shrill scream. Miss Wang opened her Little Red Book reflexively, like a nun opening her breviary as the *Titanic* goes down. The two panels of the door opened. The ceiling light came on, throwing the compartment into harsh brightness. Two men came in, young, their hair cut short. One of them grabbed the passport Georges held out, leafed through it, obviously not understanding a thing. The second took Miss Wang's orders, nodded his head, and gave a sharp command.

"Everybody down? The train has been stopped? Is that it?" Georges asked.

She looked at him curiously. "Oh, you understand Chinese now?"

"There are things I catch on to by instinct."

They took their baggage and got off the wrong side of the car. The train disgorged its passengers. A light rain was falling intermittently.

Five or six hundred people, stumbling over the ballast and ties, looked about for a place to put down their bundles, their babies, their suitcases, flags, and portraits of Chairman Mao. From inside the cars a faint light was thrown on the scene. Everything went on in silence except for the cries of babies which their mothers and big sisters tried to hush with rocking and patriotic songs.

From the south bank of the river a beacon swept along the train, then searched the opposite bank, lighting factories and warehouses. Two men made a step with their hands and boosted a third to the roof of the car, where he began to harangue the crowd through a bull horn. Some of the passengers asked questions in angry voices. "They're asking," Miss Wang explained, "when the train will go again, when they'll get where they're going." A man came up on a bicycle, certainly an important cadre of the local committee. He got up on the roof with the other man. Both of them began to reassure the passengers and reason with them in what seemed a rather frank exchange. People protested that they were on important missions for Chairman Mao, holders of essential jobs in production or for the Revolution that could not suffer any delay. But the cyclist, a man from the army, ended by admitting that the train had been stopped because of troubles that had flared up in Wuchang; the counterrevolutionaries opposed to Chairman Mao's Thought, pushed on by the turtle eggs of the local Party ex-command, had tried to wipe out the masses.

Pursuing its search, the beacon swept the length of the bridge again. And it was a very long one, more than a mile, with two decks—the lower one reserved for automobile traffic, which was totally nonexistent. And then the beam stopped itself over the car, directly on the two speakers who simultaneously fell flat on the roof. The beacon immediately switched off and tracer bullets came at them from out of the north. The familiar crepitation of automatic weapons mixed with a kind of collective exhalation of astonishment. For the first time since the advent of the regime, the crowd was facing the realities of combat. In an instant, Georges, once again the journalist, searched his pocket for pencil and paper. But he changed his mind. It was no time to risk being taken for a spy, and, who knows, thrown into the Yangtze.

On the north bank explosions reverberated and a warehouse went suddenly up in flames, throwing clusters of sparks into the black sky. The reddish flames gained height rapidly. Some tracers shot quite low over the train.

A young woman flattened herself to the ground, just beside Georges and his partner, protecting her baby with her body. Everyone did the same. By the dancing glow of the flames, all these silhouettes falling down one after the other called irresistibly to mind a file of dominoes, the image so dear to

158

American strategists. Georges took off his jacket, put it on the ground, and, pressing firmly on Miss Wang's shoulders, made her lie face down. Then he got down himself. She turned her face to him. He could not make out her expression but he was sure she had a look of astonishment and gratitude for this unwonted protective familiarity.

Georges felt absurdly happy. "Miss Wang," he whispered between two bursts of fire, "I love you." Her only answer was to press his hand very hard.

Whistling mournfully, the train started up slowly, northward, in the direction it had come from, revealing squeezed against the bridge railing on the incoming side a crowd almost as dense as the one far beyond on the other side. The firing died down and the passengers stood up after some hesitation. But a dozen bodies on the other track lay still. Sobbing and whimpering could be heard. The wounded were picked up howling in pain. A group took up the corpse of an old man and, over this victim of the counterrevolution, they held a session of readings from the works of Chairman Mao and took vows of vengeance in heroic attitudes reminiscent of statues by Rude.

People talked among themselves, waiting for instructions, not knowing what to do or where to go. A skinny woman, trembling all over, loaded down with bedding, spoke to Miss Wang. A little girl of three or four clung to her blue slacks. A big sister of about ten held the baby of the family in her arms, wrapped warmly in a red quilt with yellow dots.

She explained that she was a lower-middle-grade peasant of the people's commune of South Peking. She left when the cadres disappeared in protest against the harassment of a group of young Tientsin activists. The cadres abandoned their jobs, distributed or threw away the reserves of seed and rice and millet, and killed all the hogs. Her husband, the joint-chief of a work brigade, had probably been arrested; she had no more news of him. But, since he beat her in the old feudal manner, she felt it was good riddance. She had

159

finally decided to go down with her children to the Nanning area where one of her uncles lived. Now she didn't know what to do anymore and the provisions for the trip were used up.

Mouths agape, her two girls stared at Georges, the first non-Chinese they had ever seen, whose strange features were made even more terrifying by the flickering light of the fire. The youngest burst into tears and the oldest asked her mother a question and was told impatiently to be quiet. Miss Wang laughed.

"She asked," she translated, "if it was a sickness or if you were born this way."

Again the sound of whistles. The crowd retreated toward the north bank, fleeing from the south bank, which had by now fallen into the hands of the reactionary monsters. Walking was very difficult over the cobbles of ballast in the dark. Sounds mounted from the river—a motor, and then a kind of signal from a siren, short and mornful. A salvo of four shots reverberated and, by the light of fires that raged on the south bank, Georges could distinguish the silhouette of a gunboat. Chairman Mao had called on the navy to crush the counter-revolution. Georges, who had stopped to watch, had the feeling that his presence in this place, at this particular moment, would not be especially appreciated by the authorities in Peking. If it became known, there could be a real uproar.

They were pushed from behind because the refugees—and that was the only term to use—filled the entire breadth of the bridge as they slowly inched along. They resumed their march, stopping now and then along with the group they were part of, to catch their breath or to put down their baggage, happily quite light—a suitcase and a portable typewriter for him, for Miss Wang a red zippered bag, imprinted with a white airplane with red stars and the word "Beijing"—Peking in Latin characters.

Georges held his peace, abstaining from any comment on this civil war that might well mark, after all, a temporary new rupture in Chinese unity, the renewal of fighting between the

160

"warlords." If not his mission—the meaning of which still escaped him—his reportage at least began to take shape. Even macabre touches were not lacking. Right in front of them four men walked along carrying a rigid corpse wrapped in a blanket, from time to time emitting a harsh panting sound from their chests. Thus, Georges thought, this new stage of the trip took on the look of both a funeral procession and the Long March.

All of a sudden they stopped, hemmed in by the crowd; the ground under their feet had lost its metallic resonance. They had reached the bank; the double track of the railroad divided into a number of branches and sidings. They were able to walk faster, to pass the Red Guards with their macabre burden and the woman with her three children.

They found themselves separated from the rest of the passengers by a string of freight cars. Miss Wang stopped, squatted down on her heels, opened her bag, and took out a floral print thermos bottle, two cups, two bowls, a rice-filled sausage, like the ones the soldiers of the People's Army of Liberation carry in battle, dried fish, and two pairs of chopsticks. The meal washed down by green tea seemed delicious to Georges, and even more delicious was the intimacy and solicitude of the girl who treated him a little like a comrade, a Red Guard with whom she would have made a team. At least that's what he wanted to believe.

A tap on the shoulder made him start. Coming from around the freight train, five soldiers had sprung up behind them. Their approach had been muffled by the sneakers they wore. The one closest to him, the one who had touched him on the shoulder, aimed the barrel of his tommy gun at him. Miss Wang put her bowl of rice on the ground, nonchalantly wiped her chopsticks against the leg of her pants, stood up, and addressed him with something that sounded like vigorous protest and was studded with what must have been Chairman Mao's name. But the man shrugged his shoulders and demanded she be silent.

"He doesn't understand Mandarin," said Miss Wang. "I don't know what they want us for. But we have no choice. We're obliged to go with them."

This seemed quite evident to Georges, since one of the soldiers was already tying his hands behind his back. At least he wouldn't have to carry the baggage anymore. Two other soldiers of the squad picked it up. The leader made a sign for them to move out. He must have been a sergeant or corporal before the discontinuance of ranks, unless, thought Georges, not wanting to underestimate his own importance, he was even a colonel. He had the good round face of a peasant. The capture of a dangerous spy and imperialist saboteur—how else could one interpret his presence in a switchyard in the center of China at the very hour a battle of unforeseeable consequences was taking place?—left him totally indifferent. It was almost as though he had expected to find them here. Georges studied his partner, hoping for a sign, some indication that could reassure him. After all, it was she who had organized this trip, which now threatened to take such a bad turn. But the girl avoided his eyes. She walked at his side, carrying her little bag, which none of the soldiers had offered to take from her. He couldn't even figure out if she was also under arrest.

Spurred on by harsh commands and occasionally by shoves on the back so light they might have been accidental, they crossed the switchyard laterally almost at a run stepping over the tracks, stumbling over the switches.

At a grade crossing a truck was waiting, covered by a tarpaulin with a machine gun mounted on the cab. Georges was helped aboard. He found himself on the floor up against a pile of papers and posters, guarded by three soldiers. Miss Wang had not followed him. Maybe she had taken a place up front with the driver. Maybe he would only meet her again in front of a People's Tribunal, the principal accusing witness, while a selected audience would lend shouting approval to her denunciation of the imperialist agent Benachen.

162

The truck jolted to a start, throwing Georges against the chest of one of the guards, who took him by the shoulders and reinstalled him against the pile of papers. Were they Maoists or anti-Maoists, Georges wondered. In fact, he had the feeling that, given the confused situation, his fate was not necessarily linked to this question, but more to the humor of some local commander who would see him as a political ace in the hole, or as a danger to be removed immediately.

The engine knocked desperately; the driver, faithful to the rules of economy inculcated at driving school (in accordance with the Thought of Mao), poked along at fifteen miles an hour in high gear.

On one side the tarp was badly tied and whipped around in the wind. The moon was up and Georges could see interminable suburbs filing by, big brick buildings covered with posters, and a very wide street of two lanes, both empty. There was no sound except for the hiccupping of the mistreated engine of the ancient Molotova.

Trees soon replaced the bricks in open and sandy country. For half a mile he saw the reflection of the moon on a river, maybe the Han, a tributary of the Yangtze. Georges thought that nothing, absolutely nothing, made it impossible for these soldiers to stop the truck at any time in the middle of this empty country and put a bullet in the back of his head. Who would ever know what happened to him? The sergeant would write in his report in the classic manner: "Shot down while attempting escape." Why would they complicate things with the public trial of a foreign journalist, especially a "progressivist."

And then he regretted having had such an idea. It was, he reasoned, contrary to the whole philosophy of the Chinese Revolution, which was founded on persuasion, education, and conversion, not on punishment. It was the Nazis, the fascist legionnaires of Algeria, the Green Berets of American Special Forces in Vietnam, and their fathers and grandfathers, the gangsters of Chicago, who resorted to such methods. He

163

should not really let himself be dragged into blind anticommunism, he reminded himself virtuously, forgetting everything that had brought him here into this truck.

The trip went on and on, monotonous and uncomfortable. The vehicle had left the macadam road for a trail riddled with potholes. Georges ended up asleep.

When the truck stopped, as abruptly as it had started, Georges was thrown against the same soldier who, this time, pulled him to his feet and, with a punch in the back, shoved him toward his comrade at the back of the truck. They sat him down, his legs dangling. He had hardly time to glimpse a high wall surmounted by barbed wire and a closed gate. They put a blindfold over his eyes, one of the guards knotting it very tightly at the back of his head. The idea of a firing squad became insistent and more vivid in his mind—the wall, the weapons, the blindfold, the whole works. He found it strange, nevertheless, that no one had demanded a complete confession beforehand.

A new push projected him into empty air. Blind, his wrists bound, forgetting that he had just left the floor of a truck, he had time enough to think that his executioners had finally opted for defenestration. A fraction of a second later, however, he was on grassy soil, then seized under both arms and almost lifted off the ground. A long and heavy squeaking told him that a gate was opening. Irregular pavement replaced the lawn. He heard only the sound of his own steps but felt against his neck the breath of the soldiers who had eaten garlic at their last meal. They climbed a steep stairway—he counted three stories. A door opened. He had the sensation of being in a room with a high ceiling and of a certain coolness not like the outdoors.

His blindfold was removed and his hands untied. Two naked bulbs hanging from the end of their cords partially lighted a vast room in which strange shapes were silhouetted. But this was not a torture chamber, simply a gymnasium.

164

Basketball nets and backboards were at either end. A trapeze, a horse, and other apparatus made up all the furniture, along with a few chairs and an unpainted table.

Behind the table a man stood up and, in a French a little too precise in inflection, said, "Comrade Benachen, I hope your trip has been pleasant. Perhaps the last stage of it was a little unexpected?"

The man came up to him in rapid steps and shook his hand. He was rather tall, pale-complexioned, square-faced, probably a North Chinese. He must have been about forty years old. He wore a well-cut khaki uniform, ornamented by a Mao button and the green and yellow ribbon of the Korean volunteers.

Georges was wondering whether he was here as a prisoner or as a guest when Miss Wang appeared behind him. Things began to appear in a plainly more favorable light. The man—Georges nicknamed him "the Colonel"—curiously reminded him of certain heads of the OAS whom he had known during the last phases of the Algerian war. He went back to the table where he spread out documents he had taken from a leatherette briefcase. At either side of him, like judge's assistants, were the two young soldiers they had met during the Peking meeting. Apparently this was the rendezvous Miss Wang had arranged.

In a quiet voice the Colonel explained, "We've had to take certain precautions. I hope you'll not be offended. We preferred that you not identify too precisely the place we've brought you to. Our enterprise, though motivated entirely by patriotic concerns, love of peace, and a right appreciation"—he stressed the last two words—"of the Thought of Chairman Mao, runs the risk of being misunderstood. It involves certain other risks too. There's no need to add to them, don't you agree?"

"You speak a remarkable French," Georges said, conscious of the absurdity of the compliment under the circumstances.

"Well, I thank you very much. I lived a long time ago in your beautiful country. But, excuse me, you're not French, I believe?"

Georges made a gesture as vague and ambiguous as his present national status. But the Chinese continued.

"Our comrades"—he pointed to the two young officers leaning stiffly against the gym horse—"told you in Peking the outlines of the operation called . . ."—with a weak smile, perhaps to excuse the too poetic imagination of his compatriots—"'Operation East Wind.'"

He realized then, or pretended to realize, that his guest had been standing in front of him, like a prisoner under questioning. He shook his head a little unhappily and clapped his hands. A soldier rushed up to him on the run, stood at attention, and executed an impeccable salute—a far cry from the casual attitude of the Red Guards. The Colonel gave an order. The soldier faced about and left on the run. Everyone waited in awkward silence for about two minutes until five soldiers reappeared. They trotted in on their felt-soled shoes, each carrying two chairs. It was like an act in the Chinese circus. They arranged them in a semicircle around the table. A sixth carried a teapot and cups on a tray. Miss Wang, very much the young lady, did the honors. Everybody sipped politely. And then the Colonel threw a commanding look at one of his young subordinates—the one who in Peking had accused Georges of taking prohibited pictures with the phantom camera. The man picked up from the floor a kind of tube rolled around a stick of wood. He climbed onto a chair and hung the tube on a nail. It unrolled with a crisp snap.

"Do you like modern Chinese painting?" the Colonel asked point-blank.

Without conviction, Georges waved an affirmative. In fact, he was totally insensitive to any kind of plastic art. He looked without a word at a traditional Chinese landscape, a temple, sketched more than drawn, perched high on a rock. White clouds floated at mid-point. In the valley a river wound its

166

way through high reeds. Birds soared, each a V, two strokes of the brush. The whole thing showed an extreme economy of means. In the upper right corner were three black ideograms on a vermillion cartouche.

"It's an authentic Fu Pai-chi," the Colonel said, taking on the air of an antique dealer trying to sell a valuable piece. Of course you know Fu Pai-chi, one of our great contemporary artists. He died at a very advanced age, unfortunately just at the beginning of the great proletarian Cultural Revolution."

"I know the name," Georges answered.

"I would like," the other went on, "to make you a present of this modest work of art. In memory of our meeting in Wuhan, to make amends perhaps for our rather unusual methods. Oh no, I insist!" he added before Georges made the slightest sign of refusal. "Don't worry, you won't have the least problem with customs; the exportation of these paintings, which testify to a decadent bourgeois taste in contradiction to Chairman Mao's revolutionary line, is authorized. . . . It might even be true," he concluded in a whisper, "as some people say, that our Chairman himself had once been an admirer of Fu Pai-chi's works. But that's a secret, a big secret."

"I don't think," Georges cut in, "you have me brought here, at considerable risk to you as well as to me, as you have just admitted, only to talk about painting."

The Colonel nodded agreement. He clapped his hands. His subordinate, whom Georges had nicknamed to himself the "Aide-de-camp"—he had rather the obsequious manner of a well-trained orderly with the evident ability to read his chief's every twitch—climbed up on the chair and hung the scroll facing the wall. He took a little flask out of his pocket, dampened a sponge, and began to rub gingerly on the blank side.

"Please come closer, the Colonel suggested.

Out of politeness as much as curiosity, the journalist stood up.

The outlines of a map, with place names in Chinese characters and arrows doubtlessly symbolizing aerial vectors, began

167

to emerge from under the rubbing of the sponge on the white slightly rough surface of the parchment. He recognized the profile of the island of Hainan, the Gulf of Tonkin, the coast of North Vietnam, the dotted lines of the demilitarized zone on both sides of the seventeenth parallel.

Automatically Georges took out his pad and pencil. Miss Wang tapped him on the shoulder.

"Are you crazy?" she whispered. "Where do you think you are? At an Intourist press conference!"

"The comrade is right. No notes," the Colonel commanded stiffly. "And it will hardly be necessary."

He had supplied himself with a long ruler. Professorially he began a lecture in his precise French which lasted more than an hour. For a layman like Georges the project seemed perectly plausible, terrifying in its simplicity. Under the baton of the master, details unfolded one after the other. The plan specified possible objectives in order of priority: the base at Daning, the base at Nha Trang, a carrier of the Seventh Fleet, the Tan Son Nhut complex with its airport and American headquarters (little recommended by reason of its proximity to a dense civilian population). Seven IL-21 planes, only two of them carrying miniaturized nuclear bombs with payloads of one hundred kilotons. Flight at over one thousand feet from Hainan across the Gulf of Tonkin. Operation to coincide with massive sorties of all planes of the second, fourth, and fifth air wings of the People's Army of Liberation, in order to scramble to the maximum enemy radar protection. Cyanide pills for the crew, automatic destruct mechanisms for the plane in case of ground contact other than "normal" landings. A long portion dealt with the recruitment and political orientation of crews chosen for the operation.

"The ideological aspect is of course the most important," the Colonel concluded. "The problem, as a matter of fact, is to weld the socialist bloc now so badly divided, to solidify it once more under the enlightened leadership of Chairman

Mao Tse-tung, by exposing publicly the shameful capitulation of the revisionist leaders of the Soviet Union."

He sat down visibly satisfied.

"Any questions?" he asked Georges.

"Yes, many."

It had not been easy for Georges to keep silent and immobile during this speech. He was terrified. The plan seemed to him both dangerously realistic and extraordinarily childish.

"First, why have you taken me into your confidence?"

"Let's say that we hope that through you—after all, you're a well-known journalist I believe, and not a common imperialist spy—responsible elements in the outside world would be warned and be able, before it's too late, to take whatever measures are required—notably to bring the Paris talks between representatives of the United States and of the Democratic Republic of Vietnam to an end, talks that are nothing but a crude trap of the imperialists assisted by their Soviet revisionist allies. If these talks were to end, we would obviously have no more reason to pursue the preparations, for they are aimed above all to prove the glorious determination of the great peace-loving Chinese people under the leadership of Chairman Mao Tse-tung to checkmate the imperialist attempts of obtaining by intimidation, around the conference table, what they have been unable to attain on the battlefield where their mercenary troops have suffered defeat after defeat."

Georges found himself once more disconcerted by a conspirator's apparent praise of the very politics he was working so hard to crush.

"But now, if you agree with this project," he risked, "why do you seek to subvert it by having me pass the word to your enemies?"

Miss Wang leaned toward him. Like a teacher unhappy with the answer of her pupil during the visit of the Inspector General, she whispered: "You understand nothing of dialectics.

169

Believe me, the reasons are perfectly clear. You're making the comrade waste his time."

True, he made a show of looking at his watch during their brief exchange; however, it was Miss Wang whom he took to task. "Let our friend ask any question he wants," he said. "We—certain responsible comrades and I—realize that such a policy, justified in its principles and in its goals, involves considerable risk. And moreover, that it would certainly be falsely construed by other comrades, inside and outside the socialist camp. It could, for instance, be faulted as adventurism. You see, even the responsible comrades of the government of the Democratic Republic of Vietnam and the Lao Dong Party (Vietnamese Workers' Party) have not been told of the existence of the plan, the realization of which could lead, for both their country and party, to reprisals even more serious than those that might afflict our own country. More than that, we profoundly disapprove, like all peace-loving peoples"—his voice, Georges noted, took on in intoning the ritual formulas a metallic sonority very different from his normal diction—"the use of atomic weapons. That's why," he concluded, "it seems preferable to us that, from the discreet warning that we expect to accomplish through you, our Vietnamese friends, like our American and Russian enemies, will understand the dangers for everybody that come from pursuing the farce of the Paris negotiations. But they must know too that the just rage of the great Chinese people cannot be eternally contained and that they must adopt without delay the only right line—that of pursuing the war until victory for the Vietnamese people, and, for the imperialists and their accomplices, that of accepting shameful defeat. Is that clear now?"

He seemed triumphant. Georges wasn't at all convinced. "If the real goal of the operation was to torpedo the Vietnamese-American talks," he thought, "its denunciation could only have precisely the opposite effect because it would throw into full light, for Hanoi as well as Washington, both the aggres-

170

siveness and the impotence of those in office in Peking." But he preferred to keep these reflections to himself. After all, the recipients of this intelligence would be able to try at their leisure to decipher the hidden intentions of his interlocutor. He had just to confine himself to his already perilous role as messenger, even if he retained some doubts about the authenticity of the message.

Meanwhile, the "Aide-de-camp" had climbed on the chair again and busied himself, with the help of a new mixture, with removing all trace of the markings that had been carried on the back of the scroll. After that he took it down, rolled it up, and gave it to his chief. He himself tied a red ribbon around the parchment, with the delicacy of a pastry clerk from the provinces wrapping the Sunday cream puffs. To bring the job to perfection he stamped a seal to one side of the knot.

"Marco Polo," he said. "One of the great antique dealers in Peking. The price is on it too. Look! Three hundred and fifty yuans. It's a little expensive, but worth it, don't you think? In any case, I bestow here a document perhaps less scientific than a microfilm but surely more agreeable to look at and less dangerous to carry. Am I right?"

"That's not the problem," Georges said. "What I'd like to know is what makes you think that my . . . chiefs—supposing that I have any, and that's your idea, not mine—would agree to change in any way their position, and even their plans, only on the basis of this . . . work of art?"

"That's your concern, and theirs," the Colonel answered after a moment's reflection. "If your story doesn't interest these gentlemen, they'll just have to wait two or three weeks and then they'll know for sure. And you and I would simply have wasted our time, which is not terribly serious. But I don't think so. To me, in any case, what counts is that I will have done my best for the cause of peace, and for the revolution, that is to say, objectively, the cause of Chairman Mao."

Georges admired once again this subtle distinction that

171

allowed everyone in China to pretend, perhaps in good faith, to be fundamentally in agreement with the Thought of the Guide.

"May I ask another question?" he asked.

"Please do."

"Who will give, or cancel, the order to proceed?"

"The military commission of the Central Committee in liaison with the Committee of the Cultural Revolution in the army."

"Has a date been set for the operation?"

"The units are to be placed on a state of alert beginning next Friday. Flight orders may then be issued in a few minutes, thirty-three to be exact, before takeoff. The crews are sleeping these days at the side of their planes, but this delay is necessary to allow for a last 'operational briefing' in order to reveal the targets as affected by meteorological conditions and possible modifications in the political and strategic map." He smiled, visibly satisfied at the precision of his vocabulary. Georges noticed that steel crowns capped two of his incisors. "Possible cancellation or postponement," he pursued, "has to come from the same leading bodies and under the same conditions. They can intervene up to one minute before H hour."

"But you don't expect me to believe," Georges protested, "that all the members of the Military Commission, certain of whom are having trouble now, and the Committee for the Cultural Revolution in the army, which now seems to be dormant, will have to meet in order to make, in a minute, a decision of such scope!"

"You know perfectly well, Mr. Benachen, that in spite of what the professional detractors serving imperialism and revisionism pretend"—he stared with embarrassing insistence at the man he talked to—"all decisions are taken by a college of leaders. Of course, certain people can at certain times play a more important role than others. It's futile to try to pierce their identities, it's a perfectly vain exercise. Content yourself—and perhaps reassure your superiors—that there is no

172

such thing as a 'little red button' in our country that someone can push in order to set off the worst atomic catastrophe.
There is the Little Red Book, the Thought of Mao Tse-tung,
the biggest spiritual nuclear bomb of our time, which by itself
assures us total security against potential threats from our
enemies. This is enough for us."

He stopped to catch his breath and Georges wondered
whether this return to Maoist orthodoxy, in this confirmed
and avowed traitor, were sincere or an affectation. And he saw
once more the vanity in this kind of speculation in an adventure that, everything considered, he had not yet got a
hold on.

"In this book," the Colonel went on, "there is a quotation
among many others. It will be read over Radio Peking during
the six o'clock morning program the day the operation is to
take place. It will immediately put the crews on alert while
giving them an hour and a half before takeoff. And if the
operation is canceled at the last minute, then we'll simply
repeat the quotation two times. See how easy . . ."

"The Chinese speak to the Chinese . . ." Georges interrupted.

The strategist looked at him wide-eyed. Plainly, this allusion to the great hours of Radio London escaped him.

"Nobody," he stressed, "would be surprised to hear a quotation of our great guide repeated." He allowed himself a bit
of a smile. "I would go so far as to say that it's rare if a quotation is not repeated at least twice. So your chiefs would waste
their time trying to decipher our message. After all, if they
were capable of understanding the Thought of Chairman
Mao, they wouldn't be doing their dirty jobs of spies and provocateurs. Isn't that so? What do you think, Mr. Benachen?"

As if ready to arrest him again, the two young officers came
up on either side of Georges, making it clear that the meeting
was over. The Colonel came around the table and put the
famous scroll with its ridiculous red ribbon almost by force
into his hands.

"After all," he said by way of concluding, "if these gentlemen refuse to believe your story, they will just have themselves to blame for the consequences of their stupidity, which will surprise none of us. They will have, I repeat, only a few days to wait before they find out. Then they'll give you a nice reward, the Legion of Honor—most probably posthumously."

Before Georges left, the Colonel could not resist making one last crack. "You have one string left in your bow," he said. "You can sell the picture in Hong Kong. You can get, let's say, ten thousand dollars, Hong Kong. What do you think, Comrade Wang?"

"Nothing," she said drily. "I don't know prices in capitalist markets for works of art stolen from the Chinese people. And I'm positively not interested."

Georges had the feeling—but he was no longer sure of anything—that she hated this soldier who gave such a frightening image of his country and its army to a foreigner. The tension in this strange gamelike setting had become unbearable. Yet neither he nor the Colonel could make up his mind to turn a farewell into the point of no return in their transaction.

"One last question, if you please!" Georges almost had to shout because more than fifty feet already separated him from the Colonel. "What will happen if I'm arrested at the border, if the message on the back of the scroll is discovered? Who can say, after all, that you're not ready to turn me in, if you haven't done so by now?"

"No one can say, absolutely no one," the Colonel answered sharply as he turned about. "In that case you'll be shot. With your charming interpreter"—saluting her with some mockery. "And I would be too, if that's any consolation. You tell yourself you're subject to denunciation, Mr. Benachen. You're perfectly right. But we are too, at least as much as you. And we have infinitely more to lose. Something entirely foreign to you—our honor as communists, as Chinese, as companions of Chairman Mao. So don't talk to me about danger. Danger

174

is everywhere. From the moment you entered the territory of our country to carry out your mission, and got yourself involved in the internal affairs of the People's Republic of China and of the great Chinese People, you made yourself liable to summary execution. I hope for your sake that your motives were as honorable as ours."

There was nothing further to add. The door closed noiselessly on the Colonel. The two soldiers put the blindfold back on Georges and escorted him in silence to the truck. This time he was sure that Miss Wang was beside him. From time to time, she would brush against his shoulder for reassurance.

2 ● It was not easy to leave Wuhan, this city only partially "revolutionarized," where the still so recent battles on either side of the river seemed already to be ancient history.

In order to get air travel permits they had first to find and then to lay siege on the proper offices. They were sent, in the course of one day, from Security Services to regional headquarters of Wai Shao Pu, the Ministry of Foreign Affairs, the only place authorized to take care of foreigners. Everywhere they faced incredulity, annoyed shrugs, and cautious groans. At a time of total revolutionary upheaval, nobody—cadres more or less suspect, Red Guards more or less in favor, soldiers more or less sure of being on the right side—would take the trouble or assume the responsibility either to arrest this "long nose" who never should have been there in the first place or to permit him to continue his journey.

A ceaseless crowd came and went in these offices, arguing for a place to sit, for the telephone, for the official seal. All were armed and wore on their red brassards group insignia which Miss Wang translated: "Rebel Regiment of Red Rebels for the Liquidation of the Bourgeoisie," "Wuhan Committee of Young Intellectuals who carry the Revolution into the

175

Mountains and the Plains," "Red-Flag Headquarters for the Thought of Mao Tse-tung."

As in any bureaucracy, after Miss Wang had unwound her little story for the *nth* time—the train stopped on the Yangtze bridge, the necessity for Georges to leave the Chinese territory before the expiration of his registration certificate in two days, his status as "progressivist," as a friend of China and guest of the government—they usually ended up being told in a dry or regretful tone: "Go somewhere else . . . Come back tomorrow . . . We're not the ones . . ."

Strangely enough, they were free to wander through these offices, to pace the dusty corridors where sometimes whole families slept, to open squeaky doors at random. They had some surprising encounters: an old gentleman with glasses who happened to be—according to a janitor also suspect—a repentant rightist, expelled from the Central China Party Bureau but who had "turned a new leaf." He offered to take them, for a slight charge, to the Revolutionary Museum. Miss Wang took it upon herself to decline this offer politely.

Then, in a broom closet of the Army Committee they surprised four people playing bridge. Scandal! "These are," Miss Wang explained, "wayward functionaries, fallen under the influence of the sinister Tao Chu. This ancient proconsul of Kwantung, rightly purged for having followed the capitalist line, was, it seemed, a passionate devotee of this repugnant pastime. According to the Red Guard press, when he would stop at a station during trips through the province, where the comrades expected enlightenment on the latest decisions of the Central Committee, he would send as a messenger whoever was dummy in the bridge game he was playing. The influence of this monster was already visible in the north, as far as Wuhan.

None of this brought Georges closer to his goal—a plane, Canton, and from there, with luck, the border, a "free world" that faded deeper and deeper into a phantasmagorical fog. At loose ends, still dragging the suitcases, the typewriter, the

176

precious scroll, they ended up appealing to the Commission in Charge of Putting the Revolutionary Committee of the Province on its Feet. It took them three hours to find it, walking through Wuchang, passing by three lakes, admiring— tourism never loses its power—the ancient Square of the Horses and the pyramidal monument to the memory of the heroes of the 1911 Revolution.

Georges' case, a young officer explained complacently, was hopeless because the competent authority was not in Wuchang but in Hankow, on the other side of the river in the dissident zone. "Unless," whispered Miss Wang, "they are the ones in the dissident zone and the other bank has remained loyal to Chairman Mao."

It was a delightful surprise when at last they found a familiar face—the "Aide-de-camp," from Peking and the gymnasium, who never before had opened his mouth. He pretended not to recognize them but showed a certain eagerness to issue them a vague document sealed with numerous stamps. He advised them to make tracks to the airport without delay, cynically adding, "We don't need foreigners around here right now."

They spent the night on a bench in the waiting room of the airport amid a continual coming and going of passengers. Early in the morning, as the Ilyushin took off, Georges observed to his partner that the Colonel could very well have thought of giving them a pass that would have avoided all the tiresome and dangerous running around. Really, these conspirators lacked any idea of follow through.

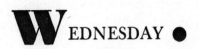

WEDNESDAY ●

● ● ● Canton was a spectacle of confusion far worse than
● ● ● Wuhan. It took a lot of telephoning for Miss Wang
● ● ● to get a room at the Ai Chun Hotel—"The Love of
the Masses"—and then a car to take them into town.

Canton seemed to be in a state of siege. Tarpaulined army
trucks in convoy, lights on in daytime, moved bumper to
bumper, horns bleating continuously, portraits of Chairman
Mao on their radiators. The crowd, blank-faced youths
mostly, made way grudgingly. Rival loudspeakers, on the
trucks and on the roofs of buildings, engaged in bitter alter-
cations, answered here and there by punches from the Red
Guards. Georges questioned his companion.

"I don't understand a thing. It's Cantonese politics," she
answered irritably.

In the lobby of the hotel, while she was talking with the
clerk at the reception desk, he looked at her and was moved.
"I'm in love like a schoolboy," he thought. He was in love
with a girl whom he had reason to believe was using him.

"You are in 314," she announced loud enough to be heard
by all the personnel. "The dining room is on the top floor.
I'm going to Intourist to arrange your departure tomorrow
morning by train up to the border at Chum Chum. I'll drop
by after dinner to give you your ticket and to see if you need
anything. But the menus are written in English and you can
even have European dishes."

In the dining room, immense and deserted, he nibbled
without appetite on sugared pork and was watching the
muddy waters of the Pearl River when a familiar voice surprised him.

"Bon appétit!"

Chen had just taken a place three tables away. He made a
sign for the newsman to join him. Georges obeyed.

"Don't be afraid," Chen said. "I'm perfectly safe here with
the 'East Wind' Regiment—at least as long as I don't wander
into the northern sectors," he added smiling. "You see, Liu

180

Liang-fu, Vice-Chairman of the Preparatory Committee of the Revolution, is a friend of mine—I got him his job—and he's posted his men all around the hotel to protect me."

"But what are you doing here?"

"The same as you. I'm getting out. First to Hong Kong for only a few days and from there to Pnom Penh. You see how things work out finally," he said, alluding to their conversation in Algiers long ago. "Not always, of course, the way one would have wished."

"But do you have an exit visa?"

As soon as he asked the question Georges realized its absurdity. It did not seem to strike Chen, who answered quietly.

"Yes. But I won't use it. They are certainly waiting for me at the border." He indicated the riverscape at their feet. "One of those junks will take me over to Macao without any trouble. But it'll be later, once I'm out of here, that the real problems will start. Your friends," he shot out violently, "are such idiots! They don't understand a thing. They'll never understand!"

This explosion reminded Georges in a way of the Colonel. But Chen returned to his usual manner and said with a smile, "By the way, I'm taking your interpreter with me. I know she's here with you. She has become too involved in this unhappy business, just as you have—and I'm sorry—for her to risk getting back into Peking."

"But she doesn't know you're in Canton," put in Georges.

"Don't worry. I'll have no trouble reaching her. Maybe we'll meet again in Hong Kong, Mr. Benachen. You should stay at the Mandarin. I've been told it's one of the best hotels in the world, even better than this. I won't ask you," he said standing up, "how your trip was. I hear you had to stop in Wuhan. It's not much of a city for tourists but I think you might have found it . . . interesting. You can tell me all about it in Hong Kong, unless by that time you've tired of giving your report to so many people."

181

With that he was on his feet and put one yuan and fifty-two fens on the table, the exact amount of his check.

"Did you see your uncle?" was the first thing Georges asked Miss Wang when she came as promised to wait for him in the lobby of the hotel.

"No," she answered with no show of surprise, "but I know he's in Canton. Did he talk to you?"

"Yes."

Her placidity bothered him and gave him more and more the feeling of not holding a single thread of the plot.

"He even told me that he was leaving China, exiling himself, and that he was taking you with him."

"It's out of the question for me to go! I like him well enough. Politically I think he's right, in part anyway. But I can't separate myself from the masses, whatever happens to me, even if I have to face the consequences and be justly punished." She sighed. "And then there's you; I like you very much. I'd hate not to see you again."

This near declaration enchanted Georges. It made him sure now that he could persuade her to join him. However formidable, the practical obstacles seemed suddenly negligible to him—the risk for him of being intercepted at the border in possession of evidence that was out-and-out incrimination, and for her the even greater risk of having the Red gunboats sink the escaping junk in the Macao waters.

He noticed that she had prettied herself up. Because of the heat, still very intense in Canton at the end of October, she had changed from her eternal blue tunic to a white blouse with nice little pink flowers, which gave her more than ever the look of a schoolgirl.

"I could be arrested for abducting a minor!" he said. "At this point wouldn't that be something! Really too much."

She looked on, uncomprehending. For once her French was inadequate.

He was dying to take her in his arms, to embrace her. He

182

refrained, not without effort, less out of a desire not to "compromise" her than because such demonstrations are looked upon in China as the height of ill breeding and lack of culture among foreigners.

They went out. At a lovers' pace they crossed a footbridge over a canal. They found themselves on the island of Chamien. With its immense banyans in place of Parisian acacias, its houses built for the English and Portuguese traders at the beginning of the nineteenth century, it evoked images of a kind of phantom Ile-Saint Louis, haunted by a past forever lost. They stopped in front of a gracious mansion made into a warehouse, from which they could hear the laughter of children.

"The old French consulate," Miss Wang said.

André Malraux had set some of the action of *The Conquerors* on this island. But all the girl knew about the writer-minister was that he had been received by Chairman Mao in Peking a few years before.

At one point about a dozen children dogged their heels, all of them very small, a friendly and silent audience. They leaned their elbows on the parapet of the quay. She was quiet and a little sad. Every sign of tension had gone from her face, as if she had made herself a part of this landscape, peaceful to the point of being anachronistic.

"I'd like to show you Paris," he said.

She turned on him, suddenly furious.

"You're out of your mind! I wouldn't go to Paris unless my government sent me. But . . ."

He insisted. "I need you, Wang."

"Don't call me that. I'm not 'Wang,' and besides, forget the whole thing. At a time when imperialism redoubles its threat against our country, against the great proletarian Cultural Revolution, and when you have been assigned a mission that you obviously don't understand a thing about, but that should nevertheless serve the cause of peace in the end, all you're interested in are your rotten little bourgeois feelings! The cult

183

of personality! What do you think? That I'm going to follow you to Paris or Tunis? That you're going to show me off in front of your little friends, all of them stinking intellectuals just like you? Look at her—a real Red Guard who came with me out of love! Love! Maybe Hollywood will make a film of our story and we'll make a million dollars . . ."

"We'll live wherever you want, in Hong Kong, in Cambodia. We'll fight in Vietnam if they'll accept us . . ."

The shoulders of the girl shook. Was she laughing at his naiveté or was she crying? He would never know because at this moment she started to recite in her most official voice: "It was right here, comrade, that the French and British imperialists, with the aid of the compradors and other feudal traitors and Chinese hoodlums, set up what they called their 'concessions.' Complying with the principle that was to be spelled out many years later by the Chinese Khrushchev, the number one figure who, although a member of the Party, follows the capitalist line, they proclaimed endlessly: 'Exploitation is good!' Thanks to the profit they extracted from the misery of the Chinese people, they led a life of luxury and debauchery in these palaces, in the company of their concubines, drinking fine wine and gorging themselves on spicy food, while the workers collapsed of starvation on these quays where, every morning, hundreds of emaciated cadavers were picked up and thrown pitilessly into the canal. The exploiters —in order to gain ever greater profit and to deprive the Chinese people of all will to resist oppression—also forced them to poison themselves with opium. But a few years ago, inspired by the Thought of Mao Tse-tung, the Chinese proletariat took up arms against the British and French mercenaries who were under the orders of American imperialists and inflicted a decisive defeat upon them. This stone slab commemorates . . . And now, stop talking nonsense. It's time to go back to the hotel."

She had recovered her usual tone at just the moment a group of three Japanese businessmen walked off, escorted by

184

one of her colleagues who had delivered in English almost word for word the speech she had been giving to Georges.

"Listen," he said, "I have a date with Chen in Hong Kong at the Mandarin. When you get there you can decide between you what you want to do, what is still the best way for you to serve China. It's certainly not in being shot or in carrying manure in a people's commune in Sinkiang."

She broke in vehemently. "What do you know? Can't you just see me in Hong Kong?"

She made a derisive gesture to evoke the split dress and the impudently exposed thighs of the creatures of capitalism.

"You'd like to corrupt me, you'd like me to become—how do you say it?—a Sing Song girl. I saw one at the movies once, in one of those decadent films Chairman Liu Shao-chi was so fond of . . . I mean the Chinese Khrushchev."

Georges tried to stop her, but it was no use. Under the dumbfounded but fascinated eyes of the Chamien children, she flounced around like a Hong Kong movie actress, swinging her hips, rolling her eyes, and letting out a series of high-pitched caterwaulings which proved she had been a regular spectator of the old-fashioned Peking Opera.

For the first and only time of their brief period together he showed some authority. He turned on his heels and said, "Let's go. Let's get back to the hotel. You're acting like a fool and you know damn well that this isn't the point at all."

In a rush of sincerity which was becoming too much of a habit with him, he recognized that she had touched a sensitive point. Beyond the Chinese borders they might soon get to hate each other. After the first surprises, and for him the joy of seeing her dressed up, adorned and made up, with her hair fixed (maybe she would be as hideous as a defrocked nun), they would just be runaways with no illusions.

"Since we can't live together in China, at least let's try somewhere else," he went on in a very low voice, as if he wished unconsciously not to be heard. "Love isn't a sin, even in People's China. Is it?"

185

"Yes it is, yes, if what you want to do is to turn me into a capitalist whore, like you . . ."

Sick at heart, he understood that everything had been said between them. In silence, like estranged lovers, they continued to walk. Chamien became again an assemblage of worn-out warehouses reflected in the greenish waters of the canal under a leaden sky. The island had lost its magic.

Their steps brought them back to the hotel. Georges still hoped her resolve would weaken; he thought that she would let herself be convinced. But the spectacle that greeted them cut short his imaginings.

Thirty Red Guards, all of them very young but officered by four or five older men, rushed out of the three army trucks and a jeep and entered the hotel. Against all caution, Georges and Miss Wang fell automatically into step with them.

Crowded in front of the elevator, the hotel's staff recited stanzas from the Little Red Book under the direction of one of the "Little Red Generals" dear to Chairman Mao's heart. A colleague, seated at the reception desk, looked through registration forms and threw them one after the other onto the rug. Young men ran up and down the stairs shouting. The Japanese they had seen earlier in Chamien gaped, their Leicas over their shoulders, berets tight on their heads, until their interpreter drew them authoritatively into the rooms at the rear. Georges understood vaguely the violent shouts that came from the upper floors: "Rebellion is legitimate! Death to the imperialist dog heads!"

He turned to check this with Miss Wang. She was no longer at his side. Georges did not have long to wonder—the elevator door opened and the "imperialist dog head" came out. It was Chen Wu-hsieh.

He must have been beaten, because the right half of his face was bruised, his cheekbone swollen, one eye half-closed. But he remained impassive, just as on that long ago day in the Peking stadium. Maybe the reason for this rough handling was that he had refused to lower his head in repentance even

186

though they had fixed the cord from a curtain around his neck. The youngest of his guards held it proudly, like a dog's leash. Another Red Guard triumphantly waved the prisoner's briefcase—it was all they needed to prove his ignoble class crime.

Someone brought a chair. Chen was forced to straddle it, and a circle closed in on him. The imprecations began to break out against the devil and monster finally exposed.

A cadre finally became aware of the European's untimely presence and told him to leave. Georges made a show of not understanding. The man took him by the arm and rushed him to the door. The journalist cast his eyes about desperately for Miss Wang. Had she been arrested? If so, wouldn't it be normal for him at least to be held for questioning? But what was normal any more? Despite the cadre's injunctions and the circle that was starting to form around him (a true biological process: healthy cells surrounding the sick one), he succeeded in stopping at the reception desk. The cantankerous clerk had got back into her place and was picking up the scattered records to the accompaniment of much jibing and raillery.

Georges, throwing caution aside, asked her straight out if she had seen Miss Wang, his interpreter, who had registered him at the hotel earlier in the afternoon. The woman studied him suspiciously. "I don't know this comrade," she said at last in English. "If you want an interpreter for touring the city you'll have to fill out an Intourist form." She slid some literature toward him. He put it in his pocket and went away.

He wandered about in the hot night of Canton, found himself back on the other side of the footbridge in Chamien where he walked all over hoping to find his partner. He understood then, with certainty, that he would not see her again, that he had lost her forever.

Without haste, without illusion, without hope, he returned to the hotel. He looked at his watch: after midnight. The lobby was empty, cavernous. The cranky desk clerk threw him

187

a reproving look through her glasses. No, there was no message for him. Did the foreign comrade expect one? And from whom if you please? He left hastily. In the antique elevator, its walls lined with white cloth (clean but patched, like the clothing of the honest poor in the moralizing novels of the last century), was a totally decrepit operator who had apparently cut his tunic from the same cloth. He had a toothless smile. He looked like the last eunuch of the court of Peking as immortalized by Cartier-Bresson.

Alone in his room, Georges felt lost in unbearable anguish and despair. The scroll was waiting for him on the bed seemingly intact. For the sake of this message, most probably phony, certainly useless, he had lost the girl he loved and what little self-esteem he still had. "At least I have never betrayed a pal or a cause I thought just," he used to tell himself before "The Journey to China." He realized that mentally he placed "The Journey to China" between quotation marks, as if it had been made by someone else, as if it were the title of a book.

He went to the window and watched for a long time the few little lanterns that bordered the Pearl River, which was here just the width of the Thames downstream from London toward Greenwich. Did the British merchants, the "Taipans" of the nineteenth century, think of that when pinching the buttocks of their concubines? A ferry-boat let out a desolate lowing which drowned the indistinct recitative from a loudspeaker and some distant gunfire.

The words of a song he had heard over and over from all his friends the day before he left for Peking came back to him. "China nights, caressing nights, nights of love, nights of raptuuuuuuuuure and tenderneeeeeeeess." He hummed along, hoping that someone, someone like one of the judges in Kafka's *Trial,* would hear him and wonder.

If tomorrow, by some miracle, they let him past the frontier —he whose guilt was so evident—because of some obscure political consideration or because the confusion in South

188

China surpassed even the estimates of American specialists, he realized he would have nothing to take with him of the woman he loved. Not a picture, not a thing. Maybe she was not even called Wang, nor really related to Chen; maybe she was just a niece of circumstance.

He tried to rouse himself. Maybe after all she would appear, any moment at the break of the day, quiet, serious, efficient, the ideal interpreter, to take him to the station, to make him understand by a shake of the hand that she was ready to attempt the escape. Maybe he would find her at the end of the week in the lobby of the Mandarin, among the blue-haired widows from Iowa, poured into dresses with necklines plunged down on floppy tits, exchanging in grating voices the names of their dressmakers ("In pure silk for only twenty-five dollars, and three fittings in two days, Mrs. Mc-Fadden!"). Maybe . . . Sick at heart, disgusted with himself, he fell across the bed.

Thursday ●

● ● ● THERE WAS A knock on the door, at first soft, then
● ● ● pounding. Georges knew at once it was not, that it
● ● ● could not be, Miss Wang. He sat up in the bed. He
was bathed in sweat. The ceiling fan, languishing just a few
moments ago, had now stopped. For an instant he relived
some snatches of his nightmare. He was in the middle of a
vast arena, which looked like the Palais des Sports in Paris
and the bullring at Nîmes. Lead balls rained on him, thrown
by an invisible crowd. Michel Loriot, Zagachvili, Garrison
were there, somewhere among his judges and executioners.
Miss Wang herself remained absent, hopelessly absent, and,
on regaining consciousness, he recalled that in fact the morning had come for a definitive separation.

It was still the black of night. So it couldn't be for the train
to the border, which didn't leave until nine in the morning,
that whoever it was had come to awaken him. Maybe it was
the police, or the Red Guards.

It was a girl who came into the room alone—stiff, graceless,
authoritarian, just like Miss Wang when they first met at the
Hsin Chao.

"I'm your interpreter," she said in French. "My instructions are to take care of you until your departure from Canton."

These were the very words Miss Wang would have used.
Was this some kind of parody they cooked up for his benefit?
Was this some brilliant demonstration of "brainwashing" à la
Chinoise? No, the Canton brass, in the middle of an insur-
rection, certainly had other problems.

"I'm waiting for my interpreter who has accompanied me
since Peking and who's supposed to come and pick me up this
morning to take me to the station," Georges ventured.

As if she had not heard, she repeated without changing her
tone, "I'm your interpreter. My instructions are to take care
of you until your departure from Canton."

She was really very ugly with none of the grace, none of the
192

sweetness of Miss Wang. She stood in the doorway, sober as a judge. Was she on the side of "East Wind" or "Red Flag"?

"We must go, the car is waiting," she insisted.

He wrapped a towel around his middle, took a quick shower. The water was barely lukewarm. Tonight he would know the luxurious bathrooms of the Mandarin, or the dusty basins of a prison cell.

It was 2:35 by his watch. He had slept less than two hours.

"I thought the train didn't leave until nine o'clock," he said.

"For technical reasons, the time of departure has been advanced."

She turned her back to him while he shaved. The "explanations" were over.

Once more he picked up his suitcase and the typewriter and put the scroll under his arm. (It would be even worse to leave it here and have them run after him to give it back, and at last give them something to nail him with.)

Downstairs, she would not allow him to stop at the reception desk where the same clerk was still on, his last link with Miss Wang.

"I paid your bill," she said. "You can pay me back in the car."

He put himself into the old black Pobyeda that waited with its motor running. She sat down beside the driver who started off right away.

At this early hour the quays and Tai Ping-Lu were empty, quite deserted. The tired engine of the car roared like a jet airplane. After a few hundred yards Georges heard shouts and saw red flags waving from behind the closed gates of the Park of Culture. At the intersection, dozens of people surged about with their arms in the air. And, with a sharp sense of déjà-vu, Georges suddenly realized the car had been blocked by a dense mob. It was strangely calm, and this silence made it even more menacing than the crowds in Peking.

193

The driver began to blow his horn and the interpreter, leaning out the window, began to quack out explanations in a falsetto Cantonese. No use. The masses said nothing, did not listen, did not budge. They paid no attention at all to the car or its occupants. It was enough for them to passively block the road. Giving up the battle, the driver decided to U-turn. They went by the Love of the Masses Hotel again, threaded the quay eastward, then turned left onto Sun Yat-sen Street. There a barricade of sand bags and two half-tracks stopped them. In the beam of the headlights Georges saw helmets shining and bayonets glinting. It was not the Red Guards this time but the People's Army of Liberation.

The interpreter got out to talk things over. She crossed the barricade ornamented by the inevitable portraits of Mao with An Men Tien in the background. As soon as they found themselves alone in the car, the driver turned to his passenger and whispered in a passable English, "You going to Hong Kong?"

"Yes, I think so," answered Georges a little surprised. Actually, he was less and less sure.

"Look around carefully on the way to the station. You'll see what the counterrevolutionaries, opposed to the Thought of Chairman Mao, the devils and monsters of the East Wind Regiment, have done to our city! This must be known outside, so the Hong Kong comrades can prepare for the fight . . ."

The interpreter's return interrupted these confidences. An army man accompanied her. He grabbed the journalist's passport, examined it from front to back, and put it in the pocket of his tunic, which he buttoned carefully. He then got in beside the driver, while the girl (but Georges couldn't honor her with this title, which he reserved for Miss Wang) sat down beside her client in the rear seat.

The car moved away quickly between walls plastered with posters—even the windows were covered with them. The roadway was matted with printed and calligraphed paper—the truth of the day before—which rustled under the tires.

194

Suddenly Georges was thrown forward. The driver had slammed on the brakes. Was it so that the tourist would miss none of the scenery? On either side of the street two corpses swung, hanging from lampposts. The feet of one of them, in felt slippers, were just at the height of Georges' face.

The tortured victims carried the usual placards telling their names and their crimes. The nearest one still seemed to be moving. It must have been an illusion, because nobody was in sight.

The officer gave a brief command. The driver steered quickly to the right, but he could not avoid having the feet of one of the dead men nudge the car. The interpreter pursed her lips. She turned toward Georges expecting his questions, ready, if not to answer, at least to impose silence. But he did not say a word, putting on the innocent expression of someone who had not seen a thing. He thought he saw in the rearview mirror a satisfied smile on the face of the driver. What game was this guy playing?

The car left the center of the city, entered a doubtful area where little factories of brick and mud were soaking in half-flooded rice fields. Over little wooden bridges and then over one of steel they crossed numerous canals and a wider river which must have been a tributary of the Pearl.

A few barefoot peasants with big conical hats, their shoulders protected from the rain by capes of woven straw, watched them pass. Children waving their arms, letting out piercing cries, ran to catch up with the car but soon abandoned the chase.

At last—almost two hours had passed since encountering the hanged men—they arrived in front of a rural station. It was under military occupation. Members of the local people's commune squatted on the platform beside baskets of vegetables and poultry, bundles, and children. One could see from their expressions that they had been waiting for a very long time for permission to get on the train. Two little pigs escaped, chased by yapping children.

Escorted by the interpreter and the officer Georges walked the length of the train—fifteen cars. The driver led the way carrying the suitcase and the typewriter. Real VIP treatment. He had kept the precious scroll himself. He showed it, smiling apologetically, to the interpreter.

"It's a work of art. I have the highest admiration for your modern painters."

All she said, more by way of reflex, was, "Our great guide and great helmsman, Chairman Mao, stood up against the remnants and relics of the feudal past. Those of us who build the future don't give a damn for such things and we don't understand why our foreign friends are so concerned with them."

But it was clear she did not want to take the trouble to begin a last-minute discussion on the subject.

The little group Georges was a part of came to a stop at the head car. He could as well be some guest of honor being bade goodby with regret, or some undesirable being got rid of as quickly as possible—one not necessarily excluding the other. The farewells were brief and cold. Standing stiffly on the station platform, the girl was already thinking of the report she would write (the driver would certainly be blamed for his error in driving) and of the calumnies this "foreign friend" was going to disgorge in the imperialist press, describing "the clusters of hanged men swinging from every lamp-post in Canton."

Georges felt nothing, nothing but an extreme lassitude and a great haste to have these unfriendly shapes erased. "Right now," he said to himself, "Chen is revealing my name to the investigators. Orders for my arrest are already on the wire to the border station in Chum Chum." He accepted this idea without really believing it, a little to exorcise the evil spell.

He held out his hand. Nobody took it. The driver put the suitcase and the typewriter on the ground and turned on his heels. The officer gave back the passport and nodded. The interpreter murmured, "Bon voyage." Georges climbed the two steps, opened the door, and held his ticket out to the conductor. The first-class car, without compartments but with fairly comfortable seats, seemed empty. Solemn music came out of the speakers above the benches—"Socialism is good." The train lurched to a start. The interpreter finally made a move. Through the open window she held out to Georges a thin red pad with the title printed in white: *Decision of the Central Committee of the Chinese Communist Party on the Great Proletarian Cultural Revolution*. So, she did not yet despair of his ideological perfectibility.

"*Hsieh Hsieh ni* (thank you!)," Georges said. (It was one of the rare Chinese words he had learned from his mistress.)

It was seven-thirty in the morning. He prepared himself for a long, lonely trip, for a long wait—at best—at the border where his baggage would be examined minutely. The scroll, that terrible piece of incriminating evidence, rested in the net above his head in its wrapping of gray paper and its red ribbon. He was tempted to get rid of it, to toss it out the window into the river the train was crossing so noisily. But junks circulated close to the bridge. The risk of being discovered would be increased. The dilemma was immediately resolved by the appearance of a traveling companion whose presence he had not noticed at the other end of the car—Peter Garrison.

He came and settled himself without ceremony at Georges' side, unwinding his long legs, propping his elegant suede ankle-boots on the facing bench. He had exchanged his flamboyant boubou for a gray, fairly shiny drip-dry suit. A thin dotted blue tie brought out the white of his shirt.

"So good to know that I'm not alone in this crummy train!" he burst out by way of greeting.

Apparently he had forgotten their stormy session at the Valley of the Mings and the accusations he had leveled at Georges.

"My God, what a trip!" he went on, not bothered by the silence of his companion. "Canton is a madhouse! I could just as well have been in Detroit or Watts on a beautiful day of rioting."

His face lighted up at this evocation.

"We have much to learn from these Chinese, but not everything," he said. "I mean, the Chinese are true revolutionaries; that no one can deny. Even so, they are whites."

Georges started. Was Garrison pulling his leg? Was he trying to get something started?

"I don't follow you. If that's how you feel, what brought you to China?"

"I ask myself the same question. I mean, the Chinese have never been colonized, not really. So, down deep, they don't understand our problems at all, they simply look for ways to use us to their own chauvinistic political ends as a great power."

The door squeaked open. Two girls in blue overalls, the ideological brigade of the train, made their appearance.

One of them carried a tray with two steaming cups which were decorated with the image of Mao. Tea leaves floated in them. The other girl carried a tambourine. The first put her burden on a table, effusively shook Garrison's hands, and kissed him on both cheeks.

"Brother!" she cried.

She ignored the pouting, bitter European with the tired face and the rumpled suit marked by spots of sweat under the arms. She minced back a few steps to rejoin her partner. Their made-up lips traced coquettish smiles. They took each other by the waist and with their free hands held the Little Red Book from which they recited some passages. Then the tambourine-girl threw down her book and began to tap on the instrument that hung from a shoulder strap.

The first, slightly plump, moved away from her partner and executed a little dance by herself. Two steps to the right, two to the left, one step forward, one step back. She said in English, "This is the march of all the people of the world, freed from the yoke of imperialism, and expressing their joy

198

under the leadership of Chairman Mao Tse-tung, the big Red Sun in our hearts."

She took Garrison's hands again and drew him into the dance. The black became himself again. Standing up to his full height he executed a frenzied tap routine. Between the empty seats he glided gracefully, holding his lengthy torso perfectly rigid. Only his feet moved, hitting the floor with machine-gun percussion. The girls watched awe-struck. They had to wonder whether all this was ideologically correct. But then, taken by the rhythm, they began to clap their hands and, with a touching awkwardness and in spite of their felt shoes, they sketched out a few steps of the tap-dance.

A deep clearing of the throat brought the dancers up short. Two stern-faced cadres had just entered.

One would have thought them schoolgirls caught by the headmistress in the middle of an orgy in the high school dormitory. The girls stood immobile, each with a hand and a foot still upraised in a graceful gesture. Only the black's tap-dance rattled on for a few moments, like a tired gag in an old film.

One of the two men, his collar decorated by the crossed hammers of the railroad workers, whispered a few words to the girls and, shaking his head, pointed toward Garrison. The four Chinese then turned immediately and disappeared without a backward look. Garrison rushed to the door and tried the knob, in vain.

"We're locked in!"

He grabbed a cup of tea and threw it full force against the door, where it broke. Then he attacked a pile of magazines, *China Reconstructs, Peking Review, China Pictorial,* Chairman Mao smiling on the covers of all of them. For good measure he added some issues in French of *Albanie Socialiste,* and tore them all in one motion.

After that, somewhat relaxed, he came back to his seat and with his expensive-looking, capitalistic lighter he lighted a Peking cigarette.

"Did you see that?" he said in a choked voice. "Did you see how they treated me, Peter Garrison, the man who offered them twenty million Afro-Americans on a silver platter?"

"They've treated me exactly the same way," Georges said.

"It's not possible that Chairman Mao is aware of this," put in the black. Suddenly he stroked his brow. "It's the CIA for sure, they're behind all this! One of their agents, Chen Wu-hsieh, has finally been exposed. He was arrested yesterday in Canton. But there are others, plenty of others still active! They're the ones who decided to expel me, to turn me over to the Ku Klux Klan's executioners!"

Georges could not be surprised by anything anymore. He only thought that if Garrison was judged *persona non grata* he had little chance himself of getting through the net.

"After seeing you on the job at the Workers' Stadium against your compatriot Sydney, I certainly thought you were following the line," he remarked with more than a trace of irony.

"I've told you, they behave like whites!" Garrison replied. "They're throwing me out because I scare them. And I scare them because I try to realize in the very heart of the imperialist fortress what they preach here at home. They didn't want to take my plan seriously."

"Oh, so you have a plan too?"

"Yes I do—I mean the Afro-American Council of the Revolution does. For the generalized insurrection in the United States next summer. The signal can be given by any development, the assassination of any one of us, for example, or of a Black Power leader, or of a white politician who is a little too closely identified with our cause."

He winked his eye, alluding to Martin Luther King struck down on the balcony of the motel in Memphis, or Robert Kennedy agonizing in the Ambassador Hotel kitchen in Los Angeles, dramas that, however, Georges thought, had just provoked sporadic uprisings, not a global coordinated revolution. As if responding to these objections, Garrison added,

"So far we've just had rehearsals, maneuvers to train our troops. But the next time . . ."

He took the gold lighter out of his pocket.

"The next time, pfffffffft!"

The flame shot up and he let it burn, thoughtful, until the revolving fan blew it out.

"Chairman Mao has said, 'A spark is enough to light a prairie fire.' Right now, back home, the situation is ripe or will be ripe soon, just as soon as I get back in touch with my brothers. And no one will be able to put out that prairie fire!"

He stood up.

"I gave them a very precise plan—the creation of Black Revolutionary Committees in every ghetto, made up of cells including a responsible soldier recruited from among the veterans of Korea and Vietnam; someone responsible for ideology; a teacher; a student; an intellectual; a union man, and even a clergyman. That last really made them explode, which proved that they know nothing about the history of our movement, that they're not interested." He was talking to himself, paying no attention to his interlocutor, going over and over his grievances. Voluntary contributions from black capitalists, based pro-rata on their income tax returns. Armaments? No problem; you can buy mortars or bazookas easily enough from the white imbeciles. If necessary, if they're suspicious, we can use American connections. Effective takeover of power, first in the black or majority-black universities, like Howard or Tuskegee, then, say, Michigan State or Columbia, followed by the expulsion of white students. And in the last stage, a power takeover in the ghettos themselves and the creation of pockets of insurrection throughout the country. And none of this nonsense about a 'separate black state in the South.' This sort of thing is petit-bourgeois intellectual daydreaming."

Without giving Georges a chance to get in a word, he asked, "You know what they told me when I presented these

201

ideas—which are not only mine, believe me—in front of their new commission for Brotherly Aid to Peoples against Imperialism, the one that replaced the Committee of Afro-Asian Solidarity?"

"No," answered Georges, learning for the first time of this organic change inside the apparatus, which was probably owing to Chen's disgrace.

"That it was 'premature'! Yes, that's just the word they used. They accused me of 'adventurism,' they contended that the black movement cadres were still insufficiently revolutionized, that we had first to perfect the ideological education of the black masses by spreading Mao Tse-tung's Thought among them, that the plan presented aspects that were 'leftist, opportunist, and petit-bourgeois, as plainly proved by Guevara's failure in Bolivia'! As if the proletariat in Harlem and Watts was comparable to the goitered Indian peasants in the Andes! . . . Can you feature that!"

"Well," Georges said, now in his element, "they've treated you the way the Russians treated Mao Tse-tung in the twenties, when they accused him of leaning on the rural masses for the overthrow of imperialism in China rather than on the urban proletariat, just as they are treating Castro and the Cubans now."

The other exploded. "You too! You don't understand anything! They simply treat us like niggers! Besides, they even told me Chou En-lai had been so disappointed by the bourgeois black leaders during his tours in Africa, that he put us all in the same basket. That Mao Tse-tung is no different from de Gaulle or Nixon. Even to him we're nothing, you see. Niggers! We don't exist!"

He squatted in the middle of the car and went on, assuming the inflections of the "good nigger" of American musicals. "Yessuh, yeh Dad. OK boss. Yeh we burned a few little stores in the Bronx, but it was just to have a little fun. . . . Well, boy, it's OK this time, but don't do it again. You do and we'll have your ass! . . ."

202

He went on in a normal voice. "This time they'll have to take us seriously. They'll have to be scared, really scared! They'll have to arrest thousands of our brothers and throw them in the concentration camps all set up in Texas and California, almost everywhere. We know what we're talking about. We have precise information on it. Whites understand only one thing—terror. They'll get it. And I count on you to inspire it because you, you've come back from China, you know what it's all about. Let them burn, let them hang! Preferably the innocents. Because if blacks are innocent to them, they are traitors to us. . . . Let them begin their genocide, and quick! You'll see . . ."

He intoned the cry of the ghetto revolt: "Burn, baby, burn!"

"It will be the greatest massacre in history! Hitler, the Jews, the concentration camps, I never believed it myself—it's just a story whitey made up."

He had become again the inspired prophet back at the Ming Tomb. Georges forgot his too elegant suit, his gold lighter, his affected manners. He even found him beautiful, with his short beard of an Omdurman dervish, his deep looks, his long eloquent hands.

Listening with half an ear to this course in revolutionary violence—much more virulent than anything he had heard yet in China, not to mention among the petits-bourgeois of the Algerian FLN or in the entourage of Bourguiba—Georges succeeded in almost forgetting Chen, Miss Wang, the fate awaiting him perhaps in one or two hours. The train moved inexorably toward the border through a landscape of tender green rice fields, of yellow reeds, of steel-blue hills; at each of the little stations they lost more of the Chinese passengers.

Georges observed once more that he attracted confidences. Maybe after all he was gifted for the job of a spy. "Beginner's luck," Mr. Marcel would say.

"But why me, why tell me all this?" he finished by asking Garrison. "Not so long ago you called me a spy."

"That's the very reason I tell you. I haven't the slightest doubt that you're a spy, an *agent provocateur*. I've seen hundreds like you in the United States, so-called 'journalists,' so-called 'liberals,' so-called 'whites who understand our problems.' As soon as you're back among your kind, in Hong Kong, you'll make a report on me to the FBI. But I don't care. If the British hand me over, as the Chinese hope, my brothers will avenge me. And they'll listen to me at my trial! Then our revolution will break out all the sooner! And believe me, it won't be Chinese style revolution! Blood will flow, a lot of blood! But first the whites must be scared; they must know that from now on the Black Revolution has a chief and his name is Peter Garrison who is not just a shitty little 'non-violent student,' or an Uncle Tom who organizes 'poor peoples' marches' and leaves like a good boy when the beautiful people of Washington ask him to. And who's going to make me known all over the world, known by our friends and our enemies? Who? You, Mr. Spy; you're going to play a useful role for once by denouncing me. After all, you're also a De Gaulle agent, aren't you? And De Gaulle, what excites him in life? To bother the Americans. So, objectively, we're allies, like our Chinese friends would say."

He sat down, satisfied with his demonstration. Stroking his goatee, he added, "Anyhow, I'll soon disappear. Like Guevara. I can assure you, once I'm among my brothers, they'll have a hard time finding me. You can tell anybody anything you want to. Even the fact that I have been expelled. Nothing wrong with that. Just the opposite. It'll prove that I'm independent, from everybody, like Che was. Maybe one day, after they kill me, you'll write a book about me. Not so bad, eh? This trip can bring in a lot of money, and that's all you're interested in. Right?"

With this insult, he moved ostentatiously away from his future biographer and buried himself in looking at the scenery.

The train slowed down and soon stopped. The loud-

204

speakers blared out *The Great Helmsman*. On the side of a big lattice-work shed, both in ideograms and in Latin characters, Georges read "Chum Chum." It was the border, the end of the journey.

He seized his suitcase, his typewriter—as in Peking, as in Wuhan, as in the fifty airports of North Africa or the Middle East he had dragged himself through these many years. His companion went to the door—now unlocked, their captivity ended, at least temporarily—his hands in his pockets. With a slight and embarrassed smile, the black explained "I always travel this way. Suitcases, a change of clothes, shoes. They're for the whites. Me, I have a toothbrush. And my lighter . . . to set America on fire." He smiled at last at his own bragging. "Look at me . . . Doesn't this remind you of something? Lenin, the armored train!"

This time he burst out laughing.

"Very frankly," he confessed, "I do have some linen, my African costume for the ceremonies, and above all some books. But I left Peking in a little bit of a hurry. The comrades of Revolutionary Committee Security didn't let me go back to the hotel to pick up my suitcase. Well, what counts is *here*"—he knocked his forehead—"and they can't take that away from me."

They took a few steps on the platform, led by a silent customs officer. Someone was running up behind them—it was the plump little Red Guard.

"You forgot something!"

She held to Georges the scroll from Wuhan he had left in the baggage net.

Unconsciously? To make restitution to the Chinese people or to give up the role everybody expected him to play?

Half-grimacing, half-smiling, he held out his hand; but Garrison took it instead.

"I carry it for you, boss!" he said, mimicking the accent of blacks in a comedy.

They moved along a platform with giant posters on one

side—a Chinese worker smashing the imperialist hydra, its face twisted by helpless hatred; little Pioneers, their faces radiating health, their arms loaded with flowers, running up to Mao all chubby and paternal; Mao again, among representatives of all the peoples of the world, black, yellows, browns, and even whites (maybe some Albanians).

In the same direction but on the other side of a fence, several hundred Chinese climbed down from other cars and walked toward customs—border people, Hong Kong residents going back home after visiting their relatives, political agents assigned to bring the gospel to the masses persecuted by British colonialism.

The two travelers were ushered into a small room furnished by a table with a lace cloth, a steaming teapot on top, and chairs in Holland slipcovers as in the parlors of provincial convents. An official took their passports, left them without a word, and came back ten minutes later. The two open passports showed the "liberating" stamp in red. How easy it all seemed! Formalities had certainly been reduced to a minimum.

There was still customs to get through—three men and a woman seated behind a table under Chairman Mao's portrait. Georges was shown in first while Garrison waited, still carrying the scroll. "With this, at least it looks as if I had some baggage," he whispered smirking to his companion. Nothing like a trip to cement friendships.

A form was held out to Georges. *Foreign bills?* He handed them the printed form given him when he arrived at Peking Airport, in a past now quite nebulous, and the 2,500 Swiss francs he had then declared and which he had not touched. *Camera?* He wrote "none," remembering the set-to in Peking that had preceded his first encounter with Chen. *Weapons? Ammunition?* "None." All this was routine, no problem. He hesitated only at the question, *Works of art purchased in the People's Republic of China?* But, after all, wasn't Fu Pai-chi a "turtle egg" whose decadent production could not decently

206

claim status as a work of art? "None" he wrote again at the risk of having to pretend, if necessary, that he had forgotten about this miserable scroll that Garrison had agreed to take charge of.

The search of his suitcase by the customs woman was perfunctory. Everybody seemed in a hurry to be rid of him. The oldest of the officials advised him not to waste time if he wanted to catch the English train leaving in forty-five minutes. He went out by the other door (to "freedom"?), resigned to wait for Garrison as long as he had to. The black appeared two minutes later. He still held the scroll under his arm and the red ribbon, apparently, had not been untied.

"It helps to be without baggage," he said. "They didn't ask me a thing."

They started off on their way again, preceded by the station employee, to take their last walk on Chinese soil. They ran into an Indian diplomat coming from the British "New Territories," who seemed downcast, and two Scandinavians putting on a show of importance, carrying bags sealed with red wax.

"So, they're having a hot time in Canton?" asked one of them as he passed.

"Less than in Chicago, you bastard!" Garrison fired back.

His hatred of whites grew the more closely he approached the world where they make the law.

The platform took an L-turn, beyond which was another station, glass-paneled, and a train, its engine in full steam. In front of them, under a big red flag emblazoned with five gold stars, the last two Chinese sentries in soft caps, khaki tunics, dark blue pants, and armed with submachine guns walked their posts.

Georges stopped a moment to catch his breath. He put down his suitcase and turned back toward the country he would end up betraying. He was leaving there the only woman with whom he might have been able to find a kind of peace, and the few illusions he had brought with him.

207

Garrison grabbed the suitcase and gave back the scroll in exchange.

"It'll give me some dignity in the eyes of the colonialist cops," he said.

They moved on toward the sentries. Dominated by the Chinese banner, a little "Union Jack" hung loosely against the leaden sky. Georges put down his typewriter and groped in his inner pocket for his passport stamped with the Tunisian crescent. Garrison already held his American passport in his hand. He would not see it again soon, certainly, if he were to be shipped back to the United States.

A whistle blew. Robotlike, the two sentries aimed their tommy guns at them while five soldiers came running out from a guardhouse to the left of the tracks.

Barbed wire fences blocked both banks of the twenty-foot wide stream that marked the border between People's China and "New Territories," an area leased to Great Britain after the Opium War.

The scene had something unreal about it, like one of those dreams you seem to be remembering even while you dream them. Georges waited, resigned. James Bond, he took the time to think, would leap over the barbed wire to the other bank under a volley of fire, and offer, once safe on the other side, a little toss of the hand to his pursuers. So this is how things were to end. Maybe he would see Miss Wang again when she came to finish him off at his trial.

But it was upon Garrison that the five men hurled themselves. They spun him around and led him on the double in the direction of customs. One of the soldiers carried the journalist's suitcase. The black struggled desperately. He shouted in English, maybe to those on the other bank who waited to make their own arrest: "Long live the Afro-American Revolution!" It was the last look Georges had of him—a black Gulliver tied up by Lilliputians, an ultra anti-imperialist arrested by the only serious champions of his own cause. Already, with much circling of their guns overhead,

208

the sentries signaled for Georges to hurry. The Chinese didn't even look at his passport. They shoved him onto the bridge. The metal flooring sounded under his footsteps. If he looked back would he be turned into salt?

A Chinese policeman, in khaki shorts, a freshly ironed shirt, in a cap with Her Majesty's coat of arms, leggings, Victorian stiffness, studied carefully the Hong Kong entrance visa obtained a month ago at the British Embassy in Tunis.

"Is that all the luggage you have?" he asked pointing at the typewriter and the scroll.

"I just lost my suitcase," Georges said.

He went to wait for the train in the bar of Lowu station. He ordered a scotch and soda, just as James Bond would have done.

2 ● TWO MEN, OBVIOUSLY journalists, one Chinese, the other perhaps American, waited at Kowloon station for the daily train from Lowu to arrive.

A dozen European travelers and a great many Chinese boarded the train at the many way stations during the trip that lasted a good three hours from the border, but Georges was the only passenger coming from "the other side." The Chinese he had seen at Chum Chum had probably been held too long to catch the same train.

In his compartment a red-faced English family, with their bathing suits rolled in towels, talked about a fishing party they had been on, about a pleasure junk they would have to put into dry dock. The daughter, a girl about seventeen, with long red hair still wet, did not stop laughing at the pleasantries whispered to her by a boy her age, who sported a college blazer. All British discretion, none of his neighbors paid Georges any attention. The China of the Cultural Revolution could have existed tens of thousands of miles, or, better, decades away.

As soon as the train stopped Georges lost this brief ano-
nymity. A Chinese photographer, his press card stuck into the
band of a straw hat, like reporters in old American films, adjusted his Leica, took a dozen shots of this tired character,
his face blue with a growth of beard, his nails black (the
plumbing was on the blink at the Love of the Masses Hotel),
which had made the little English girl stare at him with
curiosity. The Chinese then came up to him and called out
(he must have had friends at Lowu Control): "Mr. Benachen,
welcome to Hong Kong, welcome to the free world!"

He chuckled a bit. This greeting obviously made everybody
laugh. He hauled out his card with his name in English and,
on the back, in ideograms: "Yang Kuo-ming—Press Photographer—45 Wishes Road, Hong Kong."

"What hotel are you staying at? I'll send you the pictures
there. Can I help show you around Hong Kong?"

Maybe he was really a photographer, a free-lance, a little
bit of a pimp who on occasion peddles information from the
Red Hell to British intelligence in the colony, or to the U.S.
Consulate General. But then an Englishman came up, pad
and ballpoint pen in hand.

He mouthed the name of a newspaper, the *Hong Kong Star*
or *The Sun* (Georges paid little attention), then began a
regular interrogation in English. Two or three colleagues,
American or British, joined in.

"What's going on in Canton? Is it true that the blood oozes
all over South China? That the railroads have been cut?"

Georges pretended not to understand a thing.

The pack of them invited him to dinner, offered him hotel
rooms, and, right out, even to pay him for an interview, each
putting in the name of his own paper—*Time Magazine,
Philadelphia Inquirer, Asahi Shimbun*. . . . He fended them
off with good humor.

Well, he had expected something like this. He was changing some of the Swiss francs for Hong Kong dollars when he
saw the understrapper's head of the man from the Batignolles,

incongruous in a tropical jacket that he must have had whipped up here by one of the famous Hong Kong ultra-quick, ultra-cheap tailors. Mr. Marcel wore dark glasses—in the tropics it was not necessarily a distinctive mark of his profession. He must have lain in wait for Georges for several days, because no one could have known what train he would arrive on, or what day.

Mr. Marcel followed him into the first-class section of the Star Ferry of the island of Victoria.

Their elbows on the railing, they turned their backs on the group of journalists, on the cute and nearsighted Chinese typists whose well-starched sheer white blouses disclosed padded brassieres, and on bank clerks who, in their behavior and their walk, so much more resembled their counterparts in London and New York than their cousins in Canton that their Asiatic faces seemed to have been pasted on.

"I knew right off that you were French and that you had come from the other side," Mr. Marcel said, loud enough for the others to hear.

"I'm not really French," Georges answered playing the game. "Tunisian, to tell the truth. But when you're so far from home it's almost the same thing, wouldn't you say?"

The other agreed with a solemn nod of the head.

"Do you smoke?" this not-very-secret agent asked.

Georges had given up smoking long since, on the insistence of his ex-wife. Mr. Marcel knew it. Georges took the cigarette offered him anyway. The other struck a match and handed him the little flat pack.

"Keep it," he said, "and have a good stay in Hong Kong."

He went off and sat down at the other end of the first-class lounge, beside a big-bellied Chinese. On the pack, under the gold characters of "Hilton Hotel," Georges read the penciled message "Room 812, 7:15." He was back in tow.

With a grinding of cables and pulleys, the ferry tied up at the Connaught Road dock. The passengers prepared to leave with the automatism of subway riders. Mr. Marcel shrugged his way into the crowd, panting. He did not do too well in this climate.

After having allowed him to enjoy the view of the bay in peace, the Chinese photographer and his Anglo-Saxon colleagues, who were pursuing Georges, resumed their attack.

"Listen," he finally told them in English. "I'm a journalist, I do the same kind of work you do!" He liked this ambiguity, which probably characterized pretty well the real activities of some of his questioners. "You shouldn't have any trouble understanding that I prefer to keep my own material for my own paper. I invite you to read it, by the way, in *African Will Power*. All right, now I'm going to the Mandarin so I can take a shower and clean up. If you insist, look me up there in an hour and I'll answer a few questions."

Not used to air conditioning, Georges shivered in the gold bar whose fake Chinese style recalled the "Pagoda" theater in Paris on the Rue de Babylone. His fellow journalists stuck to their guns; they must even have drummed up some of their comrades, because the contingent had grown to a good dozen. A solemn young page, dressed in a Mandarin robe of a cherry color, brought them a long, immense wine list. Two scotches, added to what he had had at the border station, made him euphoric.

"China, it's marvelous!" he began without waiting for questions.

He limned an idyllic picture. The Cultural Revolution had become a kind of permanent national holiday. The young Red Guards danced in the streets, singing for happiness. Chiang Ching, Chairman Mao's wife, was Joan of Arc, the Passionaria, Louise Michel, and Eleanor Roosevelt all wrapped up in one. The posters told the touching stories of heroes rewarded and a few villains justly chastised. In Canton, a joyous, fraternal disorder reigned; the diverse factions vied with one another in healthy emulation, just to see who could best apply the precepts of Mao.

212

The more he ground out this baloney, the more his listeners' faces fell. Finally one of them, a professional "China watcher" from a big American magazine, interrupted. "If I understand you, Canton is a much more peaceful place than Hong Kong."

He took Georges over to the window. Seventeen stories down, hundreds of Chinese waved red flags and portraits of Mao. Helmeted police, armed with clubs and tear gas cannisters blocked the street that led up to the United States Consulate.

"For three weeks we've been having demonstrations like this every day!" the American cried. "There have already been five deaths and hundreds of arrests. And it's all your peaceful little friends from Canton, your red boy scouts who have provoked it!"

To Georges who, some hours ago, had found himself in the middle of crowds twenty times more numerous, it seemed strange to watch this agitation from so high up, in this comfortable milieu, in these sterilized surroundings, his glass constantly refilled by the page with the face of a cynical old pimp.

"I don't very much like having my fucking leg pulled!" snapped the American. "I don't know who you're really working for, but I hope for their sake you'll report to them a little more seriously. Count on me to publicize your next book!"

He took off, followed by his colleagues, leaving, by way of reprisal, the bill—not bad considering all that these sponges had soaked up. Georges signed it abstractedly. He'd put it on Mr. Marcel's account. The little Chinese photographer was the only one not to take part in the exodus. Sipping an orangeade, he waited patiently for Georges to take some notice of him.

The journalist tried to avoid him, but he persisted. "Do you know Hong Kong? I can help you, show you the city."

"I don't need anything or anybody," Georges answered.

This was not true. But the only person whom he needed

213

was separated from him forever, by an impassable distance, a closely guarded border, maybe the walls of a prison, barbed wire, or even by a firing squad.

Not in the least discouraged, Yang followed him into the elevator where another page, this one in a saffron robe, operated a control panel worthy of a Boeing 707. Yang was still at Georges' heels as he bought shirts, a razor, some light slacks in a store in the hotel's shopping arcade, to replace the incriminating evidence that remained in the hands of the Chum Chum police. The photographer even haggled with the clerk, got a lower price for Georges and ended up giving him the name of a tailor on Gloucester Road.

"Tell them I sent you, they'll give you a good price," he declared.

Disarmed by all this openness, fearing his own solitude, Georges let himself be coaxed back to the bar.

"I have friends who are dying to chat with you," the Chinese said amiably. "Don't be afraid, they're not journalists but people much more serious who have considerable means and who are quite obviously interested, like all of us here, to know what is going on in People's China. If you want, if you're free of course, come and join us this evening, any time even very late, at the Blue Dragon. It's here on the island, all the cab drivers know it."

His wink was almost obscene, as if he were offering to show him dirty movies.

"There will be pretty girls. Lots of pretty girls," he added as he said goodbye. "And also one of your colleagues, who you must certainly have met in Peking, Mr. Yoshiwara of the *Hokkaido Shimbun*. You'll be able to trade impressions. It will be very interesting for us all."

Georges had only to cross the square to go from the Mandarin to the Hilton. Meanwhile the confrontation had taken shape. The soldiers' bayonets glittered from behind black police vans. The crowd shouted in Chinese and in English:

"Down with imperialism! *Mao zu chi wang tsuei!* (A thousand years of life to Chairman Mao!) Over a loudspeaker installed at the top of the Bank of China building a woman with a voice a little like Miss Wang's explained unexcitedly, articulating every syllable, "English imperialists! This rally made up of all strata of the people of the Chinese city of Hong Kong, inspired by Chairman Mao's Thought, the great big Red Sun in our hearts, will not tolerate your provocations any longer. The time when imperialism and colonialism could make the law for the great Chinese people is gone forever. This is a solemn warning. Liberate our imprisoned comrades. Apologize while there's still time to the great Chinese people and indemnify them for one hundred years of brigandage."

From a neighboring roof, that of the Hong Kong and Shanghai Bank, a respectable survivor of an era when colonialism had a good conscience, another loudspeaker tried to sink this propaganda under a flood of insipid music. Only chopped quotations could be heard: "Like . . . Tse-tung . . . every Communist . . . power grows out of the barrel of a gun."

Georges heard the noise of breaking glass. A stone had just hit a lamppost. There was much running in a nearby street. He just missed being hit by a paddy wagon that zoomed away down the street, preceded by cops on motorcycles, their sirens howling. The faces of the new martyrs pressed against the reinforced glass of the rear door of the van. The Red Guards of Hong Kong, bourgeois communists, fornicators, players of Mah Jongg, always feeding their faces, at last were paying their dues to the Cultural Revolution.

Georges had no problems getting through the police lines. Here—at least for now anyway—a white face was its own passport. He held the precious scroll very tightly under his arm. He was anxious to be rid of it.

The key to 812 was in the door. He entered without knocking. Mr. Marcel dozed in a chair. Keeping him company were two men, one of them quite young, skinny, and stooped, the other older, with crew cut gray hair and a very military look.

215

The three of them stood up as one when Georges entered the room. Mr. Marcel took both his hands and shook them effusively. He oozed good will. His smile expressed the relief of the chief for the miraculous return of one of his men from a suicide mission.

They offered him a seat and forced another drink on him. Mr. Marcel looked on, on the verge of tears.

"You see, my dear fellow, I couldn't resist the temptation. I had to see you myself right away, to get your impressions while they're still fresh." And then, with a conspirator's smile, "I took advantage of this and arranged a little trip to Hong Kong for myself on the house. Our friend Tillard can tell you, he lives here all year round; it's not unpleasant to be in this country so blessed by the gods."

The one called Tillard, the gray-haired one, rose in his chair and made a rather stiff salute. He obviously did not take part in his chief's ecstasy.

Mr. Marcel switched to beer-hall banter. "What about them, these little Chinese? I've heard you didn't manage too badly in some angles . . . the horizontal for instance! Ha!ha! ha! At least that's"—adjusting his glasses to look at the dossier, suddenly serious—"what our friend Michel L. has told us."

Why, Georges wondered with annoyance, didn't he come right out and say, "Loriot told us you slept with your interpreter. Give us the information you got from her." But no, that would be too simple. One must respect the forms, even—especially—in this profession.

"Do you have tangible proof that Miss Wang is really the niece of Chen Wu-hsieh?"

This time, it was the young one who spoke. Drily, incisively. Here's one guy you couldn't accuse of tying things up with pretty ribbons.

The interruption seemed to bother Mr. Marcel, perhaps because it disregarded the chain of command—unless it was all part of a scenario prepared in advance, as in a police in-

216

terrogation. In fact, Georges thought, this conversation resembled certain sessions at the Quai des Orfèvres or in the security offices in Algiers, where he had been summoned many times during the French period and after.

"Am I supposed to answer this gentleman whose name I don't know?" Georges asked eyeing the youngster.

"Paul, one of my assistants," Mr. Marcel hastened to introduce. "A boy of great merit."

"I think it'd be better to let Mr. Benachen tell us in his own way," Tillard said.

Paul went over and turned on a tape recorder and took out a notebook.

"So you arrived in Peking on the twenty-fifth. Today is the third. Let's proceed day by day. It'll be easier for you. Don't get mad at us, but we're maniacs of precision."

Mr. Marcel had given up his debonaire tone. He was again the professional agent, the "old man" of spy fiction.

The questions revealed a perfectly tuned system. Every encounter, every conversation had to be reported, commented upon, explicated, every person described and placed. The stadium episode and the clandestine meeting interested them particularly. On the other hand, they wasted no time with Zagachvili.

"We know, we know," Mr. Marcel put in. "You were right not to get too involved with him. That was all a line, of course, that we had made common cause with them. Whatever our American friends think, we're not at that point yet with these gentlemen from the KGB."

Georges spoke at great length. He was not really unhappy to be reliving his adventures—it helped him see things more clearly. However, he mentioned his encounter with Garrison only briefly and kept to himself the last confidence of the black. After all, the poor man was having trouble enough with the Chinese right now. When he talked to him in the train he did not know he was going to be arrested at the border. And any kind of publicity—Georges had no illusions that intelligence services were leakproof—would do nothing but delay his eventual release.

The questioning went on.

> *Q:* "When Chen told you about the plan of attack, how did you react?"
>
> *A:* "I was surprised, of course."
>
> *Q:* "And? How did you show your surprise?"
>
> *A:* "I said that I needed more precise information."
>
> *Q:* "Was it then that Chen brought in the two army men, or the characters who pretended to be?"
>
> *A:* "Yes, Miss Wang went to get them."
>
> *Q:* "What makes you think that they were really from the army?"
>
> *A:* "The way they were dressed. The red patch on their collars. But more than that, because Chen introduced them as such. After all, he had no special reason to make anything up."
>
> *Q:* "Maybe we don't have the same confidence you have in the word of Sir Chen and his charming niece. She was his niece, wasn't she?"
>
> *A:* "That's what she told me. She didn't show me her birth certificate. And, there again, I can't give you any guarantee. It's up to you to make up your own minds. I couldn't care less, as a matter of fact."

When they got to Wuhan, the stopped train, the battle as seen from the bridge, the phony arrest, the gymnasium, the appearance of the "Colonel," he noticed that his questioners exchanged looks more ironic than interested. In a heavy silence he completed that part of his story which outlined Operation East Wind.

"And there you have it," he concluded, "you know as much as I do now. It's your turn."

Mr. Marcel tapped his pipe against the cleat of his shoe. He packed it meticulously and lighted it after three tries.

218

"And you, do you believe it?" he asked.

"I neither believe it nor disbelieve it. I've told you what I learned there. It already goes beyond the bounds of the mission, or rather of the message you commissioned me to deliver. I took considerable risks and I still wonder how they ever let me get out."

"To be frank, we ask ourselves the same question," Tillard put in almost whispering.

Georges ignored the interruption.

"All this," he said, "is worth much more than the miserable hundred and fifty thousand you promised me. Now, if it doesn't interest you, OK, there's nothing more to say."

He made as if to leave, taking up the scroll which he had placed on the bed and whose importance he hadn't mentioned, more out of forgetfulness than by design. Now he congratulated himself on this.

"Wait a minute, just a minute, don't get worked up, old man."

Mr. Marcel laughed, a forced laugh obviously. Paul got up and placed himself nonchalantly in front of the door. From this vantage point he watched the scene, his hands in his pockets.

"I've told you my story. But I certainly don't want to make you waste your time."

Georges felt big enough to knock out this flatfoot lieutenant if he tried to keep him from leaving. The alcohol, the fatigue, and the excitement made him combative.

"Oh come on, you are too much!" Mr. Marcel exclaimed. "You come here, hands in your pockets, you casually tell us that the Chinese are ready to blow up the planet next week; after which, you put on your hat—so to speak—and so long folks! It's enough to make me believe that you take us for altar boys, or that you're one yourself, which I refuse to admit. Right, Tillard?"

Tillard started. Apparently he was not used to having his opinion solicited. He nodded thoughtfully.

219

"Come on," Mr. Marcel resumed, "sit down, have some more scotch and let's talk this over like friends. Let's go back, if you will, to what Chen told you in Peking."

Georges went back over his story, adding new details. But this second go-round caused even more skepticism than the first.

"Now really," protested Mr. Marcel, after listening in silence, "you must have some proof, some kind of document to bridge what our fine American friends—they'd be very interested, wouldn't they, Tillard?—would call the 'credibility gap'!"

Georges tried desperately to think. He did not feel at all like releasing the scroll to these idiots without trying to make some money out of it somewhere else. But the way he had, during his aborted exit, snatched up the silk scroll had sounded the alarm.

"Maybe Mr. Benachen," Paul insinuated, "just happens to have brought the document you spoke of, Chief. . . . Do you mind letting us have a look at this work of art that carries, if I'm not mistaken, the stamp of 'Marco Polo,' the great Peking antiquarian?"

Without waiting for permission, Mr. Marcel's assistant grabbed the scroll. Georges gave up any idea of protest. In this world of professionals he was, after all, nothing but an amateur. To save face he was content to say, "I brought this proof, yes. But since my whole story seemed so farfetched, I didn't think it would mean so much to you."

Paul undid the ribbon with dexterity and spread out the scroll.

"Very pretty," he said. "An authentic Fu Pai-chi. It's on the back, isn't it? Will any chemical developer do?"

"I think so," Georges answered. "They didn't tell me exactly what they used."

The young man took off his coat, rolled up his sleeves, and went toward the bathroom.

220

"Maybe you're hungry?" Mr. Marcel asked by way of conversation.

Sounds of running water came from the bathroom and of cloth being brushed lightly.

Georges was not hungry. All he had in mind was to be in the open air again, far from the three of them, at once over-familiar and hostile.

Paul returned to the room in fifteen minutes. He held the scroll by the ribbon and showed the back covered with ideograms.

"We're going to look this over right away," Mr. Marcel said.

His skepticism had vanished. He was in a hurry to be rid of Georges for a while so he could confer, evidence in hand, with his associates.

"I reserved you the room next to ours. You'll be better off here than in the Mandarin and we can resume our talk in the morning. This will take us all night. Do you need any money right away?"

Georges was tempted to accept. But to take a handful of bills on the spot in exchange for his treason seemed to him entirely too dirty.

Tillard went out into the hallway with him and opened the door of the room next door. Georges was sure that they'd lock him in.

"I'd like to get some fresh air," he said. "And besides, I'd prefer to go back to my hotel."

"I'll go with you," Tillard said.

In the lobby, a bus had just let out a fresh supply of tourists—most of them women, Americans for sure. They were exactly what he had expected—blue hair, pince-nez attached to the cord of their Sonotones by short strings of pearls, the tired walk caused by age, varicose veins, hemor-rhoids, prolonged emptiness, and shopping more than any-thing, in this city which is nothing more than one big store

221

loaded just for them with the loudest of brocade, the most twisted of imitation jade, and the most pinkish of cultured pearls. They cackled away, massaging their haunches. Some wore tight Chinese dresses that clung to their flaccid breasts and bony shoulders.

Georges pushed his way through them, knocking down packages, setting up a gabble of indignation. He performed a slalom course, spinning a Kansas City widow around, clutching at the neck of a matron from Lansing. Tillard tried to follow him but found his way blocked by the only male of the group—someone who had managed to survive the voracity of these praying mantises, or maybe he was the guide—who checked him severely. Above an ocean of falls and flowery hats stirred by a swell of anger, Georges shouted at Tillard, "Call me up tomorrow morning at the Mandarin! Don't be afraid! I won't vanish. You haven't paid me yet!"

He had lost all his inhibitions. The sight of the Americans had suddenly restored his good mood.

Outside the demonstration had ended. An imposing deployment of police, some broken lampposts, and an unusual peace were all that was left of it. Georges heard Tillard running behind him. He saw a taxi. He jumped into it. "The Blue Dragon," he ordered. If he was going to this new appointment, it was under no illusion about the level of those expecting him there, but childishly to rile Mr. Marcel.

The door opened at the first ring. An old waiter in a white jacket showed him up a rather steep stairway. In a large room, three-quarters empty, Mr. Yang Kuo-ming sat beside a heavily made-up Chinese girl. Facing them, a young, athletic man, with a crew cut, was caressing the neck of another girl just as heavily made-up. Even though the room was air conditioned, Mr. Yoshiwara sat at the end of the table making short strokes with a fan adorned with a blue dragon. He had taken off his shoes, and his chubby feet in violet cotton socks followed the syncopated rhythm of a Philippine orchestra. His welcome was as warm as it had been at the Hilton.

222

"Delighted to see you," gabbled Mr. Yang (he must have had a lot to drink), "let me introduce Miss Mary Lou and Miss Betty Ann."

The two girls smiled. They were very pretty with their silk dresses, one red, the other blue, split up the thighs but severely buttoned to the neck. Mr. Yang pointed toward the American: "Doctor Alexander Gehring, from the Center for Asian Research of the Massachusetts Institute of Technology. Dr. Gehring is a distinguished sinologist. You have certainly read his *Introduction to the Study of the Evolution of the Politico-Economic Structures of the People's Communes in Shensi.*"

Mr. Yang delivered his little panegyric in almost one gasp. It rang out unexpectedly in the smokey room, which seemed a combination brothel and railway waiting room.

Gehring protested, "Yang is always making me out to be a bookworm. Call me Alex. Hi, George!"

He shook hands vigorously. Yoshiwara bowed low, head almost to his toes. His breathing whistled noisily as he exclaimed, "Welcome, welcome to Hong Kong! This is a far cry from Peking, wouldn't you say?"

That whinnying laugh. He seemed especially cheerful, maybe because his wife was not here.

"Dr. Gehring," Mr. Yang resumed, "is dying to hear the story of your trip. With him, you needn't worry about reading your story on the front page of *The New York Times*. Dr. Gehring is a university man, discreet by profession."

"I was born in Peking," the American explained to put him at ease. "My father was a missionary there, and also a doctor."

"Oh! Is that so?" Georges said politely.

He couldn't have cared less. He was busy watching the girl next to Mr. Yang. She resembled Miss Wang a little bit; maybe it was the pouting mouth. He realized that he was looking everywhere for the face of his lost friend.

"Do you want to dance?" he asked.

223

She stood up readily.

"You must buy tickets," she whispered.

But Mr. Yang took a handful out of his pocket and slipped them into the girl's hand.

Georges took the taxi dancer in his arms. He had not danced for years, but the girl led him.

"Is that your name? Mary Lou?" Georges asked just to make conversation.

"Yes, of course," she answered, indignant. "I'm a Christian, what'd you think?" Then, to get the dialogue back on the track: "Yours is Georges, right?" she asked. "Before you came they were talking about you all the time. Is it true that you came back from there? Have you seen Chairman Mao? Do you know him?"

"Not intimately," Georges admitted, "but I saw him."

She pressed herself against him. His prestige shot up a few degrees.

"I'm from Shanghai myself. Have you been there?"

"No."

"Neither have I. I was two when my parents left. So I don't remember."

"You'd like to go back?"

The girl hesitated. She was not used to active cerebration. Her pretty forehead wrinkled in a violent effort to concentrate. Finally her lips opened half way, but this time unaffectedly, not playing the professional. "Yes, I think so. I'd be a little scared by the Red Guards. I've heard that they kill people and even cut the girls' hair. I wouldn't like that"—she shook her studiedly wavy hair. "And then, to work the soil and get your hands all dirty, to go to rallies or carry buckets full of . . . well you know, what they use for the harvest. . . . But, even so, maybe it'd be better there than here."

For an instant Georges was tempted to convert his pretty partner to Maoism, to push her to go back home. Maybe this way he would make up to some extent for his abandonment—which was how he saw it this evening—of Miss Wang.

224

But she had already changed the subject.

"Are you a friend of theirs?" she said, pointing with her head toward the table.

"Not really," Georges answered.

"Well, they scare me. Especially Mr. Yang." Then, under her breath in his ear: "He's not a real photographer you know. And people say he's from the police. Well, a kind of police, I don't know which one. And the American, he speaks Mandarin, but so badly! . . . And then they always put on such a mysterious front. With you it's not like that."

Georges was not familiar with taxi dancers, B-girls, and part-time whores. He mostly picked up his mistresses among students, intellectual liberals, or wives of militants he worked with. But he found this one nice, refreshing in her naiveté. Like the three other couples dancing in the dimly lighted room, they were very close to each other, following the slow rhythm of a sort of Philippine blues. Under the brocade of her blouse, he felt the firmness of her breasts. Unlike the typists in the ferry, she didn't seem to need a padded bra. She gave off a rather vulgar scent which made him miss Miss Wang's cheap soap.

The music stopped and the Philippine musicians packed up their instruments. They were the last customers in the place.

"We're not going to let you just go to bed on your first night in the 'free world,'" Mr. Yang said. "Let's go somewhere for a nightcap. I have an idea!"

He whispered something to Mary Lou, who shook her head vigorously. But he insisted and then announced with a triumphant voice, "Our charming friend will take us to her uncle. We can have a nice time there. OK? Everyone agree?"

Georges hesitated, torn between fatigue and his desire not to go back to his hotel where he was sure one of Mr. Marcel's cops would be waiting for him. Mary Lou took his arm and led him toward the exit. Alex, who insisted on calling him "George," which he found totally unpleasant, took his other arm. Could he be too drunk to walk by himself? The group

225

went down the stairs, Mr. Yang in the lead, Yoshiwara and Betty Ann bringing up the rear. They sank into a taxi. The ride was very short. The car stopped along a dark and deserted pier. There wasn't a breath of air. In the harbor, the green and red lights of the freighters turned about slowly as the boats got underway. From deep inside the nearby junks, moored at right angles to the pier, came a kind of machine-gun sputtering.

"Mah Jongg," Mary Lou explained. "They play until morning. I've been told that on the mainland it's forbidden. I really wonder what they do at night."

Mr. Yang had disappeared a while back, but now he came toddling back.

"I found a walla-walla," he said, "a little motorboat that can get you across to Kowloon after the last ferry has gone. Because this pretty young thing is going to take us to the mainland."

"Mainland" was the term the people of Hong Kong and Taiwan used in referring to China herself.

Georges wondered if this was a kidnapping, if he wouldn't find himself back in Canton to be tried at the side of Chen, Miss Wang, Garrison, and the Wuhan Colonel; or aboard that Seventh Fleet destroyer whose long, gray silhouette he had seen that afternoon, where he'd be given the third degree by the CIA; or simply at the bottom of the sea with a stone around his neck. He jumped aboard. He almost fell down and clung to Mary Lou's neck. She made him sit beside her in front and looked at him smiling.

He had nothing but a vague impression of an endless taxi ride through the wide streets of the Kowloon shopping district. On the balconies he could see forms lying on beds, red flags, laundry put out to dry. The building they finally stopped in front of looked like suburban low-income housing, a little more decrepit, and much more foul-smelling—a stink of garlic, urine, soya and dead rats. Two fleshless men dressed

226

in shiny black Cantonese pajamas slept under the porch, and Yoshiwara swore when he stumbled over a prostrate body.

By the time they had silently climbed the five stories of a dark and sticky stairwell, there was nothing left in them of the jolly pub crawlers. Mary Lou made them wait at the landing while she went down a hallway alone. A door opened. They could hear whispering. The girl came back.

"My uncle invites you to come in but he warns you not to make too much noise, because of the children," she said in a low voice.

In the entry three urchins between two and five years old, their underwear up revealing plump bellies, rested on a cot. An old woman lying beside them on a mattress woke up growling. On the wall a big calendar in color showed an artist of the Peking Opera with a sort of gold miter on his head, his face made up in white ceruse.

They adjourned on tiptoe to the next room, a little larger, where the "uncle," a fat little chap wearing glasses and a bathrobe, was clearing away bedding and dishes. He came up to shake hands, ceremoniously, and with many protestations of hospitality. No, no, they weren't disturbing anyone. On the contrary. In three minutes the apartment was emptied of its rightful occupants; the sleepy children, rubbing their eyes with their little fists, had been taken out by the grandmother to end the night at some neighbor's. The glaring ceiling light was replaced by the flickering gleam of a tiny oil lamp. Georges found himself seated on a plank, alone with Mary Lou. She was making a translucent ball stuck to the end of a long needle sputter as she held it in the flame of the night light.

Georges knew very well what was expected from him. He inhaled deeply from the opium pipe. Mary Lou approved. "It's not bad for the first time." She was already preparing a second pipe. The scent, at once acrid and sweet, spread all over the room and filled his lungs. He recognized one of the components of the odor he had detected but had been unable to identify around the junks of Victoria Island and in the streets when they got out of the cab.

He lost all notion of time. Vaguely somnolent, he breathed in and exhaled the smoke, stopped, drank some tea, smoked a cigarette. And then, against his face, he felt the undone hair of the girl squatted beside him. He searched for her lips, but she turned her head and it was her cheek, covered by a light sweat, that he kissed.

"Wait," she whispered. She gave him another pipe, prepared one for herself, and then came to lie close beside him. He was not touching her but he was feeling all the curves of her body. Without his brain ordering it, his fingers unhooked the first button, then the others of her Nehru collar. Under the rather rough fabric, he found the nipple of a small, round breast. About the size of Miss Wang's.

She raised herself, pulled her dress over her head, then helped him to undress. A wheezing fan stirred up the hot air to little effect. The noise vaguely reminded Georges of the train, and he thought for a moment that he was back with Miss Wang in the compartment traveling through the plains of North China.

He needed several tries before penetrating her at last because she was so tight. His sensations were all muffled and prolonged. He was not making love to Mary Lou but to a kind of fleecy entity, a synthesis of all the women he had known. The flesh of the girl was soft, damp, enveloping. But he did not really want her, and the state of permanent erection was not bringing him at all to a climax. Perhaps he fell asleep inside her. When they pulled apart finally, gently— or rather, unglued from one another—their bodies were covered with sweat.

Then he began to talk. He could not stop. The phrases interlocked with a marvelous ease and precision. Did she know that opium, which produces a different reaction for each individual, would have this effect on him, or had she

228

given him some other kind of drug too? For the fact was that he was reliving and retelling, for the second time today, everything that had happened to him. Mary Lou said hardly anything to draw him out, although sometimes, with her fresh and dreamy voice, she'd put his story back on the track. The Hsin Chao Hotel, the improbable conspiracy, the Wuhan Colonel seated in the gymnasium between the trapeze and the horse, the last walk with Miss Wang along the Chamien quay, all again took shape and consistency.

The scroll interested the little taxi dancer very much. She would have been so pleased to see it! She was very disappointed to learn that it was at the Hilton in Mr. Marcel's hands.

"This Miss Wang," she asked, "was she prettier than me?"

He had the feeling of again betraying his vanished friend. Seized by a sudden fury against the little whore who dared compare herself with Miss Wang, he wanted to hit her, but she had stood up in a supple twist and Georges' hand slammed down on the floor and closed around something metal at the end of an electric cord. In spite of his torpor he understood immediately—a microphone. But this neither surprised him nor made him unhappy. All had been foreseeable and he had to admit the means they used had been, all in all, very pleasant. Nor had he particularly wanted the French intelligence to be the only ones in on his secret.

He realized, too, that Mary Lou had talked to him in French, that their conversation had been entirely in French. The part-time whore of the Blue Dragon had turned into a very sharp agent with a very pronounced Vietnamese accent.

"What do you think of Miss Wang?" she insisted. "Is she your friend or your enemy?"

"And what about you?" he asked. "Are you my friend or my enemy? . . . You work for them?"

He pointed to the door behind which the group from CIA—he had no further doubt about it—would be following the playback of the magnetic tape.

229

He did not wait for the girl to answer. Stupidly he caressed her chin and said, "That's pretty soft skin for a flatfoot! Why do you work for them? Out of liking, out of need, out of pride? Or because you don't want to have an honest job, like a whore, for instance? Because you take pleasure in this rotten world where everybody betrays everybody else, including himself? Because it's easier for a girl like you to sell political and military information, more or less dubious, than to sell fabrics, dirty books, or just your body?"

He raised his voice. "Listen to this, the rest of you!" he cried into the microphone. "We're all whores here. But not her, not Miss Wang! Even if she turned me in, even if she turned Chen in, she did it for a cause. And all those I encountered in China, the Maoists, the anti-Maoists, the Red Guards, the soldiers, the little kids, the elevator boys, all, all serve a cause! If they want to blow the American bases in Vietnam sky high, or the Seventh Fleet, they're damn right. So now, fuck off, you piles of shit, with your stinking tape recorder and all your fucking information! If your bosses in Washington don't want it, you can always offer the tape to the whorehouses in town. They might like to hear me making love to your honorable agent!"

He stood up, staggering. In the grayish light that filtered through the dirty windows he could see all the details of the filthy room. The plank, the cracked teapot, and on the wall a photo of the "uncle" when he was young, in Sunday clothes at the side of a little bride who must have been the old lady he had seen.

Mary Lou, unperturbed, buttoned her dress. She seemed much less attractive, her features drawn and hard, her hair dull. She was watching him with some curiosity, perhaps mockery. When she was dressed, she rose up on her toes and kissed his forehead. She wanted to pick up the microphone, but he pushed her away.

"Just a minute! I'm not finished. Listen all of you. All that

230

you try to do against China will turn against you. The Cultural Revolution, it's already had its victory in your country and in mine! At Columbia and at the Sorbonne, in Harlem and at the Renault plant, in front of the White House and at the Odéon Theater!" By now he was really shouting. "Your world is done for, our world! It's coming apart at the seams!"

His eyes caught a little mirror that stood on the only furniture in the room—a night table. He made a face. A greenish complexion, minuscule pupils in unblinking eyes, rumpled shirt streaked by slobber—this vision of himself sapped him of all energy. He collapsed quietly onto the mattress and fell asleep right away.

The door opened. Yang came in in his socks, followed by Yoshiwara.

"Did he faint?" the fake photographer asked the fake taxi dancer in Cantonese.

"Yes, I think so. In any event, he'll be unconscious for a while. It often has this effect the first time, the opium and the rest. At first they spill everything they know, right off, with no fear of the consequences. And then, sometimes immediately, there's a great crisis of indignation, a metaphysical disgust. And then suddenly it's over, they're all gone."

Standing around the inert form on the plank they looked like so many undertakers.

"We can't stay here all day," said Alex, who had just come in with the tape. Then grinning: "This looks entirely too easy to me; it must be a trap. The scenario must have been written by the SDECE. The French have only one thing in mind—to get us involved in an adventure. They're scared to death to see the Vietnam War end. Their interests coincide with those of the Research Center. Anyway, our chiefs at Langley will listen to this little masterpiece a hundred times. And afterward, maybe six months or a year, when what our friend has said will be totally out of date anyway, they'll decide very nicely to do absolutely nothing."

231

The American stretched, yawning mightily. He was the only one in the group to look pink, fresh, and clean. He kissed the girl on both cheeks.

"Thank you, Nuang," he said gravely. "If I went for women and if both of us were in a decent profession, I'd ask you to marry me."

"And I, major dear, would decline your offer," she answered with a little bow.

Friday ●

● ● ●　IT WAS DAYLIGHT when Georges regained conscious-
● ● ●　ness. Compassionately, Mary Lou had wrapped him
● ● ●　in a blanket. On his chest he found a piece of kleenex
on which she had written in lipstick: "No hard feelings, colleague!" The suggestion was superfluous. He felt rather a
vague tenderness for the little Vietnamese. He credited her
with feelings toward her American employers similar to those
he himself entertained toward Mr. Marcel and his subordinates.

He went down the stairs, his hand holding the rail. Once
in the open air he was seized by a violent nausea and vomited
profusely against a garbage can.

He was on Canton Road, the main street of Kowloon. He
looked vainly for a cab to take him to the ferry slip. All he
wanted was to get back to his room in the Mandarin, to take
a long shower, and to sleep after putting the "Do not disturb"
sign on the door.

The traffic seemed remarkably light. The crowd seemed to
have deserted the streets. Behind him a merchant was quickly
putting his stock of mangoes and watermelons inside, and
then closed the iron shutters of his little shop with a bang.
Other merchants did the same and mothers stridently called
their children home.

He hurried on. People looked at him with curiosity. Maybe
they were not used to an unshaven European wandering the
streets of Kowloon at nine in the morning, unwashed, hag-
gard. Maybe they just took him for someone out on the town,
struggling back to his hotel after a wild night in the arms of
one of the local whores—which, after all, was almost the case.

Ahead of him, a row of red double-decker buses was
stopped. Passengers stepped off in bunches and ran off in the
direction opposite his.

Then everything happened at once. Windows flew out in
splinters. Demonstrators, under cover in a side street, threw
stones at the buses, maybe because they were operated by
scabs in defiance of strike orders issued by the Maoist or-

234

ganizations of the city. Thirty seconds later they rushed into
Canton Road. Like those Georges saw the day before in front
of the Mandarin, they seemed curiously middle-class by com-
parison with the "true" Chinese masses of Peking, Wuhan, or
Canton. Most of the men wore short-sleeve shirts and, some
of them, ties; they even had pot bellies—Georges realized that
in all his time in China he had not seen a single fat man. But
there were among them, in the mob, some starved and ragged
individuals—neither had he seen any of them there, where
cleanliness and neatness were among the cardinal virtues of
the regime. They were probably rickshaw boys, unskilled
workers, and, worse, the unemployed of Kowloon City, this
terrifying shantytown where the British police never ventured and where the old secret societies, with Peking, Canton,
and Taipei struggling for control, made the law.

Georges found himself fifty yards from the first bus when
he saw a long, yellow flame leap out of it. In an instant the
big vehicle was nothing but flames and the fire spread to the
second, which exploded, sending debris all the way up to the
top stories of the buildings. Hit by a stone, a dog let out a
pitiful howl, his back broken. In China there are no dogs, no
pets, Georges recalled. What was it Miss Wang had said on
the subject, the day after he arrived, when their relationship
was still the normal one of interpreter and foreigner, and
when she irritated him so much with her doctrinaire tone?
"In People's China, where we build socialism under the enlightened leadership of Chairman Mao, we have other things
to do than to concern ourselves with useless animals. It's in
America that millionaires feed their dogs from gold plates
while the little black children die from hunger in the gut-
ters!" A little black child had just got his revenge.

Far off, he heard a police siren, then two others converging
on the scene of the demonstration. It grew in intensity. Four
buses were on fire. A dozen men overturned a car. The barricade decorated itself with red flags and portraits of Mao,
just like those he had seen brandished on the other side of

235

the border. "At least this is a demonstration that is directed against a really present 'imperialism,' " Georges said to himself. Before his trip to Peking, he would have been on their side, the side of the exploited against this hateful symbol of colonialism—the white-directed police, the police in general.

And they appeared at last. Three hundred yards away cops jumped from their vehicles even before they had stopped. And, adding itself to the odor of burning gasoline, was the familiar stink of tear gas.

Georges put a handkerchief to his eyes. He was right in the middle between the demonstrators and the forces of order. "Between the revolutionary masses and the cops—what a symbol of my new life!" he thought out loud. He was a little delirious from the opium.

He began to run, the way the others had. He was not frightened. He felt no curiosity. He had been in dozens of demonstrations of this kind in the Latin Quarter, and also at the beginning of the Algerian War, during the time of the raids against the Arabs, just before he committed himself to the side of the FLN, back to Tunis, and for a short time with the Willaya 5 guerrillas. He was not a bastard then, even though the Algerian brothers never totally overcame their suspicion of him, as if they had foreseen the future.

Georges took refuge in a small street with booths on either side. He felt secure. On Canton Road the helmeted policemen marched slowly toward the barricade and its defenders began to scatter, throwing stones that fell in the no-man's-land or hit the iron shutters of the shops.

He noticed a form that rose up behind him, and he just had time to think, "Ah, here is another fool to keep me company."

The police found him twenty minutes later, after they had put out the fires and arrested and beaten up a dozen rioters.

He was lying flat on his face, over a crate of scattered tomatoes, his skull smashed. His blood was mixed with the produce in a happy array of colors.

236

It was only in turning him over that they discovered he was dead, and not Chinese. Sergeant Wang—there are so many Wangs—called his superior by walkie-talkie.

Lieutenant Russell came thirty minutes later. He was a fat and heavy fair-haired man. The sight of the European who had come here to be killed, as if for pleasure, during a demonstration he obviously had nothing to do with, put him in a rage. As if he hadn't trouble enough with the governor's instructions ("Above all, do not provoke the natives") and pressure from the banks, the Chamber of Commerce, even from his friend, the submanager of Jardine and Mathieson, who was always repeating that, if order was not restored "with the utmost rigor," Hong Kong was done for—the colony would share the fate of Macao!

"Did you search him?" Russell asked.

"Yes sir," said Wang.

He held out a strange passport; its green cover was stamped with a gold crescent and carried, along with some Chinese visas, a British visa of admittance through Lowu, dated the day before.

"He doesn't look like an Arab," the lieutenant grumbled, vaguely relieved. "Take him to the morgue!" he ordered.

He wondered if there were a Tunisian consulate in Hong Kong. Since the affair looked like a real stickler—a fellow who managed to be killed the day after his arrival from the other side—he decided not to wait to submit the case to the governor's diplomatic advisor. "That'll keep him busy, that creep who spends all his evenings at the Hong Kong Club!" Russell had not slept for four days.

2 ● xcerpt from the *South China Morning Post:*

Journalist Killed
in the Line of Duty

We must deplore the first death of a European since the series of riots provoked by the Maoist elements in our city started.

During a violent confrontation on Canton Road, in Kowloon, between the police and the striking bus drivers joined by irresponsible elements from Kowloon City, a journalist of French origin but of Tunisian nationality, Mr. Georges Benachen (35 years old), was knocked down, probably by the blows of an iron bar. His body was found in a pool of blood, a few minutes after the demonstrators had been dispersed by the police wielding tear gas bombs.

The physicians of the YMCA Hospital, where the victim was taken, could do nothing but confirm the death.

A well-known newsman, an expert in the problems of underdeveloped countries, Mr. Benachen had come just the day before to Hong Kong after a trip through People's China. His death, in such circumstances, seems all the more tragic as he did not hide his sympathy for the Communist cause. Interviewed as he stepped off the train, Mr. Benachen expressed his admiration for the accomplishments of the Cultural Revolution and denied that it amounts to a wave of violence and repression.

It is likely that, pushed by professional curiosity, our unfortunate colleague was anxious to see for himself, while in Hong Kong, the situation of the colony, and that the rioters thought they were dealing with a British policeman in plain clothes.

Mr. Benachen is the first journalist to be killed in the dis-

238

charge of his duties since the beginning of the disorders in Hong Kong.

3 ●   <small>R</small>ADIO <small>C</small>ANTON <small>B</small>ROADCAST

Our respected leader, Chairman Mao Tse-tung, has taught us that "many representatives of the exploiting class, disguised as sincere Communists," frequently adopt a strategy consisting of "hiding in the furls of the red flag only to tear up the red flag" and perpetrate, until they are unmasked once and for all, the most shameless provocations.

Along this line, under the protection of the Chinese Khrushchev, the number one member of the party who follows the capitalist road, a certain Chen Wu-hsieh, had succeeded in infiltrating and making his way in the Party.

Following the appeal of the Preparatory Revolutionary Committee of Kwantung, the masses, representing all strata of the province's population, held a rally in the Cultural Park to judge and condemn this traitor and *agent provocateur* who, blinded by his impotent hatred of the Thought of Mao Tse-tung, the big Red Sun in our hearts, had offered his services to the American imperialists and the Soviet revisionists.

For that purpose, he went so far as to entirely fabricate a so-called "plan" of the People's Army of Liberation, according to which our country was to launch a nuclear attack against the imperialist forces occupying heroic Vietnam.

An ex-cadre of the People's Army of Liberation, Tseng Tsien-min, who had been Chen's accomplice in this absurd plot, had been unmasked and was tried with him.

All the peace-loving peoples of the world know perfectly well that the 750 million Chinese, united more than ever under the great red banner of the Thought of Mao Tse-tung, will never launch an attack and will never be the first to use

239

the weapons they have forged. On the other hand, every aggressive attempt against China from American imperialists or Soviet revisionists will lead them to a crushing defeat. They would dig their own graves.

Piteously, their heads low, these two criminals and their accomplices tried to deny everything in front of the masses. The people imposed silence and forced them to recognize their crimes.

With a revolting hypocrisy, Chen and Tseng admitted "having committed certain ideological errors," and particularly, having imposed by ferocious oppression a bourgeois dictatorship on the masses they had under their orders. They confessed to having derided the use of the Thought of Mao Tse-tung as related to the political and military problems which they tried to "solve" by opposing the mass line and behaving like feudal lords of the Ming dynasty.

They grasped at all kinds of absurd excuses to minimize their role in a plot destined to bring down on China the reprisals of the wild beasts of American imperialism who have at their disposal, in heroic Vietnam, all kinds of supposedly advanced "weapons."

Wang Shao, a relative of Chen whom he had drawn into his treason but who, moved by belated remorse, had confessed her crime and helped to unmask the criminals, came, weeping profusely, to implore the forgiveness of the masses.

Rightly indignant because of the wickedness of Chen and his accomplices, they asked a merciless chastisement. "Break the dog's legs of these lackeys of the Chinese Khrushchev, these accomplices of the number one man inside the Party who follows the capitalist road!" the masses shouted. "Kill the enemies of the people, the mad dogs! Death for the turtle eggs in the service of imperialism!"

Stricken by fear, Chen, Tseng, and their accomplices hid their faces and implored in vain the forgiveness of the masses. The time is long since past when, like the shell-buttoned Mandarins, they could impose thei law with arrogance and pretend to be the only true Communists everyone should respect and obey!

But the masses were not fooled by these pretenses. To the applause of the fifty thousand comrades present, they were shot immediately. Considering her tardy repentance, Wang Shao heard her execution stayed. If she gives proof of her redemption before the masses, if she really turns over a new leaf, Wang Shao will be allowed to rehabilitate herself through work.

4 ● Dispatch from the New China News Agency (NCNA) Peking

A responsible member of the Chinese Ministry of Foreign Affaires has sent the following communication to the USSR chargé d'affaires:

Alexandre Vassilevitch Zagachvili, First Secretary at the USSR Legation, has behaved in a way incompatible with his diplomatic status. He has given way to all sorts of provocations against the great Chinese people and even against Chairman Mao, the great guide, the great helmsman of the Chinese People.

Consequently, Alexandre Vassilevitch Zagachvili must leave the territory of the People's Republic of China within twenty-four hours.

SATURDAY ●

● ● ●   "WELL, WHAT DO you think?" Mr. Marcel asked.
● ● ●   Tillard put on the table the transcript made by the
● ● ●   U.S. Consulate in Hong Kong of the Radio Canton
broadcast. He shrugged his shoulders.

"It's hard to understand a thing! It seems to prove that
Benachen fed us some lies, or had been fed some himself. He
himself was partly convinced he had been the victim of a
double-cross."

"Let's have a little exercise in dialectics," interrupted the
network chief with evident self-satisfaction. "Let's study the
hypotheses one after the other. Then we'll see which one is
the best, or the least unlikely. . . . First. Let's imagine that
the plan to attack Vietnam had been conceived by the Military Commission of the Central Committee or by some of its
members without the knowledge of the others. It would then
have been the adversaries of the project who would have
notified us, through this eminently suspect character that
Benachen was in their eyes, in order for us to warn the Americans. Why?—to lead the Americans to effectuate a preventive
attack that would raise worldwide opinion against them,
would force the USSR to intervene, and would decisively
put an end to the talks with North Vietnam."

"Objection!" Paul launched in a shrill voice. "The Chinese
aren't crazy enough to expose their territory to atomic bom-
bardment, which in the present state of disorganization of
their political structure could lead to unforeseeable upheaval."

"Objection sustained!" Mr. Marcel allowed. "But only to
a certain extent. So, hypothesis amended—it cannot be a
project emanating from *responsible* people in Peking. On the
other hand, we can admit that there are, inside the army,
military chiefs who are so firmly set on toppling the regime
that they are ready to risk anything."

"Objection!" Tillard also put in. "In that case, why
wouldn't Peking simply arrest or neutralize the authors of
the plan and not bother with a foreign network which would

244

only let the outside world discover the existence of such dangerous dissensions?''

"Because," Mr. Marcel answered, "right now the balance of forces is necessarily in Peking's favor. Let's say that for the responsible in the Canton Committee to be convinced they needed real proof, especially in Canton, where—if we are to believe our late departed friend"—an unhappy smile—"there's nothing but a monumental mess. We get back in the end to the hypothesis of provocation. Benachen would in fact have been the victim of an out-and-out trick. But then, not a trick aimed against him, or us, or the Americans, but against certain political forces in China herself. Therefore the plan truly existed. Certain army men would have been encouraged to set it up, without completely being given the green light to it or the logistical means to carry it out. After which they would have arranged for Chen and his friends, whose pacifist sentiments were notorious, to know the whole story. And, thanks to Miss Wang, whose role in the affair is essential—she pulled all the strings—they facilitated a Chen-Benachen meeting. After the reversal of opinion Chen achieved at the stadium, it became vital to put him down, to discredit him, to bring about his political disgrace—even at the cost of certain risks, but limited after all. I say 'limited' because it was highly unlikely that the Americans would carry out a preventive operation based solely on the intelligence brought back by Benachen. As a matter of fact, we have nothing but fragmentary elements of this conspiracy—a political one, not military, I insist—mounted by Chen and Tseng Tien-min. By the way, did you find the file on Tseng?''

"Yes," Tillard said taking a paper out of his pocket. "He didn't make Yenan and the Long March, but he had been attached to the Party Bureau for North China in '35 and later had worked in the Kuomintang zone, where he was arrested and tortured. He escaped in '37 and went to Yenan, it's not known how. Then . . ."

"No use going any further!" Mr. Marcel was jubilant.

"North China in '35. Zones controlled by the Kuomintang. You know who his boss was at that time? Liu Shao-chi, the Chinese Khrushchev, who else? There's the thread. Just wait a few days. He's the one they want and, to get him, no doubt they're ready to take a certain number of risks in Peking that short-circuiting Chen wouldn't be enough to justify."

"That sounds pretty involved to me," Tillard said, "even for the Chinese."

"And what if it's true?" Paul put in suddenly. "If some fine day the Chinese really attacked the Seventh Fleet, or Danang, or some other base in Vietnam? We'd look great. Don't you think we ought to warn the Yanks in any case?"

"Don't worry—we already have," Mr. Marcel said. "We know very well where and with whom Benachen spent his last night. Mitchell, alias Smitty, alias Doctor Gehring, is the CIA man especially in charge of Chinese internal affairs. The fact that he's the one who has debriefed our poor friend"— he sighed again, at least for appearances—"through the charming personal mediation of 'Mary Lou'—on whom Saigon has just sent us a very instructive file—clearly shows that the Americans themselves don't take the military aspect of the affair very seriously. In fact, I'm going to invite him to lunch this week. We can compare notes. In a case like this, it's in everybody's interest to play an open hand, insofar as our own interests are not directly engaged."

"Have they ever been?" Tillard asked. "Was it really worth Benachen's hide?"

"And don't forget Loriot's hide. The embassy in Peking informed me that he had disappeared with a group of foreign experts and that he was 'probably in custody.' I'd be very surprised if they let him go, poor man. . . . But I'll answer your question—a question, by the way, that someone in our profession should never ask. Yes, it was worth it. Because, as a matter of fact, I have intelligence in my possession far more precise than Benachen could have furnished while getting his kicks in bed with the girl they call Mary Lou. So this gives us, as far as the Americans are concerned, a certain advantage, money in the bank. All that's left is for me to decide what to do with it. I haven't thought about it yet. Maybe I should consult Paris. And I've got to send them this damn report. They're raising hell for it. And I really can't send them just guesswork, without nailing it down to the facts! . . . Let's go back to the beginning."

He seemed very tired suddenly—the climate definitely didn't suit him. He dipped his old clerk's pen in the inkwell.

"Case . . . What'll we call this case?"

"Benachen, we owe him that much," Paul remarked. "By the way, Chief, do you have the results of the inquest?"

"Yes. It doesn't prove much either. Anyone could have done it. Hong Kong intelligence is convinced we did it and they're looking at us fishy-eyed. They even talk of expelling Tillard, which could be really ugly because he just bought a house here. Right, old boy?"

"That's right, Chief, but I think things will settle down. The way I look at it, I think, by a process of elimination, that the Chinese did it. He had accomplished his mission and Peking had little interest in having him tell his little story to the papers. As long as it stays in our files or in the American files, they're not so concerned. But I think they don't want any publicity."

"Wait a minute, Tillard, it wasn't you, was it, who had him killed? That couldn't be!"

Mr. Marcel gave his subordinate a look of some severity, touched by inner amusement. But the other took the accusation quite to heart.

"Oh come on, boss! You know I wouldn't have acted without orders! Besides, we still had things to ask him. Not a lot, but still, some details . . ."

"Incidentally," Paul asked, "what if it was just accidental —he happened to be there at a demonstration where he had

247

no fucking business and was killed? Poor Benachen, he was a born victim. If I'm right, he died as he lived—purely by chance."

"You really believe in that—in chance?" asked Mr. Marcel.